Walk
Like A
Man

*We are destined
for greatness! I believe
in everything you stand
for. This is your story!
Enjoy!*

Laurinda D. Brown 8/07

Walk Like A Man

By
Laurinda D. Brown

Q-Boro Books
WWW.QBOROBOOKS.COM

An Urban Entertainment Company.

Published by Q-Boro Books
Copyright © 2005, 2006 by Laurinda D. Brown

ISBN 0-9776247-8-1
First Printing October 2006

10 9 8 7 6 5 4 3 2 1

This is a work of fiction. It is not meant to depict, portray or represent any particular real persons. All the characters, incidents and dialogues are the products of the author's imagination and are not to be construed as real. Any references or similarities to actual events, entities, real people, living or dead, or to real locales are intended to give the novel a sense of reality. Any similarity in other names, characters, entities, places and incidents is entirely coincidental.

Cover Copyright © 2006 by Q-BORO BOOKS all rights reserved
Cover Layout & Design—Marion Designs
Editors—Chandra Sparks-Taylor, Candace K. Cottrell

Q-BORO BOOKS
Jamaica, Queens NY 11431
WWW.QBOROBOOKS.COM

Dedicated to the loving memory of

Mr. James Earl Brown
August 20, 1949–November 18, 2004

It was the eighteenth of November, a day I'll always remember.
That was the day that my daddy died.
I didn't get a chance to see him. Driving down the highway
I could only think good things about him.
Now that he's with my mama, I feel better knowing I knew
Almost all of the truth.

My papa worked damn near every day of his life
Looking for a legacy to leave his three children
Plus the two he had with his wife.

My papa called himself a jack-of-all-trades
Chasing bitches full of paper painted jade.
That was what sent my papa to an early grave
Folks say Papa would beg, borrow, and steal to pay his bills
Spent so much time being the pimp and playa he was
That he screwed everybody when he left no will.
Yeah, he chased women but was never into drugs and drinking.
Now, I'm sitting here thinking . . .
My papa was a rolling stone
Wherever he laid his hat was home
And when he died, all he left me was alone.

Peace out, JB.

ACKNOWLEDGMENTS

First, I give all my thanks to God for this gift He has bestowed upon me. Words flow from me like water in a stream. Sometimes I don't even understand them, but I keep going. Sometimes I write so deep and so passionately that my own heart bleeds, and my soul explodes with an outpouring of words that surge onto the paper. And that, I've come to realize, is no one but God allowing me to do what He put me here to do.

Charlotte, thank you for the love you give me every minute and every hour of every day. You do it unconditionally and unselfishly. It has been because of your effortless support and faith in me and my writing that I've been able to trudge on when I couldn't think of shit to write. Thanks for the many nights you've stayed up editing and proofing this book and the many "you can do this" speeches that have made this all come to fruition. Poo-kay, I love you with every fiber of my being.

Jhoilan and Cydney, thank you for taking this journey with me and loving me for who I am and not for whom I love. You're the reason my days are joyous and fulfilling.

Nyree, thanks for being a great sister who shares the same sense of humor as I do. Daddy hooked us up with that. Sorry, though, that you'll never have that brother-in-law you been dreaming about. I just don't roll like that anymore.

Karen, my sister in blood and "in the life." We're walking this path because this is what's most comfortable to us. Don't ever be afraid to be who you are, and, in your woman, make sure she's with you for who you are and not for who she can change you into. Know that we walk like men in representing what James Brown brought to our lives.

Kathleen B., words cannot express the overwhelming gratitude I have for your kindness, love, and sincerity. You have been an inspiration to me and a Godsend to my family. If nothing else, you've taught me to do my damn thing.

Chastity, you are a fabulous soror and an incredibly remarkable friend. Thank you for being there for me during all of my moments, good and bad. You and your handsome house of men have been wonderful additions to my extended family. I appreciate you for accepting my life just the way it is.

Gina, thanks for your insight on "the life" and the women we love—or try to love. Your assistance and glowing friendship have been bright spots in my life as of late, and I wanted to tell you that...right here. You have been one of the few women who demands nothing from me emotionally, mentally, or physically, and I love you for that.

Liz Mitchell, you are the coolest woman I know. Thank you for the quiet space you have made for me in your L.A. home. Our talks have been entertaining and thought-provoking. You have a radiant smile and a magnetic personality, and I look forward to the growth and prospering of our friendship.

Lee Hayes and Darrien Lee, you guys have been great in this creative journey. Thank you for comforting words and support. We are here for one another to share our imaginations and live our dreams.

Leon and Arwen, thank you for loving my children the way you do and for being parents to them when I'm not around. Thanks for taking care of them in my absence and showing *me* what it really means to be family.

Ms. Vicki, Soft 'n' Wet Afternoons was the beginning of my journey into exposing same-sex-loving women to the world of alternative literature about *us* and giving them an opportunity to experience what *our* lives are really about. Thanks for those mini-field trips to the dressing room (wink and smile).

Zane, thank you for giving me the chance to be what I am today and for supporting me in my decisions as a mother and a writer. Your advice has been tremendously helpful, and I sincerely look forward to working with you on upcoming projects.

Lisa Cox, thank you for providing me with numerous opportunities to showcase my work and for your marvelous support. Your events are off the fucking chain.

Zandra, watch what I say when I tell you that we're about to make some shit happen. Thanks for doing a tremendous job as my publicist and friend.

Until the next time,
Peace

For Daddy

FOREPLAY

The first time I lay naked with a woman I was nervous but anxious to get it on. I had no idea what we were supposed to do. All I knew was that my vagina was throbbing fiercely, and she, in her nude state, looked so good to me. But hell, she had the same thing I had, and I felt, since she was older, she would give me some direction. As I sat waiting for her to make her move, she was lying there waiting for me to make mine. So I leaned over and kissed her. It was a passionate kiss, full of tongue and juice, but there was no way that this could be what gay sex was all about. She kept whispering for me to stick my dick in her. *What dick?*

In my youthful innocence and desperately not wanting her to stop kissing me, I slowly slid my fingers between her legs and entered her. She started moaning. *Oh, that dick.* I quickly found out that I could imitate a man's thrust with just my fingers. She wiggled on my index and forefingers like a big worm, and I, amazed with this newfound pleasure—because it did feel quite nice—moved my lips from hers and redirected my passion to her breasts. Caressing them with my lips, I did to her what I knew had felt good to me whenever a man had sucked my nipples. She moaned some more, and, before I knew it, she'd had an orgasm.

What about me? As she lay there stretched out on her mother's bed, I watched her chest rise and fall during her sudden slumber. Her nipples were still erect. She seemed comfortable. I, believing I'd done my part, rolled over into a fetal position and covered myself with the blanket. *What about me?* Maybe an hour or so later, after I was no longer aroused, I felt a kiss on my neck. It was soft and gentle, wet and tender. The kisses continued down my spine, along my thighs, and ended at the tip of my toes. Flipping me over, she moved her lips up the front of my calves and spread open my legs. Her kisses, now longer and more succulent, generated this vibration in my lower abdomen that I'd never felt before. My eyes, fixated on her slender body as it slithered toward me, watered as she drew near. Anticipating her lips touching my private button, I jerked away and told her I wanted to stop. I couldn't envision getting any pleasure from someone pulling and tugging on that thing between my legs.

Sitting in a huge wet spot created by my own moisture, I knew I wasn't ready for that kind of sex. I wasn't seeking my own gratification that night. I was merely satisfied with knowing I could get a woman off just like a man could—and with no dick!

I will say that our lovemaking was one of the most intense events of my life, but during the whole thing, I found myself wanting to be a man with this huge dick planted inside her nature. I was on top of her, like my past boyfriends had been on top of me, working it and stroking it like a champ. And when I came, the muscles in my back tensed up as I released myself in her. That whole night I felt this power . . . this aura about myself that I'd never felt before. Resting between her legs while embracing her torso, I tickled her breasts with my tongue. She begged for me to enter her again, and I did, but not with two fingers. Try three.

The butt of dawn caught me racing through the streets across town trying to make it home to get ready for work. And then, as I pulled into my driveway, it hit me. I'd spent an entire night with a woman consumed with the idea of me being a man;, the idea of me having a dick; the idea of me fucking her with something that God didn't give me. The irony of the whole thing is that I felt like I had one; I felt that shit like it was real. I went into the house and took a quick bubble bath, and afterward, I sprayed myself with perfume. I put on my tightest skirt and my highest heels and strutted back out to the car with my face beat. On the way to work, I thought about my new sexual freedom and quietly laughed to myself. I checked my lipstick in the rearview mirror as I reached in the backseat for my purse. Delicately picking the lint off my skirt, I admired my gentle strokes against the fabric. Every part of me was meticulous, down to the color of my lingerie that was forever on point with my outerwear. My nails were always punctiliously manicured and polished to coordinate with my toes. On the outside I walked on the tips of my toes—dainty and self-assured—bouncing my long, thick hair from side to side. I looked every bit of a lady to the world. I had it eating out of the palm of my hands. But on the inside, though, down beneath the smooth skin and soft fragrance, I walked like a man.

"A" IS FOR ASHLEY

Standing in the mirror with my mascara wand gently separating each lash and shading them brownish black, I thought about the many cards she'd sent me, the flowers, the love. By the time I finished stretching each hair that protected my hazel eyes, I realized just how much flattery and compassion she had bestowed upon me. Every aspect of my eye makeup that morning reflected my thoughts of the previous evening. Without a single blemish in my makeup, I had unintentionally achieved supermodel status with my creation. Every thought of her made me strive even more toward perfection.

This mental façade I was putting on was killing me. I saw them—Ashley and her acquaintance for the evening—dancing body to body, swaying so tightly to the reggae music that I felt the movement. I leaned when they leaned; I crooned with them. My mellow demeanor melted when I saw them kiss. Tongues entangled, their passion was evident. Nervously, I adjusted the Ralph Lauren silk blouse I'd finally bought after eyeing it for months at Dillard's. I knew it would be perfect for this late May event I'd attended for ten years in D.C.

My plan was for her to see me in it and revel in my couture. But she didn't. Instead, she merged with this woman. She intertwined our lives at that moment. Ashley had once meant the world to me, and it was like in a mysterious instant, that world had come crashing to an end.

"You wanna dance?" a leaning figure with a soft voice whispered in my ear.

"I'm not dancing right now," I snapped. Whoever she was turned and walked away, obviously observing that I was preoccupied with my own thoughts. Ashley had never said anything to me about this woman she was dancing with, but I couldn't deny that I'd seen the signs.

When I was first introduced to Ashley, I was at Dover, Delaware's rendition of Black Pride. Lacy, my road dawg from my earlier days at the club, and I had ridden up together from Largo, Maryland, expecting to see Dred King and to hear the funky beats of DJ Shy-Town. The first event was an outdoor bazaar and cookout in a moderately sized park. Anticipating seeing tons of Pride paraphernalia or maybe even a book or two, I was shocked to only find this sistah selling T-shirts she'd cut strips in for thirty dollars, a vendor with incense, oils, and soaps, and a brotha selling poems he'd run off on his home computer. There were about ten women—OK, maybe thirty—out in the park sitting in truck beds, on car trunks, on the ground, or in lawn chairs. Advertised as a free food event, I expected the offerings to be below standard for a cookout—no-name sodas, chicken legs and thighs, store-bought potato salad, and generic chips. Needless to say, I wasn't disappointed. I chose not to eat.

Digging through the trunk of the car, I found a bag of chips left from when I'd gone grocery shopping. Lacy— who'd eat anything, anywhere, any time—had gotten a plate and was tossing back sodas left and right. She stopped stuffing her face long enough to say, "Girl, did you taste the chicken legs? They hooked that shit up," as she proceeded to suck her fingers.

"You know I don't do dark meat." I laughed, licking the salt from my fingers.

"Yeah, I know. That's probably why you won't touch me." Lacy chuckled. She was what I call a dark chocolate honey with beautiful white teeth who stood about five-ten. I loved her but couldn't *love* her because her friendship actually meant more to me. She and I would often lie in bed and watch TV or talk. One night things got a little heated, but I backed away, fearing that making love to her would only complicate our friendship. It was the first time I'd allowed myself to dismiss a roll in the hay for mere companionship.

"See, see, you know you wrong for goin' there with me. You and I are cool, and I want to keep it like that. That's why there'll never be any sex. We . . ." Then, in that same breath, two femmes approached the car. One of them was fine as hell—titties all bulging from her bra, tight shorts, and flip-flops on. The other was in a wifebeater, wearing jeans and Timbs. I knew she was femme because her nails were flaw-lessly manicured and her makeup was exceptional. Besides, she walked too soft to be anything else. She looked a little funny in the face, but she had an ass that wouldn't wait. That one with all the cleavage showing was going to be mine, though. I didn't care whom she was with. Lacy peered over the top of her sunglasses and began to smile. She got up from the edge of the fender and placed her plate inside the trunk. From the huge grin on her face, I assumed she knew them.

"Hey, Tommie. I didn't think you were coming," she said as she reached to hug the one with the wifebeater on. "How you doin'?"

The young lady, cheerfully hugging Lacy, was squeezing

my girl so tight I thought she was going to suffocate her. "I wanted to surprise you. You remember my friend, Ashley, right?"

Peeking over at Ashley like she was a piece of prime rib, Lacy replied, "Yes, I do. I haven't seen you in a good while around the club."

"No, my work schedule changed. Between work and school, I don't have a lot of time on my hands," Ashley responded.

I was trying not to stare, so I kept my face buried in the bag of chips. I figured Lacy would introduce us at some point. Ashley looked over at me, but I couldn't bear to glance in her direction or I'd bust out laughing. This energy was running through me that I could only describe as sensational. All I know is that I was full of giggles like a little kid who'd found a new toy.

"Dee, this is my girl, Tomika, but I call her Tommie." Tommie extended her hand toward me. "Tommie, this is Dee, short for Deidre." Taking my hand from the wrinkled bag and wiping it against my jeans, we shook hands. A pretty firm grip for a femme.

"Hi. Tomika Adams. Nice to meet you. This is Ashley, my best friend."

"OK, good to meet both of you." That was encouraging to know—they weren't *together.*

"Damn, are those chips good?" Ashley giggled.

Embarrassed, I rolled the bag closed and tossed it in the trunk. "Actually, they were. I'd offer you some, but I've been sticking my wet fingers in the bag, and . . ."

"T-M-I." she laughed again, letting me know I had given her too much information. Ashley moved closer to me and reached for my face with both of her hands. I, being a true playa, couldn't take my eyes off her breasts and stepped back in a jolt of excitement.

"Heyyyy, what's going on? What you . . ."

Ashley gently brushed her fingertips around my dimples. "You've got potato chip crumbs around your mouth." She dusted them to the ground. Blushing, I politely thanked her and wondered what was going to happen next.

Later that evening, we followed Tommie and Ashley back to the Sheraton. Tommie offered the sofa in the suite for us to sleep on that night, so we wouldn't have to pay for an extra room. That arrangement was going to be a trip because I felt somewhat uncomfortable sleeping next to Lacy. Despite my outward feelings toward her, she did make my nature rise—most women did. But this particular night I had my mind on other things—like Ashley. If I could have just five minutes with her . . . OK maybe ten minutes, I'd rock her shit, hitting it hard like a jackhammer.

Once I started unpacking my bag, I realized my toiletry case was missing. It had to be in the car. "Dayum, my bag is in the car, and all my shit is in it. I'll be right back," I yelled to Lacy who was in the bathroom unloading that nasty-ass meal from earlier.

"Wait," Ashley pleaded. "I'll tag along with you. You don't need to go down there by yourself." Milk chocolate skin . . . that's how I liked them, and, as I watched her come toward me, I knew I was about to get a cavity because I was going to eat her ass alive.

Putting on a tough exterior, I was like, "I don't need an escort. Ain't nobody gonna fuck with the Big D." I had this habit of trying to be all gangsta, but the truth of the matter was that I still had quite a bit of bitch in me.

Ashley chuckled. "I don't care what kind of hardcore front you put on for me. Your ass is still a woman, and it's late. I'm going with you."

Quietly pleased, I obliged. "Suit yourself." Opening the door, I adjusted myself—all of me—and said, "Ladies first."

* * *

That had to be the longest walk to an elevator I'd ever experienced. Ashley was in front of me, swaying in a little-ass skirt that bonded to her like glue. It moved when she moved. Her skin glistened with body oil spread across her shoulders, arms, and legs like butter. If she'd been a piece of chicken, it would've been all over but the shoutin'. I could tell from the lack of panty lines that maybe Ashley didn't have on any panties or perhaps she had on a G-string. I wondered what color it was. Did it smell as she did? I'd give up the cash to hold that muthafucker in my hand right then. I even thought about asking her for it, so I could put that bitch under my pillow at night.

Approaching the elevator, we both reached for the "down" button. Pulling away, I gave her this one opportunity to be in control. The doors opened, and there was this White couple standing in the corner.

"Hello," Ashley offered.

"Good evening," they responded, smiling comfortably at Ashley and me.

Wow, she's magnetic, I thought. The energy in that elevator was amazing. Ashley moved closer to me as the elevator stopped three floors below the lobby. Her fragrance . . . so sweet, so enticing . . . so . . . *damn.* The jolt of the elevator touching the ground floor caused her to slightly bump into me and that sent my "thing" into a frenzy. The doors opened, and I stepped aside to let her off first. I was on fire. Was her shit hot like mine? Had it melted like mine moments before when she bumped into me?

The car was parked in the very back of the garage because all of the good spots were taken. I didn't mind, though, since it appeared that it had been written in the cards for me to park that far away from potential passersby. "So, how does a girl like you afford a Lex like this?"

What? A girl like me? "What kind of question is that?" I was a bit offended.

"Don't get your panties in a wad. I didn't mean it like that. You strike me as the SUV type, not the luxury-car type."

"Oh. I've always liked them. After I saved half of the money for it, my pops came through with a matching donation."

"Oh, so you're a daddy's girl," she said, grinning. I unlocked the doors, and she made herself comfortable by getting in the backseat on the passenger's side.

Sliding in next to her, I responded, "Not really. I believe if there's something you truly want and you work hard for it, then people will appreciate and respect you more. Pops was willing to meet me halfway."

"I see." As she settled in her spot, now all the way over behind the driver's seat, her legs gapped open. She looked at me and winked. "I figured I'd meet you halfway." First, there were kisses . . . a lot of them—wet and succulent. I was startled a little bit by her pierced tongue because I didn't notice it before. But the more that damn tongue touched my skin and that little fuzz just above my lips, the more I liked it, seemingly adding a whole new level to the tryst. I kissed every part of her exposed skin, consuming myself in a milk chocolate fantasy. Slowly, I massaged her left thigh, caressing it with the palm of my right hand, which had the nerve to be tingling. I didn't care, though. I reached her crotch, and I could feel the heat off her pussy. The seat of her G-string was moist with steam . . . with lust. I maneuvered my way beneath the fabric and touched her. Moaning and shivering all at the same time, I felt her cum without me even entering her. Little beads of sweat popped from her forehead, and gallons of it were poured from me. As I realized that she had released herself, I began to pull away. Then, in between her moans, which had evolved into soft squeals, she whispered, "Don't stop."

It didn't matter to me that my windows weren't tinted and that the back passenger side door was slightly ajar. I took off my shirt and tossed it to the front seat. I lifted hers from her softened body, revealing her pierced breasts and navel. *Damn, she's got holes everywhere,* I thought. But, in my mind, there was only one hole I was concerned about, and I was going to fill it with a little sumthin' special.

Unzipping my pants with my left hand and massaging her titties with my right, I whipped *Tonya* out. I'd put her on while in the bathroom back in the room. I don't know. Wearing it made me feel like I was running things, and, just by looking at Ashley, I knew I could have her. Ashley's eyes had been closed most of our encounter, but, as Tonya dangled against her thigh, she opened them, smiled, and sucked her teeth. "Give it to me, baby," she muttered. I grabbed her panties—a G-string with an "A" made of rhinestones in the middle of it—and rubbed them against my nose.

"You know I'm keeping this, right?" Ashley laughed and pulled me to her. Tonya slid right in without a struggle, and I went to work. I tapped that ass like she was a hooker from the red light district, and I was her pimp taking her on a test run before she hit the streets. As my hips gyrated against her closely shaven bikini area that night, I can't explain what I felt. All I knew was that my cavities—my decay, my pain from this sensuous, milk chocolate delight, would someday cause my entire feminine existence to decompose and wither away. I felt like I had this man thing going on.

Afterward, with her phone number and address in my pocket, Ashley and I walked through downtown Dover and noticed a tattoo parlor across the street from our hotel.

"I've always wanted a tattoo," Ashley smiled at me. Her smile was irresistible.

"Really? Me, too!" I exclaimed. "I've always been too scared, though. My mom would kill me."

"We should get one," Ashley said, giggling. "You should get an A, and I could get a D."

"Girl, I don't know about that. I'm not down with putting some chick's name or initials on me. Hell, I don't even know you all that well."

"That could change," Ashley whispered in my ear as she grabbed its lobe and bit it gently. I couldn't resist her.

"OK, I'll do it. Where should it go?"

Ashley winked at me, gazing into my eyes. She replied, "Maybe on your arm. You have nice arms. Got a few muscles goin' on."

"OK. That sounds good. Where are you going to get yours?"

"I don't know. I've always wanted one on the small of my back. I think that's sexy. We'll see how yours looks first."

I straddled the stool and never thought about what I was about to do. All I knew was that Ashley was the best pussy I'd ever had, and I wanted the world to know it. Just thinking about her made my panties wet. As she stood there stroking the palms of my hands while the needle pricked that A on my right shoulder, my future, for the first time in long while, had meaning. Getting the tattoo wasn't as painful as I thought it would be. I smiled at her and realized that my life was now complete. This was going to be my wife. Once the artist was finished, I found the A, beautifully done in calligraphy, to be well worth the small amount of pain.

"So where are you going to put yours?"

Ashley looked intently at the designs on the display wall. I knew she wanted something funky if she didn't decide to get the D, so I waited patiently while the artist outlined the home instructions to care for my tattoo. "Don't take a bath or let the shower run on it for two weeks, and make sure you keep it moist with some type of heavy lotion." He then turned to Ashley and wondered why it was taking her so long to pick her design. "Got any questions, little lady?"

"Not about the tattoos," she said, "but do you have water in here?"

"Sure. I'll get you some." He looked puzzled as Ashley appeared to be about to throw up. The kind man brought her a bottle of water and asked her if she was OK.

"I don't know. I feel a little sick to my stomach."

I walked over to her and held her hand. *Was she nervous?* "Ashley, we don't have to do this tonight. We can come back tomorrow."

Massaging her stomach, she insisted, "No, I want to get this done now. Just give me a minute."

A minute turned into an hour. It took Ashley that long to get herself together. But by then, it was closing time. "Ladies, we open at 10:00 A.M." I understood the man being ready to go home, so I told Ashley we'd come back. Maybe a half hour after that, I was still trying to give Ashley Tums, Rolaids . . . anything I could find to make her feel better. It was funny, though. She was acting as if nothing was ever wrong. As a matter of fact, she downed three Heinekens when we got back to the hotel.

The next morning Lacy and I woke up to find Tommie and Ashley gone. They didn't even leave a note, and I assumed that Ashley didn't get her tattoo either.

I saw Ashley a few times after that weekend and soon realized I was unsure what I wanted from her. The one thing we never discussed was her not getting the tattoo. I was strung out over her fragrance and her sensuality. At points, when we talked, our conversation seemed endless. She would giggle at my silly jokes, and I beamed with pride that someone thought my stale sense of humor was even worth the effort. So full of excitement was I about this woman who had mes-

merized me, I completely missed the signs when things
began falling apart. Ashley sent me cards and roses almost
every day. They were cute, loving cards, and many of them
appeared to mirror what I, too, was feeling in my heart. I
arranged them by the postmarks and discovered that her
feelings for me intensified with each passing day. Every card
depicted a chapter in our love story. Then one day, without
warning, the cards stopped and so did the roses. Soon I realized that I was the only one keeping the lines of communi-
cation open, and I felt that every call from me was annoying
her. Believing I was coming on way too strong, I backed off
and gave Ashley space. But that space felt cavernous and
lonely.

One thing I'd always promised myself was that I would
never chase a woman. I didn't care how good the pussy was.
I was never going to do it. What I failed to realize was that I
was chasing Ashley. I didn't know what I was supposed to do,
so I called Lacy and spilled the beans on my little love affair.

"Dee, I can't believe you got involved with that girl."

Stunned, I asked, "What do you mean?" I was holding
back the tears fueled by my anger.

"You know she a ho, right?"

"What?"

"Girl, she's been playing you like a baby grand. Whenever
she ordered roses for you, she was ordering them for some
other trick across town. Tommie will tell you."

"How in the hell does Tommie know?"

"Because Ashley used to do the same thing for her, and
Tommie got a tattoo to prove it. She told me to warn you
that night, but shit, you'd got them panties before I had a
chance to. Yo' ass was lightnin' quick with that shit, too."
Lacy laughed.

"A tattoo? Tommie has a tattoo?"

"Girl, yeah . . . of a damn A." I would never get a tattoo for some bitch, especially one like that. The funny part is that she'd promised Tommie she'd get one for her but never did. Kept coming up with all kinds of shit as to why she couldn't get one. I'm telling you that Ashley is a—"

"Lace, I was really feeling her. I changed—"

"You don't even have to say it. I saw you wearing your hair pulled back under those damn hats. You changed your look for her, and your ass is prolly walking around with a damn A branded on you. Trying to look all hard and shit. You know you can't shake that diva style you got. I don't care how good the pussy looks. I don't know what you got going on down between your legs, but you had that ass singin' like Tweety. Girl, she told Tommie everything that happened that night at the hotel . . . all the way down to the thing with Tonya. Besides, she's got a woman . . . this old biddy who's doing time for credit card fraud. Let the story be told, it's her money that's been paying for your flowers."

There was nothing I could say after that. I desperately needed to talk to Ashley, but when I dialed her number, I found my calls blocked. *What?*

I drove over to her house and knocked on her door until my fists bled, but she wouldn't answer. My gentle knocks turned to pounds that were so hard that I missed the thunderstorm rolling in. The sky crackled with light as I called her name. "Ashley. Ashley," I cried. "Baby, please let me in." Despite my efforts, my pleas went ignored, and the rain began to pour. I knew she was home, but aside from kicking the door in or busting out a window, I was beginning to realize that I'd never get inside to talk to her. My hands were in the same knots as my stomach. In the distance, I heard a car coming, splashing through the puddles in the street. As the car approached, I turned around to see what other idiot was out in this storm. It was a police car. *Damn.*

With its spotlight beaming on Ashley's porch, the car

stopped in front of the driveway. The officer got out, reached for his flashlight, did a quick inspection of my car as he passed by it, and turned his attention to me. "Ma'am?"

"Yes, officer," I responded. Ashley had called the police on me. I couldn't believe it. All I wanted was to talk.

"How are you this evening?"

My heart hurts. "I'm fine."

He peeped around the corner and flashed his light in the front window of the house. "We got a call from the woman inside that you were causing a commotion out here."

"Me?" I said shockingly.

"Yes, ma'am. Is there a problem?"

Staring out in the street, silvery from the raindrops splattering against the pavement, I replied, "No, sir. I just wanted to talk to my friend."

The policeman was nice. He was even kind enough to offer me a towel because the wind, combined with the rain, had kicked my ass. "I think you should call it a night. She doesn't want to see you, and I don't want to have to take you in for disturbing the peace."

There were a lot of ways I could have reacted to the situation, but the best way for everybody was for me to take my dumb pussy-whipped ass home. "I understand. Thank you."

I watched Ashley and her date maneuver their way from the dance floor to the bar. All the while my stomach burned in agitation. I stood with my hands in my pockets, rolling the lint and other items through my fingers. I also watched Ashley kiss the girl on the cheek and head for the bathroom. Taking advantage of the opportunity, with single-minded determination, I followed her. I had something to give Miss Thang, and I didn't want to wait any longer.

I hesitated at the bathroom entrance and pondered for a moment if I had the nerve to go through with my plan.

Besides Ashley, two other women were inside, so I went to the sink to wash my hands. That would give me a moment to monitor everybody's position. That's when her date came in. *Damn!* I quickly dried my hands and darted back to my stool at the bar. As luck would have it, Ashley and her friend sat in the empty spot right next to me. After all we'd been through, she didn't even recognize a sistah.

Checking them out through the corner of my eye, I ordered a Cosmo and eavesdropped on their conversation. The girl asked Ashley if she had any panties on, and, Ashley, being the ho I'd come to know she was, giggled so much that it was making me sick. That's it. I'd had enough.

Taking the last swig from my glass, I cleared my throat and reached in my pocket. "Hello, Ashley," I said calmly.

She froze and nodded at me. *She can't even dignify me with a real response.* Then she rolled her eyes and turned away. But her girl kept looking at me like, "Who the hell are you, and why are you talking to my woman?"

Not wanting to disappoint my counterpart, I introduced myself. "Hi, my name is Deidre. Ashley and I go way back even though she's acting like she don't know me."

"Oh, really?" the girl replied.

"Yeah, we knew each other once, and I'm actually glad I bumped into her tonight because I have something I need to give her." Glancing at her arm I continued, "By the way, I like your tattoo." It was an A.

"Thank you," she said with pride.

I reached in my pocket and pulled out that G-string with a rhinestone A on the front—the one I'd taken from her that night in the car. Rubbing it across my nose, I took a deep breath, inhaling her aroma. It still smelled of her essence. Looking Ashley in her eyes while addressing her date, I stretched the G-string from one hand to the other in front of them both.

"This belongs to your girl, and if you've had your face as far up her ass as I have, then smell it, you'll know it's hers." I let go of it hard enough for the underwear to snap Ashley in her face. "A is for Ashley."

So here I am the morning after, on my way out the door, the diva extraordinaire Lacy reminded me about. I rubbed the faint scar to remind me of the stupidity that caused it in the first place. The laser surgery to remove the A was all behind me, and my shoulder had healed very well. I'd allowed a woman, who got her thrills manipulating people, to brand my mind, body, and spirit. Surprisingly, I'm not as mad with her as I am with myself. My skin is tough, and my heart is like a block of ice. I'm ready to start dating again now that I'm finally done going through something that made me unsure of myself. Flawless. That's what I am today because every thought of that girl made me strive even more toward a complete me. I began as "Dee," Lacy's friend; then I switched into D, Ashley's trick in the parking garage; but, for the sake of my heart, I'm Deidre again, and I'm going to stay that way.

MO

It happened at a time when there was no such thing as a sex offender. There were simply dirty old men who could have their way with little girls and dared them to tell anybody. Nobody did time, nor did anyone get counseling. Bribed with money, candy, toys, and whatever else didn't come easy, almost every girl in the neighborhood had touched Mr. Luther's dick. I, myself, had seen it, kissed it, smelled it, and touched it more times than I cared to think about.

My reflection in the floor-length mirror was disturbing at first sight. Blood was running down my legs, soaking through my white stockings. My pretty pink sundress, stained with dirt, blood, and his secretions, was torn at the shoulder straps, and the buckles on my Mary Janes were broken. I'd run from the railroad tracks as fast as I could, never looking back to see if he were catching up to me. When I got to the house, I bolted the front door and dashed down the hallway to the bathroom. There, I found some sense of security. On this blistering, hot summer's day, I'd had it. Oh, by the way, to my family and friends, my name is Monique.

* * *

At ten, I was a small girl, a little chunky in places, but for the most part, I was like the other girls my age. My areas of thickness were my breasts, my cheeks, and my rear end. My moms made me wear dresses every day with some type of matching bow in my hair. She refused to let me grow up and wear things more appropriate for my age. I had the Bobbie socks with the lace around the ankles, and my moms made sure my legs were shining from the clumps of Vaseline she slapped on my calves and thighs. To coordinate with all of my dresses, I had a pair of Mary Janes I wore with tights, necklaces, earrings—the whole nine yards. When Mary Janes came in style for pre-teens, she bought me some of those, too.

Moms and I lived alone in a two-bedroom house that we rented from some folks who went to church down on the corner. We weren't rich, but Moms made sure that I was neatly dressed whenever I stepped out of the house. She says it came from years of her playing with doll babies, imitation Barbie dolls, and those spooky-ass doll heads. From as early as I could remember, Moms never asked anyone for anything when it came to taking care of me. I met my dad once, one Friday after school, and was terribly disappointed because he wasn't this fine, debonair Black man that Moms had made him into whenever she sat on the porch cackling and gossiping with her girlfriends. Personally, I thought he was some ex-con looking for a handout. His beard was knotted up against his face, his teeth were yellow with white shit all between them, his corn-rowed hair had pieces of lint sticking out, and the stench from the stale liquor lingered in the house for days after he had left.

"Monique, this is Eric, your father. Come give him a hug," she ordered. There was no way in hell that I was going to let that man touch me. I took two steps back instead of any ones forward. "Get over here, Monique! Now. I know you ain't gonna disrespect your father. Don't let me have to beat your ass!"

All I have to say is that was the worst beating I ever got because, after having never seen me, tucked me in bed, or kissed me on the forehead, she let him spank me, and none of his licks hurt more than the pain and hurt I felt toward Moms. When he was done, I saw his hands trembling as he lit a cigarette and walked down the hall to her bedroom. I went to my room, closed the door, and fell down on my bed, sobbing for hours. Throughout the whole weekend, I made my way to the kitchen and bathroom without ever being seen. Devastated, I realized that Moms could care less about me right then because her man was at home. Closed up in my room with my music and my dolls, I was content if I never saw him again—and I didn't.

Most of my life I knew Moms hadn't really wanted to have babies. She used to tell my Aunt Penny that she'd have an abortion in a minute if she had the money, but she wasn't going to stop fucking and wasn't going to use no rubber either. Apparently, she didn't have the money when she got pregnant with me. Most of my early years were spent at Aunt Penny's house on the weekends. Moms would drop me off on Friday evening and wouldn't pick me up until Monday after she got off work. At least, I was told she'd been to work. When we returned home, there was always this stale liquor smell in the house, and the sheets on her bed were a mess and smelled like ba-dussy—a dreadful combination of ass and pussy. I never questioned her about any of it because that was grown folks' business. Moms made sure I had what she felt I needed, but, for herself, the only thing she did was to make herself available to whatever man came along. My granny believed that a woman's place was to cook, take care of the children, and be a freak in the sheets, and that's exactly how she acted. So did Moms.

Up the street from us lived this man named Mr. Luther who was like the candy man for our street. He sold twenty-five-cent sodas, freeze cups, pickles, candy, cookies, Popsicles, potato chips, and ice cream cones. Every day before school, for as long as I can remember, my cousins and I stopped by his house to buy cookies to go in our lunch. "Here, Li'l Miss Monique, take this here to your mother. She likes my sour pickles," he'd say, and I'd put it in my lunch box and give it to her when I got home from school. I liked Mr. Luther because he was always so nice, especially to us girls. Sometimes he was like the father many of us never had. Every day he asked how we were doing in school and if we were learning anything. Back then, if needed, Mr. Luther had this unspoken permission to knock us on our asses if we got out of line. I only heard about him doing that to a couple of the boys on our street but never to any of the girls.

By the time I was thirteen I was still wearing the Mary Janes, but Moms had stopped making me wear dresses all the time. It was embarrassing for me to look like Little Orphan Annie even though I was a teenager. Now I had some say in my wardrobe and wore mostly jeans and nice frou-frou blouses. I had some corduroys and a couple of pair of khaki pants that I dressed in from time to time, too. Sometimes I'd wear a dress just to change up for a bit. On one of those occasions, I bumped into Mr. Luther at our school's playground. We shared the play area with the adjacent park, so it wasn't unusual for folks to be sitting on the benches near where we played. At this point in my life, I'd starting noticing the boys, and they'd started noticing me, too. I made sure I was cute every day, and I smelled sensational. Mr. Luther would always tell me how good I smelled when he saw me, and he told me in such a fatherly way that I never thought about anything being wrong with his comments.

That afternoon, however, he'd been sitting there watching me and some of my friends gossip about the boys in our class. We'd had a special program that morning, and most of the girls had on dresses. I ignored the glazed look in his eyes and the demented smile on his face. Hell, this was Mr. Luther, the candy man, and he could do no wrong.

"Mr. Luther, what are you doing here? Were you invited to our program today?"

Looking around to see who saw him, he replied, "No, I wasn't at your program. I came up here to drop some sodas off to your principal."

"Oh, OK." I smiled. "I'll see you later."

Winking at me, Mr Luther asked, "Why don't you come by after school and get a pickle for your mother?"

"Yes, sir, I will." Since I was in middle school and class started much earlier, I didn't have time to stop by in the mornings like I used to. As I laughed and played that afternoon with my friends, enjoying my youth, it didn't dawn on me that sodas weren't allowed in our school. Later, after school, my friend Tangie and I headed toward Mr. Luther's place, but when we got there, she refused to go inside.

"Girl, what's wrong with you? You acting like you seen a boogeyman or something. It's just Mr. Luther."

Tangie's face had this look I'd never seen. Suddenly, she burst into tears. I reached for her arm, but she yanked it back. "Noooo. My momma told me to not go in there." She took off running down the street.

Nothing was going to stop me from getting my moms's pickle. She loved those things even though they gave her high blood pressure. I opened the screen door and walked into the kitchen where Mr. Luther kept the goodies. "Mr. Luther?" I called out. There was no answer. As I walked around the table that held the pickles, peppermint sticks, and penny candy, I noticed a stick of incense burning in a nearby plant. Just as I peeped around the corner into the living room, Mr. Luther came out of nowhere.

"Hey there, Li'l Miss Monique. I thought you wasn't going to make it. I was just about to get a fresh jar of pickles for your mother. Those are dill pickles in there. The sour ones are back here in the other room."

That was strange. I swore the jar read "sour" on the front. "OK," I answered and followed him to the back room. Once in there, the door unexpectedly closed. But I wasn't worried because this was Mr. Luther, the candy man. I stood in the corner behind the door while he fumbled with some boxes. Nervous, I stood gawking at the tons of shit in that room. There was enough stuff to start a small convenience store. When Mr. Luther turned around, he had his penis in his hand, and it stood out like a flagpole.

"Li'l Miss Monique, would you help Mr. Luther and touch his little friend for him?"

I was repulsed. "No, Mr. Luther, I can't do that. I just came for my momma's pickle." He asked again, and I rejected him again. "I think I better leave."

"Oh, Li'l Miss Monique, just do it this one time for me. I won't tell nobody. It'll be our little secret. I'll give you a brand-new twenty-dollar bill and all the pickles you want for your momma."

I couldn't resist that. My moms loved those pickles, and I could use the twenty dollars to go to the mall with Tangie later.

At fifteen, I was a brickhouse. I still had a small frame, but I had curvaceous hips and voluptuous breasts. I'd gotten enough money from Mr. Luther to buy a new bike, a pair of skates, a *Seventeen* magazine subscription, and a few pretty gifts for my moms. One night when Tangie and I were having a sleepover, she sat up on my bed and looked at all the nice things I had around my room. "How much of this stuff did Mr. Luther buy?" she asked playfully.

Shocked, I swiftly got up from the floor and closed my door. "What are you talking about, Tangie?"

"Don't play dumb. Everybody on this street knows you been getting money from him, and you're not the only one."

"That's not true."

"Monique, your momma works at the same plant as my momma, and they don't make that much money. There's no way your momma can afford all this stuff you got."

"Why you all up in my business?" I couldn't believe I was getting mad about this. I knew Mr. Luther was wrong, but he was giving me money, and I was able to afford a lifestyle my other friends didn't have.

"This is me, Monique. Quit trippin'."

I started crying. "Do you realize how much money he has given me since this started? Like hundreds and hundreds of dollars."

"All for you to do what for him?"

Ashamed, I began rattling off each act, none of which included him sticking it in. "Tangie, all I've done is touch it mostly."

"Monique, you need to tell your momma."

The tears began to pour. "I tried to . . . last year, and she didn't believe me. She thinks the man walks on water. Just the other night she was talking about us going to North Carolina with him, so what's the point?"

"Monique, it's only a matter of time before he asks for something else, and are you going to take money for that, too?"

I knew what she was talking about. I'd tried to stop the whole thing, but Mr. Luther threatened to tell my friends about the dirty things I did with him. I couldn't risk that and become the laughingstock of the neighborhood. "I'm going to stop it before it gets that far. I promise."

Soon after that weekend, things changed. My moms was assigned new hours at work, putting her on back-to-back shifts, which left me at home in the evenings and overnight.

She got in just before it was time for me to go to school. One morning, as I prepared my lunch, she surprised me with some horrible news. "Monique, I asked Mr. Luther to look in on you before he goes to bed."

I stopped dead in my tracks. I started trembling and felt light-headed. I was going to faint. "What? Momma, I don't need—"

"Hush your mouth. It's already done. He's going to start coming by tonight."

"But, Momma . . ." I was taking this chance to try and tell her again about the unspeakable things he'd been doing to me. "Mr. Luther, he—"

"Monique, it's done."

Maybe I should have been more forceful about trying to get her to listen. Maybe life would've been different had I done that.

That night, just as I had nestled into my bed, there was a knock at the door. I figured he'd go away if I didn't answer it. Had he been watching the house to see my bedroom light go out? He rapped at the door again, but this time I heard the lock turn. Moms had given him a key. I lay there in bed, heart pounding and unmoving, as if I'd been asleep for hours. The next thing I knew Mr. Luther was sliding into bed next to me. His dick was hard as steel when he rubbed it against my back. He stroked it up and down the middle of my spine to the tip of my underwear, and then he stopped. His breathing became heavier and his movements more swift. When he shot off, it hit my skin like hot acid. I didn't budge. "Thank you, Li'l Miss Monique," he sighed and walked back out the way he had come.

This went on for weeks, on the days when Moms worked. I'd told Tangie that I wanted to run away, and she told me they'd only find me and make me come home. She offered to let me stay with her and her momma provided that I tell her momma what had been happening. There was no way I was going to do that, so I sucked it up and dealt with it, day in and day out.

On our last day of school, the teachers and staff gave us a dance where we were asked to wear our best. Since it was sweltering outside, the boys didn't have to wear suits, but they did have to wear ties. All of the girls were expected to be in dresses. My grandmother Viola Mae had made me this pink chiffon-and-taffeta sundress with spaghetti straps. It was supposed to be for church, but I convinced her to let me wear it to school first. I had on my first pair of sheer white stockings, and some brand-new Mary Janes that had a silver butterfly on the top of each shoe. Moms knew she wouldn't be home when I got in from school, so she told me to make sure I kept the dress clean for church that coming Sunday.

"Make sure you put it back on the hanger, too, when you take it off," she yelled down the hall as I dressed that morning.

Walking home from school, I decided I wanted a Popsicle from Mr. Chu's, the Korean store on the other side of the railroad tracks. He sold the red, white, and blue firecracker bomb pops that I loved. Tangie had gone straight home because she was leaving to spend the weekend with her father and needed to pack.

Crossing the railroad tracks, I saw there were puddles of mud and oil along my path, so I took a detour through the field. I'd walked through it before and never had a fear of running into a rat or an old dog. Just as I opened my Popsicle, someone grabbed me from behind, covered my mouth, and dragged me through the weeds over rocks and broken glass. Kicking and wrestling with my captor, I realized that my screams were muffled, and no one could hear me. I was pushed face first into the ground and didn't have to try very hard to figure out who was attacking me. I could

smell the incense in his clothes and the liquor on his breath.
It was Mr. Luther trying to snatch the last bit of innocence I
had. I tussled with every ounce of strength a fifteen-year-old
could muster, but he overpowered me, ripping at my underwear and stockings. At one point, Mr. Luther snarled and
growled at me, but I didn't have time to be scared. *I've got to
get away* was the only thought going through my head. His
upper body was lying on my legs while his arms had my
upper torso pinned to the ground. He grabbed my crotch
and rubbed it so hard and rough that it felt as if it were on
fire. Then he thrust his fingers into my vagina and stuck his
thumb in my butthole. *Mmmmph. Mmmmph.* I struggled to
scream but my mouth filled with dirt. He flipped my frail
body over and covered my mouth with one of his hands before I had a chance to call out. With his other hand, Mr.
Luther released his dick and rammed it between my legs.
Noooooo!! My eyes bulged from their sockets as excruciating
pain tore through my body. He wiggled his way deeper into
my private part with no compassion or mercy. I managed to
free one of my hands as he moaned and grunted, and I
reached for a piece of broken glass that was strewn about the
ground. When he lifted himself from me, still erect, I, in one
fierce swing, sliced him across his dick. As he fell to the
ground and rolled to his back, I jabbed him in his balls with
the shard of glass one final time.

Standing in the mirror, I was faced with something I'd
come to know all too well: fear. I was afraid Mr. Luther was
going to come bursting through the door to finish his business, I was afraid I was going to jail, I was afraid my moms
wouldn't love me anymore because I'd done this horrible
thing, and I was afraid someone would know that I'd hurt
Mr. Luther.

I removed my pink dress and placed it back on the

hanger. I hung it in the bathroom with me as a reminder of what hell had been like for me. I turned on the hot water and contemplated whether I should take a bath or a shower. Taking a bath would force me to sit in my filth and allow it to soak further into my soul. I didn't want that.

As the water beat against my back, I watched the blood run down the drain with the dirt and the pain I'd experienced for years. I leaned against the tiled wall and thought about what I had allowed myself to get into. The hairbows, the dresses, the Mary Janes—all of those things made Mr. Luther like me and made him want me. I shed tears for every girl in the neighborhood at that moment. As I observed the suds swirl down the drain, I watched a part of me disappear, too.

I went to the bedroom and packed a bag with jeans, T-shirts, a jacket, and some tennis shoes, then I returned to the bathroom and pulled out a pair of scissors and cut my hair off down to the scalp. I took some wave pomade from the cabinet, spread it in my palms, and rubbed it into what was left of my straight black hair. In the sink was the femininity I was prepared to leave behind. Next to the pomade were two Ace bandages. I took them and wrapped them around my bosom until I was flat. I put a T-shirt on with a pair of jeans and borrowed a pair of Mom's work boots. I returned to the bathroom and revisited myself in the mirror.

In that moment, I'd made up in my mind that I wasn't going to stay around any longer to deal with anything that reminded me of Li'l Miss Monique. I didn't care if that bastard bled to death out there in the field. No more dresses, no more hair bows, and no more Mary Janes—ever.

I snatched up my shit and headed for the back door. Oh by the way, I'm now that niggah they call Mo.

CAUGHT UP

(Part 1)

I fell in love with a woman who didn't belong to me, and I'm ashamed to admit that I wasn't even totally free. I never thought my heart had room for the love of two, but somehow it managed. Nights were tricky because I never knew whose name I'd call in my sleep, and sex? I refrained from it, never knowing whose face I'd want to see when I was in ecstasy. She knew the strengths and weaknesses of my relationship, and she also knew what had hurt me the most in all of my and my lover's years together—something my lover didn't even know.

I wasn't looking for her. It was like one day I looked up, and she was just there. And I must admit it was a beautiful surprise. Soon thereafter, I realized I couldn't live my days without her. My lover became more of a routine, an obligation to me, and I, trying to maintain a decent level of respect for her, heard her when she talked to me, but I wasn't listening. I seemed to always be in a constant daydream and never wanted to be awakened from it. My stomach turned flips when she called my name, and I didn't care who knew it. I found myself often comparing them, weighing my options. Why be with her when I could be with *her*? But then one day, while I watched my lover carefully iron my clothes after she'd run my bath, I knew that, despite this other woman I was sure I loved, I was never leaving home.

1:00 p.m., EST

"May I speak to Tammy, please?"

Morgan and I had been grocery shopping with the kids, and we all were just walking in the house when the phone rang. Saturdays were reserved for quiet family time, and everyone in our circle of friends knew that.

"This is she."

"Hey, this is Liya. How you doing?"

Taken by surprise, I said, "I'm fine. What's up?" She and I had made rules, and the first was to never call in the middle of the day during family time. Although just the sound of her voice was soothing, a rule had been broken, and I wasn't happy.

"Oh, nothing. You busy?"

"We're coming in from the store. That's about it." Morgan and the girls were putting away the food while I took a seat in the family room. I was puzzled by this long-distance call in the middle of the afternoon. Liya and I had limited our conversation to IMs and emails. I'd been honest and very direct from the beginning, telling her I was in a relationship that was steadily approaching the twelve-year mark. Sometimes, though, I felt like it had fallen upon deaf ears. Then there was this call. I sat on the sofa staring into the empty fireplace as she proceeded to make small talk.

"Well, I was only calling to say hello and to see how you were doing. I didn't really want anything."

Hastily, I answered back, "OK." Where I usually had a lot to say in my emails, I had nothing to say over the phone, especially while Morgan was home. "I'm going to have to call you back because I need to help put away the groceries."

"OK, then. No problem." She hung up without even saying good-bye, and I despised that.

Reclining on the sofa, I waited for some hesitation in the kitchen about that strange phone call, but Morgan never said a word.

I'm a musician, and I met Liya at an art exhibit at the Mezza Art Gallery in Detroit during an appearance. After I performed "If I Kissed You," she came over to me and asked for my autograph. I was only there to help out a friend who couldn't make it, offering my services as a saxophonist. I still put out her business cards, though, so people would call her if they were looking for entertainment. I didn't play my music that often and didn't mind filling in for her.

"That was great." Liya smiled as she stuck out a slightly damp napkin and a pen.

"Thank you," I replied. "Who am I making this out to?"

Flashing her pearly whites, she said, "To Liya . . . with love." She picked up one of Belinda's cards.

I nodded, signed the napkin, and handed back the pen. "You have a great evening, Liya." I never thought twice about the encounter.

Two weeks later, I got an email from Liya telling me again how wonderful my performance was. In my return message, I asked how she had gotten my email address, and she said she had gotten it from Belinda. Friends since elementary school, Belinda wasn't about to give out my number to a complete stranger, especially a woman. I sent a return email for no other reason than it was the courteous thing to do. Then, it was as if she was sitting on top of the Send button. I got three more emails from her within the hour. In her last email, she asked if I were in the life because she knew the artist whose showing she attended was. With nothing to hide, I responded yes and later in the same email told her I

had a girlfriend. In her next email, she asked me if I was
happy.

What kind of shit is this? I don't even know this girl, I thought.

Liya relayed to me she was in a relationship as well, but
they were having problems. I shared my compassion with
her because Morgan and I were having problems at the time,
but I didn't elaborate on what those problems were. Despite
those issues, I was happy—or, at least, I was making myself
believe I was.

Morgan and I were introduced through a mutual friend
and subsequently went on a blind date. Highly intelligent,
Morgan's conversation kept me intrigued and yearning for
more. She was, and still is, an attractive woman whose ele-
gance radiated beyond my wildest imagination. And the sex?
The sex was something else.

When I arrived at her house that night for dinner, I had it
on my mind that I was going to make love to her. We'd been
talking on the phone for weeks, and every now and again, I
would say something suggestive. She thought I was being fresh,
but I knew I was being serious as a heart attack. Morgan had
prepared my favorite dinner: steak, mashed potatoes, and broc-
coli. We talked before and all through the meal. As the candlelight flickered against her brilliant skin, I felt my nature rise.

"What's on your mind?" she asked.

"Oh, nothing." I blushed. With my legs crossed to the
right, I shifted them to the left and bounced the ball of my
foot against the carpet. "Dinner is delicious."

"Thanks. I don't cook often, so forgive me if it's—"

"No, no, it's fine. Trust me. It's better than McDonald's or
Wendy's with the kids, for heaven's sakes."

"I bet," she laughed. "So do you enjoy being a mother?"

I had to be honest. "Sometimes."

Morgan rolled her eyes. "What kind of answer is that?"

I needed to clean that up. "What I mean is that I think I

don't do everything I can do for them. My last partner helped with them, but she had her limits."

"Well, I'm going to be truthful. I've never wanted to be with a woman who has kids. It's too much trouble . . . too much drama."

Well, this train ride is over, I thought. In defense of my children, I spoke up, "Well, if you feel that way, then why . . ."

"You didn't let me finish," she smiled. "I'd make an exception for you. I kinda like you."

Emotionally, I was going through some changes, and the last thing I wanted to do was to dump my baggage into someone else's life. "Morgan, look, I'm not ready for a relationship right now. I'm not relationship material."

Pouring me another glass of wine, she responded, "I'll wait for you, and I'll be here when you're ready."

At that moment, I didn't care that she was the soft stud I never wanted to be with, nor did I mind that, for exercise, she chopped trees into logs for firewood. Morgan loved the roar of a Harley, and, despite the fact I detested motorcycles, I'd ride on the back of hers in a black leather body suit any time. She smoked, but, what the hell? That was her and her little red wagon. I wasn't accustomed to what Morgan was offering me, and the only way I could accept it was if I knew how she was in bed. The last thing I wanted was to be tied up with a broad who couldn't fuck.

After dinner, we opted to sit on the sofa. I plopped my ass down right next to her—almost broke her shoulder off actually. A little tipsy, I nestled up against her like a kitten to its mother, taking in her sultry fragrance. Morgan softly pecked me on the forehead and rested her check against my head.

"So what are we going to do next?" I questioned. I was ready for this soft, studly female to lay it to me.

"Whatever you want. You're a guest in my home, and I'm treating you as that."

Please keep in mind that Morgan and I hadn't even kissed yet. My underwear was soaked. "We've been talking on the phone it seems like forever, and you're treating me like a damn guest? Can I at least have a kiss?"

Morgan chuckled, "I guess so." She leaned over and kissed me on the lips. Our exchange lasted a couple of minutes, and, I was too through. The cigarette smell took a second to get used to, but, overall, I was impressed. My pussy was popping fireballs.

"That kiss was great, Morgan." I didn't want to seem pushy, but . . . "I want you, and I want you now." She led me into the bedroom and slowly started taking off her clothes. This woman, in fact, took the time to neatly fold her clothes and lay them in the chair next to the bed. *Okayy*, I thought. And then there she was standing in front of me . . . naked. I snatched my shoes off and threw them in a corner. I pulled and yanked at my clothes until I got them off. Morgan watched me the entire time. *Wow, she's waiting for me to sprawl my voluptuous body against her sheets.* I turned my back for only a second, and the next thing I knew, Morgan had stretched her ass on her back across the bed. *Noooooooooooooo! A pillow princess?*

The first several months together were a bit difficult because, in my previous relationship, I'd been subjected to a great deal of emotional abuse and didn't trust anyone with my feelings. Morgan understood when I broke up furniture and pictures in the apartment, and she even took it in stride when I lashed out at her. Through all of my horrid tantrums, Morgan stuck with me and made herself one hundred percent available to me and my children. Since it appeared that she'd rescued me from myself, my parents adored her for being my savior.

Over the years, however, the roles in the house reversed, and I became the provider, and Morgan stayed at home. I paid the mortgage and the bills, bought the food, and bought clothes for everyone. I didn't have a problem with it. In bed, she was still the pillow princess, and I'd grown used to handling business. Whenever we did do something different in the sack, it lasted for only for that moment. It was easy to have sex without excitement because I loved her with all my heart. In our home, everything was so routine and so predictable that I'd grown bored with the house, the kids, and her. This distraction with Liya was welcomed.

Liya asked me for my address at work, so she could send me a little token of her thoughtfulness. I gave it to her, but I also gave her my address at home. Within three days, I started getting package after package, card after card—at both places. The things I got at work were easy to hide because all I had to do was to not bring them home. I felt, however, that my twelve-year relationship was solid, and the gifts would be harmless. One afternoon, I arrived home and saw that Morgan had gotten the mail before me. My mail—this assortment of greeting cards all sent separately—was waiting for me on the counter. I gathered the cards and went into the bathroom and shut the door. My lover never said a mumbling word.

I was in love with Liya. The attention continued, and I was overwhelmed by it. I got to the point where I expected something in the mail every day, and there always was. I was smitten with this woman and her way of wooing me away from home. I'd stopped helping the kids with their homework; I didn't talk to them, or to Morgan, for that matter. The more I talked with Liya, the more I wanted to share with her. I told her the things that hurt me: things my lover had intentionally or unintentionally done. I discussed with her Morgan's faults, and my reluctance to correct them. Liya, to me, seemed almost perfect. There were things about her, though, that made me glad I was in a relationship, but there were other things that made me wish I was with her.

For instance, she was a big flirt. In one breath, she'd tell me about a girl she'd met on the street and how they'd exchanged numbers, yet, in the next breath, she talked about sharing a life with me and my kids. Like Morgan, she promised to love them as if they were her own.

Something else that bothered me about her was that sending stuff to the house crap. That was mean. I'd told her Morgan rarely gave me cards, and, without missing a beat, Liya's cards almost tripled. I'd given her permission to send me things, don't get me wrong, but I began to see that she was deliberately trying to hurt my lover. She brought enough excitement for me to think twice about my life with Morgan and the kids. I, however, wondered what was wrong with having everything—Morgan, the kids, and Liya.

We talked on the phone fifteen hours a day, and I dreamed of her at night with our bodies embraced. I was infatuated with the idea of knowing her and being near her. I didn't need to touch her; I simply needed to know she'd always be there to calm my soul and spirit. Quietly, part of me was ashamed, but the other part of me was jubilant, rejoicing in this new love affair. It had completely slipped my mind that Liya had a girlfriend.

In yet another email, Liya inquired again about my happiness with Morgan, and I reflected a moment before answering. YES, I'M HAPPY, I wrote.

Her reply was, YOU'RE LYING. IF YOU WERE HAPPY, THEN YOU WOULDN'T BE MAKING TIME FOR CONVERSATION WITH ME. She had a point, and I did think it was a valid one. Liya wanted me to leave Morgan and move to Phoenix to be with her. I was tired of sneaking around, and I was convinced Morgan didn't know a thing.

But then, without warning, things starting going awry at home.

NATASHA

Fierce is what I call her. Body like a Coke bottle. Skin smooth as butter. Smile as bright as the diamond we call ice. She wore jewels that sparkled and glistened with her every movement. As she articulated her purpose to the rest of the room during orientation, I fantasized about making love to her. I envisioned a time and a place where neither of us knew boundaries. From the moment I first saw her, I knew something was wrong with me. My gaze followed her around the room like she was the mouse's cursor on my computer screen. I'd never seen grace like that . . . all in one person . . . all at one time.

Whenever her eyes met mine, I smiled and continued taking notes. Nothing I wrote reflected her words. Instead, my doodling made my feelings known. The cute little hearts that dotted my I's, and the smiley faces around her name told it all. I was in love with my boss.

"Natasha?"

She's calling my name. I'm breathless. Looking up from my pad and hoping to hide my sly grin, I responded, "Yes, Meredith?" I felt like I was going to pee.

"Would you mind—" she smiled—"coming up here to explain this organizational chart to the group? You do such a wonderful job at it."

How was I going to say no with this roomful of people looking at me? As I pulled the top sheet from my writing pad, balled it up, and put it in my pocket, I said, "Sure." When I got to the podium, Meredith was still smiling at me as if she'd been standing over me the entire time I'd been "taking notes." I took the pointer from her and proceeded to do the job the company paid me $76,000 a year to do.

After the orientation, I went to my office and fell apart. I couldn't understand why my heart was so full of affection for this woman. First, I'd sworn my heart to God that I'd fight these feelings if they ever came around again. It was wrong for me to lust after the flesh of a woman. The last time I was with a woman—a one-night stand I'd met at a bar—I almost lost my cool when, as I was lying there with her riding the passion between my legs and with my eyes closed and poised to express my pleasure at any moment, I opened my eyes to her gold crucifix pendant dangling above my forehead.

With my hands wrapped around her breasts, I stopped. I stopped everything. Tears rolled from eyes, and I asked her to please get up. In awe—because she was about to cum so hard that I believe the heavens would've opened up for both of us—she removed herself from me and asked what was wrong. In my shame and frustration, I lied telling her that I'd felt a pain shoot through my chest and needed to take a break.

We sat up in the bed and talked for hours; we never went back at it again. As the sun rose, we traveled to IHOP to get some breakfast, and then I took her home. For a while she called every week just to check on me. But after a few months, she stopped. I guess she got tired of hearing me stress about the fact that God sees everything. Sad, though, I wonder if He can see how miserable I am.

Later that night, after my aerobics class, I decided to stop by my office to pick up some papers and a file I needed. As the elevator approached the ninth floor, I could hear music. The cleaning crew had already left for the evening, so I knew they weren't around playing music that loud. It was Regina Carter I heard, the sistah who's the violinist. *Who the hell?* Instead of being nosy, I continued to my office because I didn't want anyone to see me in my workout clothes with my hair shot to hell.

A few minutes later, I heard a woman yelling at the top of her lungs. Since no other voices were audible, I assumed she was on the phone. "You know what? We're done! This is over! Don't call me for shit! And don't bother coming by the house to pick up your things. I'll get them to you!"

I listened closer to decipher the voice through the anger and the music. It was Meredith, and she was hot. *Oh, shit. Let me grab my stuff and get out of here.* I wanted so badly to stick my head in her door and ask if everything were OK, but I didn't. Instead, I walked to the elevator and pushed the button. Pacing, I hoped it would hurry up. Just as I stepped into the elevator and pressed the down button, I realized I'd left my car keys on my desk. *Shit.* Catching the elevator door before it closed, I stepped out and walked down the hallway. That's when I heard the music stop. *Fuck.* I broke into a soft trot on my toes and made it to my office. Trying to grab my keys in one swift movement, I dropped them. Almost instantly, Meredith called out, "Is someone there?" She didn't sound scared or panicked.

Damn. "It's me, Meredith. I . . ." Before I could finish my sentence, she was standing in front of me, beautiful as ever. "Wow, you got over here quick."

"Girl, don't play. I saw the elevator close just as I was coming out of the ladies' room, but I didn't know it was you."

Grinning as she leaned against the door, she continued, "What's up with the hair?"

Busted. "Tonight is aerobics night, and for some reason, I'm not tired, so, I came by here to pick up a few papers." I tried not to look at her because, if I did, my thoughts would show. *Even in the night, she's still gorgeous.* "After aerobics, I went for a swim and then sat in the sauna for a few minutes."

Folding her arms as she shifted to the other side of the doorway, Meredith commented, "You seem a little worked up. Are you stressed out about something?"

You think? I refused to lie. "Yeah, I got a few things on my mind." *I'm in love with you. I can't sleep. I can't eat. I can't do anything but work out like a madwoman because I can't even fuck to relieve the stress.*

"Oh, I'm sorry to hear that. Is there anything I can do?"

You can take me in your arms and stick your tongue down my throat while I finger you and . . . "No, I'm fine. Whatever it is will pass." With my keys in my hand, I had what I'd come for, so it was time to jet. "You know, it's getting late, and I need to head home. Come to think of it, why are you still here?"

Dressed in the same suit I'd seen her in earlier, Meredith confessed, "Girl, I'm a workaholic. I had two reports to finish, and evaluations start tomorrow."

Shocked, I answered, "Oh, really? It seems like we just had those last month."

"No, it's that time again. Speaking of which, you want to go ahead and talk about yours now?"

This is weird. "Well, I . . ."

"Trust me, it's not bad," she chuckled.

"OK. Make it quick because *Good Times* comes on in an hour."

Meredith stepped inside the doorway and jumped right to the point. "You've been doing a fabulous job around here, and I was wondering how you felt about becoming an assistant director. There's a twenty-thousand-dollar raise involved, and you'd get a new nameplate along with a couple of other perks."

You're forgetting to mention a bigger office, particularly the one that's closest to you. "I see," I responded. "I don't know, Meredith. Aren't there some other people who should be considered first? After all, they've been here longer."

"Maybe, but I don't like them. You've got what we need to move forward—personality, zest, ambition . . . looks." She smiled.

I couldn't turn that down. Single and making almost a hundred thousand a year? I'd be a fool. But when was she going to mention the office?

Meredith glanced down at her watch and noticed the time. "Shoot, it's late. Let me get out of here so you can be on your way. Think about what I said. I don't need an answer right away." As she turned out the door, she stopped suddenly, pausing to think. Then she looked back at me. "You know, I forgot to mention the office. You'd be moving down the hall in the one next to me. But you don't strike me to be the type who likes to be up under people, so it's up to you." With that, she proceeded down the hall headed back to her office.

I'd love to be closer to you and that amazing perfume you wear. I want to be next to you, so I can stand against the wall and fantasize about you being between it and me. I want to be able to see you and watch you when you work. I . . . I broke into a sprint to catch up with her. She was just beyond the elevators. "Meredith, I'll take the promotion, but I'd prefer to keep the office I'm in. I like being able to look out at the water."

Her countenance seemed to drop as she simply replied, "OK."

Pushing the elevator button, I watched her stroll down the hallway and thought, *What have I done?*

When I found out I had to go to Atlanta for a business meeting six months after my promotion, I was pissed off. I was going to miss the biggest football game of the year and the huge after party that Elaine, my crazy beautician, always throws. Allen, the other assistant director who was supposed to be going, canceled at the last minute—the very last minute—and I knew his ass only did that so he could see the game with his boys. I hadn't traveled by plane since before 9/11 and was sick as a dog. Every person with skin the same color as mine, but with straighter hair, was stopped at the security checkpoint. Some were damn near stripped down to their underwear. The only problem I had was that I'd decided to wear my Timberlands and had to take them off. Thank God, I'd put deodorant powder in them. "Ma'am, can we see your bag?"

I couldn't argue with the four of them—with their guns and badges. I gave them the bag, and, after dumping all my tampons, pads, and condoms on the counter, they found my nail clippers underneath the cardboard thing that gives the bottom of the bag its shape. I didn't even know they were down there. It wasn't like I was going to slice somebody's throat with nail clippers, but I understood the precautions. I, in my jeans, T-shirt, and baseball cap, stopped at Starbucks for a strawberry frappucino and a muffin before looking around the terminal to find my gate.

Oh my God. She looked like a dream to me. A dream where she and I were enveloped in each other's bodies . . . wet with sweat and sex. She . . . "Meredith?" I said, juggling my muffin, drink, and saddlebag.

Startled by my appearance, she realized it was me. "Hey,

you. Let me help you with that." She took my bag and placed it by her leg.

Blushing, I sat down, leaving the chair between us empty. *I'd melt if I had to sit that close to you.* "What are you doing here?"

"Duh, I'm going to Atlanta, silly. Didn't Allen tell you?"

"Uh, no, he didn't."

"My bad then. I thought he told you I was going. He canceled at the last minute, claiming his wife needed emergency surgery on her knee. I'm not stupid. I know he wanted to see the game between Georgia and UT. He's running the office pool, and I heard he's got major money in it. All I know is that his wife better have a serious limp and a big-ass bandage on her knee when I see her at the company family picnic next weekend."

I'm not pissed anymore . . . just stunned. I can't believe this.

"Actually, I don't mind going. Gives me a chance for a change of scenery." *Liar.* I sat there like a damn rock. I couldn't move. She was rambling on about us boarding the plane because it seemed that the gate attendants were running behind. In my mind, I was wondering how I was going to be able to get away to enjoy the "atmosphere." While in line at Starbucks, I'd glanced over the shoulder of the lady in front of me and had seen in the *Atlanta-Journal Constitution* where Black Gay Pride was this weekend. I figured I'd hit a Girls In The Night party, which was always the bomb, and maybe catch a movie or something. But there was no way I was going to be able to get away now.

The secretaries always booked first-class seats for management, so when our seats were called first, I immediately jumped up. Then I paused for Meredith to gather her belongings. When she bent over, I watched her and imagined the thrust of my dick into her doggy style. We walked up the jet way and on to the plane. I glanced at my ticket and realized I had a window seat. *Good.* Seeing Charlotte, North Carolina, from the air was going to be nice. "I hate the window seats," Meredith said, breaking my train of thought. "Makes my stomach bubbly. I have the aisle seat."

We're on the same row? "Um, you were going to be sitting right next to Allen? I can't imagine that because he's got a bit of a breath problem."

Meredith burst into laughter. "I thought it was just me. My plan was to have a pack of gum, some Altoids, or something for him. I wanted to go over the agenda for this meeting," she said, taking her seat . . . right next to me. I put my bag underneath my seat and sighed. My nerves were starting to get to me because they had closed the doors, and the plane was preparing to taxi the runway. Closing my eyes, I prayed to God that we take off and land OK. I opened my eyes to find Meredith staring at me.

"Don't like to fly, huh?"

"Nope. I hate it."

"You'll be fine. The flight's not even half an hour."

My knee started shaking, and my palms were sweating. "I know." As the plane lifted from the runway, Meredith grabbed my left hand, stroking it like the fur on a kitten. I was terrified, but the terror turned to joy as I creamed in the seat of my pants from her touch. I will never be afraid to fly again.

Atlanta was popping. Women were everywhere. Because I'd fallen in love with the Heavenly Bed at the Westin, that's where I insisted I have my room even though it wasn't one of the recommended hotels on our list. When the airport shuttle arrived at the hotel, there were at least a hundred women just hanging out along the curbside. All I could do was smile. Meredith, looking through the shuttle's window, seemed to be amazed by the number of women standing around. "I wonder what's going on here."

The shuttle driver chimed in, "Oh, it's the Atlanta Black Pride celebration. This is one of the host hotels, so most of the women are staying here."

Never changing her facial expression, Meredith replied, "Oh, OK. Sounds interesting."

As I tipped the driver, I could see Meredith out of the corner of my eye, watching my every move. *I wish she'd stop.* "Meredith, would you like to meet for cocktails and dinner later?"

Meredith had this expression that let me know she wasn't feeling the atmosphere. "Um, Natasha, are you sure you want to stay here this weekend? It doesn't seem like it's going to be all that quiet. I mean, couldn't you try to see if the recommended hotels still have vacancies?"

Hell, no. "I . . ."

The shuttle driver chimed in again, "It's usually a pretty good group. Never had any problems. They seem to mind their business, and outside of an occasional not-knowing-if-it's-a-boy-or-girl, the guests haven't been complaining. Besides, every hotel in the city is booked."

To hell with that. What about my dinner invite? "Meredith, I'll be fine. Now, what about dinner?" I asked as the bellhop loaded my bags on the luggage rack.

"Oh, I'm sorry. We can definitely do that. Let me get checked in, and I'll give you a call."

"OK. I'll chat with you later then."

Passing through the lobby, I couldn't believe my eyes. There were little ones, big ones, short ones, tall ones, light ones, dark ones, brown ones, and a few White ones. Some had locks, others had braids, a few wore it straight, and a couple had none at all. I knew I'd died and gone to heaven with all these beautiful women surrounding me. Pressing the elevator button, I kept reminding myself that I was there on business and didn't need any distractions. When the doors opened, the ladies poured into the lobby like milk into a kitten's bowl. *Well, maybe one teeny-tiny distraction wouldn't hurt.* We stopped on almost every floor between five and twenty, and with each stop, a different flavor of woman got on the elevator. This one chick was standing in front of me, and her hair smelled so damn good that I found myself taking deep breaths and filling my senses with her presence. I opened my eyes and saw the bellhop staring at me. *Shit, I don't care about you peeping my cards. Besides, how come there aren't any female bellhops?*

My room was the shit. With the Westin being like this huge cylinder in the sky, the room was in a curve. I'd asked for double beds, so I could dump my junk on one of them. I've never been one for organization. The Atlanta skyline was like a live mural, for the beds were placed, not against the wall, but against the window. With down comforters and pillows adorning each bed, I walked between them and admired the view. It was absolutely breathtaking.

Fifty-five floors above the world, I gazed out across the skyline and could see every mountain for miles. It was beauty I couldn't put into words, much like the emotions that I experienced whenever I thought about Meredith. Fantasizing about her, my hands began to tremble, and I broke into a cold sweat. My limp dick stood erect, and my nipples protruded through my T-shirt. I imagined her kisses falling upon my lips, and directed by passion, they rested upon my chest. *Oh, God, why do you let me feel this way? Knowing that I can't have her, knowing I can't touch her, knowing that I need her.*

In my fantasy I was standing close enough to touch her breath, but in my reality, I was standing pressed against a window yearning for something that should not be. My fingers tightly gripped my pleasure and my desire melted away. After exiting my "moment," I looked at and touched the moisture I'd inflicted upon the glass. I gathered my composure and began to undress. I needed a shower. A cold one.

Just as I passed the bed strewn with all of my clothes, the phone rang. "Hello."

"Natasha, this is Meredith." She seemed slightly panicked.

"What's wrong?"

"There are men everywhere over here, and they're all over each other! And I mean like really *all over* each other."

Laughing to myself because I knew why there were men everywhere, I responded, "Well, what are you going to do? You heard the shuttle driver say there weren't any more rooms in town."

She paused before answering. "I was wondering if I could stay with you."

Shit. I got the double beds for my bags in case I went shopping. Never had I thought I'd be sharing a room with Meredith. What the fuck was I going to do? With the way I felt about her, I had no business with her that close to me. But . . . it would give me a chance to maybe catch a glimpse of her while she was naked.

Privately, I thanked Tina Turner and Oprah Winfrey because my wildest dream was about to come true. Maybe Meredith would let me make love to her. If she wanted to walk away afterward, then I would be fine with that. "Sure, you can stay here. I'm in Room 5524."

"OK. Thank you, sweetie. I'll be there in about fifteen minutes." *Damn, she called me sweetie.*

I got a towel from the bathroom and wiped off the window. Rushing to clear the bed, I realized that an opportunity had presented itself, and I had to think about what I was going to do with it. I sat on the bed to ponder my options. *There are a lot of different ways I can play this, but whatever I choose needs to be what feels right. Meredith has to know I have feel-*

ings for her. But she isn't gay, and she doesn't even know that I am. I'm going to let my heart guide me from this point forward.

With the brisk water pounding against my skin, I drenched my sexual excitement and replaced it with calmness. *Am I going to fake who I am for the rest of the weekend?* I saturated my face with soap, cleansing it with the lily-white washcloth until it tingled. Then using the washcloth, I scrubbed my pussy until it burned. Stepping out of the shower, I grabbed my towel and dried myself all over. I sprayed a hint of eucalyptus oil behind each ear and swept it across my shoulders. I wrapped my lower body in a fresh, dry towel and watched my fluid movements in the mirror.

I see myself as a lesbian who has yet to fully come to grips with her sexuality, and the only way I've been able to deal with it thus far is through my secret sensuality. I'm not ashamed of my reflection but I am curious as to how to chisel away at the boulder called Meredith that rests inside. I have this passion for her that borders along the lines of lust. I wanted to penetrate her. I wanted to fuck her.

As I looked into my own eyes, I searched for an end to my desires, but I kept coming up short. As I heard Meredith's faint knocks at the door, I knew what I was going to do.

"Girl," Meredith started as she rushed into the room ahead of the bellhop and dropped her purse on the desk. "I'm so sorry to barge in on you like this. I appreciate you helping me out."

Closing the door after tipping the bellman, I got the sensation that everything was going to be OK. I knew for certain that I didn't want to go through the weekend faking it. Therefore, telling the truth was my only recourse. "Meredith, before you get too comfortable, I want to talk to you about something."

Puzzled, Meredith, took a seat in the chair at the desk, and asked, "What's wrong?"

"Meredith, I'm gay, and I think you should know that before you stay here this weekend."

I was expecting her to flip, but she didn't. For several seconds, she didn't say anything. Then, with her eyes fixated on me, she said, "I know."

That blew me the fuck away. How the hell did she know? I hadn't done anything to give it away. "You know?"

"Yep, and guess what?"

"What?" I asked with a bit of a frown.

"You're in love with me."

My insides screamed, *Busted.* But outwardly I laughed while calmly asking, "What makes you think that?"

Meredith sat back in the chair. "I was in love with my boss once. Her name was Nina."

What? "So, are you telling me that . . . ?"

She had this look on her face I'll never forget before she answered me. "Yes, I'm telling you what you think I'm telling you."

"And not wanting to be at the Sheraton was a front?"

"Oh, hell no. I don't like all that show-and-tell shit. I really didn't want to be over there with that. While I was in the cab, I was trying to figure out how I was going to tell you. I had a vibe about you. You know you know your folks, right?"

"Well, yeah, but I could never get a good read on you. You cover yourself very well."

"It's not a cover. I'm just being me. I like to run shit, and that's probably why I'm by myself now. By the way," she said, laughing. "One of your little sticky love notes was attached to your report last month. I thought it was cute."

"Oh, my God. I'm so embarrassed."

"Don't be. I was flattered. I do need to let you know that I refrain from mixing business with pleasure."

To me, that meant we weren't going to fuck. I was heartbroken. "I can understand that."

The entire weekend was spent working. After Saturday's sessions, I needed to unwind and decided to check out the Girls In The Night party in one of the ballrooms downstairs. Meredith, sitting on the sofa reading a novel, was cutting her eyes at me over the top of her book. A couple of times I know she caught me naked. "Who's going to be at the party?"

"Da Brat is performing."

"Really?"

"Yes. I think I'll get a drink or two and catch the show. She probably won't even take the stage until about two."

"I see." Meredith put down her book and continued watching me get dressed. "You know one thing I love?"

"What's that?" I asked as I was putting on my blouse.

"Watching a woman get dressed turns me on."

I can't believe she said that.

I wasn't wearing anything special to the party: some jeans, a casual blouse, and some sandals. "Oh, really. That's interesting." *This is my moment, and I'm taking it.* "So, Meredith . . ."

"Yes."

"Let's do a hypothetical here."

Intrigued, she responded, "OK."

"If I were to come over to you right now and blow in your ear, would you jump my bones? I mean since you're horny and all."

"Natasha."

I loved it when she called my name. Da Brat might just have to wait. I took a seat on the bed. "Yes, ma'am?"

"Bring your ass over here, and blow in my ear. I want to fuck."

"No," I replied. *What the fuck are you doing?*

"Excuse me?"

"That's a turnoff for me. I don't like demands. Sex should be sensual and not full of commands."

Meredith sighed and offered an apology. "I'm sorry. I'm doing it again. This is exactly what Donna, my ex, was talking about." She started crying.

Shit. I got up from the bed and walked over to the sofa. The view from outside was perfect. I sat next to her and took her hand in mine. "Meredith, you don't have to cry. I'm sorry if I hurt your feelings, but there's no need to be so hard with me."

She looked at me with a yearning that mirrored my feelings. *If I kiss her, to hell with the not mixing business with pleasure theory. I'm going to rock her world.* Meredith closed her eyes and leaned in to kiss me, and, with my heart pounding against my chest, I kissed her back.

The sex was incredible. We fucked all that night and into the wee hours of Sunday morning. The only break we took was to go to the adult toy store on Peachtree to purchase a dildo. When we got back to the room, I soaked it in hot water and alcohol. Then I dug through my bag for a condom, and, before strapping it on, I checked to make sure this was really what Meredith wanted to do. Her comment was, "Only if I get to do you, too."

Once back at work, our lives took a different turn. My position was more demanding than I anticipated, and Meredith, the control freak that everybody could love or hate, found it difficult to work with me and then go home and fuck me. I, in fact, enjoyed it. We moaned together; we climaxed together. Whatever I did to her, she did to me in return.

During the day at work, we never exchanged looks, making it a point to keep our schedules separate. I would see her at lunchtime, watching her thighs crossed in those hot miniskirts she loved to wear. It drove me wild as shit. I didn't need to whisper to myself anymore because I was free to tell her whatever was on my heart. In spite of all this, our days together were difficult. I had no problem working through them with ease, anticipating being with Meredith when I got home. However, I could tell it unnerved her not being able to openly love me, to break her personal rule of mixing business with pleasure. Work wasn't what it used to be for her, and the fire she once had for it was gone. Her world had slowly evolved into mine.

"I'd do anything for you, Natasha, even it means quitting my job. I love you just that much," she told me after a night of emotional lovemaking.

Six months into our intense relationship, I got the shock of my life. Meredith and I were in love. Every breath I took was because of her, and it was evident she felt the same way. We'd do anything for each other. While sitting in our usual Monday morning staff meeting, Allen got up to close the door at three minutes after nine. "Aren't you going to wait for Meredith?" I asked curiously. His ass could be spiteful sometimes.

"Didn't you get the memo? Meredith resigned this morning, effective immediately."

Leaving at that very moment would let everyone know Meredith and I had some kind of connection. I'd talked to her right before the meeting, and she never said a word about any of this. I knew she said she'd do anything for me, but did that include something of this magnitude? The main thing she never wanted was for anyone to know about the two of us. I didn't have a problem with that, but with things being so heavy between us, someone was bound to find out. Hell, I didn't care. I wanted all these tight-assed corporate freaks to know that I was boning Meredith, and she loved every fucking minute of it.

When the meeting ended, I dashed to my office, picked up my cell phone, and hurried to the parking lot to sit in the car. Soon as I turned the phone on, it vibrated indicating I had a message. "I know you're going to want to talk to me, so give me a call in the car."

I dialed her car phone number as quick as my fingers would let me.

"Hello," she answered.

Making sure the windows were rolled up, I asked, "What the hell is going on? You quit?"

"Yes, I did," she chuckled, but her tone hastily became more subdued. "I did it for us."

I wasn't sure how I was supposed to be feeling but I did know that I've never loved a woman the way I love her. Fierce is what I called her. Body like a Coke bottle. Skin smooth as butter. Smile as bright as the diamond we call ice. She wore jewels that sparkled and glistened with her every movement. I once envisioned a time and a place where neither of us knew boundaries, and now we are there. From the moment I first saw her, I knew my love was real.

DOM AND DOMMER

Katrice was cute. She was what femmes call a pretty tom-boy. Her silky, creamlike shell covered mountains of muscles on her arms, her thighs, and her calves. There wasn't an inch of fat on her stomach. Her cornrows extended from the front to the back, and the tips of each braid touched right under her shoulders. She had enough ass to just fill the seat of her pants, but for me, that didn't even matter. Oh my God, she was so cute!

Every Friday night at the club I made sure I was dressed my best, hoping she'd ask me to dance. Couldn't walk around smelling like I'd been shoveling shit all day. I wasn't feeling the dude's cologne, so I splashed on CK One. Nobody seemed to wear that anymore. That's why I claimed it as my official "chick juice." And the ladies loved it. I always wore my Timbs, some nicely starched jeans, and a new flannel shirt. Precious had braided my hair just like always. Don't nobody even know that we used to kick it in the twelfth grade. If she was into girls now, she probably coulda been my baby's momma. Instead, she chose some no-count niggah who just got out of the penitentiary. But we cool, though, and it's all gravy. I help her out with her kids when I can, and she takes care of my hair for me when I need her to.

When it comes to describing me, most fish call me dom because of the way I wear my hair and my clothes sometimes. They ain't never seen me when I get all dressed up for church, though. My mama would kill me if I fell up in the Lord's house with pants and braids, and I ain't missed a Sunday since I was born. Mama always says she doesn't care what I do during the week just as long as I'm in church on Sunday, and if I ain't home from the night before, I'd better take my Sunday clothes with me and meet her in Sunday school, or there'll be hell to pay. I try not to make her mad because when she's mad a lot of mean shit comes out of her mouth. Those are the only times that I'm a lesbian or bull-dagger. Otherwise, I'm just her baby girl.

My mama would straight-up trip if she ever saw how I stepped to a woman when I was trying to holla at her. I don't think she'd be surprised because my dad was a playa, and, even though he never had any sons, he left a legacy. I ain't never had a woman tell me no. I've been getting pussy since I was five and ain't never thought twice about it. During the first ten years or so of my life, Dad knew I was into women, but he never said anything about it. In my late teen years, I'd confided in him about this girl named Shalinda. He knew how tough I was feeling her. "Don't get no woman that ain't gonna get up and fix you something to eat when you hungry." He also encouraged me to never forget I was a lady and demand to be treated like one. "Treat them like you want to be treated," he said to me right before he went into the operating room. I wasn't expecting to hear the doctor tell my mama that Dad didn't make it through surgery. I had so many questions for him. *Do I hold her hand in public? Do I pull her chair out for her? Do I kiss her when everybody's looking?*

Anyway, I took Shalinda to his funeral, and, at the repast, I told her I wanted us to take it slow because I didn't want to make any mistakes. I bought her shit and took her out damn near every night. My peeps was always tryin' to tell me what to do and how to treat her, but I wanted to do this thang on my time. I don't know. One day she just packed up and moved to Chicago with this woman who'd bought her a ring after only one kiss. I guess I was moving too slow for her.

But Katrice, man, had me wildin'. I finally got the nerve to walk over to her one night at Faces and found myself at a loss for words. She had on a Louis Vuitton baseball cap with a L.A. Sparks jersey covering a white T-shirt. Yeah, a little tacky, but I didn't care. Surprisingly, she spoke first.

" 'Bout time."

Shocked, my mouth fell open. "What?"

She flashed those pearly whites and repeated herself. "'Bout time you came over here."

"What you mean?"

"Don't even play. The whole club knows you been sweatin' me. We just wanted to see how long it was going to take you to come over. What's it been? Three? Four months now?"

Damn, I was busted, but I wasn't about to lose this chance. "OK, well then, I guess I should skip the dumb shit. My name's Asia. Wanna dance?"

The deejay played reggae, hip-hop, rap, techno, all that shit, and we danced to all of them. Katrice is five-eight, and I'm five-ten. She's tall enough to rest her head on my shoulder. I've danced with a lot of women, and this is the only one that I actually wanted to touch me. Usually, I stand just close enough to exchange body heat because I've never been one for folks being all up in my space. But Katrice was different. I wanted her in my space. I wanted her next to me. I wanted her inside me. For some reason, embracing her wasn't enough. I wanted to feel her pressed up against me—tit to tit, crotch to crotch. I was sweating so tough that my braids were sticking to the back of my neck. My clothes were soaking wet, and so were hers. I didn't care, you know. I felt as one with this girl. Our bodies swayed in sync with each other until the music stopped.

It was 3:00 A.M., and we both agreed that breakfast was a good idea. I didn't want her out of my sight. By now, I was wearing her baseball cap and was truly feeling her vibe. I ordered the All-American breakfast that came with almost everything Waffle House had on the menu—grits, hash browns, eggs, toast, sausage, bacon, and a waffle. I was trippin' because Katrice ordered the same thing . . . a woman after my own heart.

Halfway through breakfast, Katrice skipped the B.S. and went straight for the jugular. "So why you been stalking me all this time?"

I choked on my milk and sent streams of it pouring down the sides of my mouth. I gave a hearty laugh like my dad used to whenever he was talking to Mama and was trying to impress her like he did when they were teenagers. "'Cuz I like you. I mean, I been feelin' you since the first time I saw you."

Sliding her fork from between her teeth, Katrice replied, "Are you femme or dom?"

I hated that question. "Man, I'm Asia." I despised the question because I never knew how I was supposed to answer. "I mean, I like the ladies. Don't get me wrong. Because of my mama, I know I'm a girl on Sundays, and that gives me a chance to keep my shit in check. She makes me wear a dress and get my hair done. Most times, though, I don't get into all that femme . . . stud junk."

Katrice smiled as she reached for her orange juice. Then she responded, "Me neither. I'm just me."

The way I felt about Katrice was that she rolled either way.

She sure as hell was dressed like a tomboy, but she carried herself like a lady. "That's good. You know, why can't women love each other without role-playin'?"

"What you gettin' at?"

"It's like my dad, right, he told me to treat a lady like I want to be treated and to expect the same from her. But yet, we played pool and shot hoops together. He never had a son, so he mainly worked with what he had."

"Ain't nuthin' wrong with that. It's called mutual respect," she said, sitting there chewing on her straw.

"A'ight then. So you don't mind bein' treated like a lady?"

"Asia, do your thang, OK? I'm cool."

I tossed three dollars on the table and picked up the check. I got up from the booth and stood, like a gentleman, extending my hand to help Katrice from her seat. She slid out and never noticed it. When we got to the cashier, Katrice fumbled in her pocket for some money as I was doing the same. "I got it," I said, reaching for my billfold in my back pocket.

"Naw, let me. You bought drinks all night."

"So. I don't let no woman pay my way." I thumbed through the bills in my billfold and flung a twenty on the counter. Katrice reached past me to get a toothpick, and I took one as well. Getting out the door was a trip. I rushed to open it for her, but I didn't see her. Next thing I knew she was standing at the other door holding it open for me. I'm stubborn, and I stood my ground, but so did she. I eventually had to give in.

"After all, you paid for breakfast. The least you could do is let me open the daggone door for you," she said, rolling her eyes at me. As we approached the car, Katrice shot ahead and opened the driver's side door for me after she heard the alarm disarm. I guess I could get used to that. We both sat there, right in the Waffle House parking lot, talking and picking our teeth for hours.

* * *

No matter how much time I spent with Katrice, I felt like I could never get enough of her being in my space. Her smile was infectious, and I have to admit I was diseased with every bit of her. Every Friday night we went to the club and danced like there was no tomorrow. She knew that my favorite drink was Heineken, and, when the bartender saw me approaching, she knew to start pouring the orange juice and the Peach Schnapps because I was coming to get it for my baby.

One Saturday night I got up the nerve to ask her to go to church with me. For real, though, I was expecting her to turn me down, but I was mistaken. I had to explain to her that we couldn't show up all pimped out like we usually do. My mama would have a fit. Katrice kindly agreed to respect Mama and do what was right.

When I got to her house to pick her up, my girl looked like she could do that thang on the catwalk. I was speechless.

"Damn, you act like you ain't neva seen a woman in a dress before," she smiled.

She could have very well said the same thing about me. "Well, it ain't that. I just neva thought you'd be like Christmas morning in a dress." Never had it crossed my mind to say some shit like that, but all I was doing was telling the truth. That was one morning where I wanted to look like a playa straight outta *GQ* because Katrice was fine as hell in that dress, and I wanted everyone to know that she was with me. I played it cool when we was around my mama because she hated shit thrown in her face, and she really wasn't feeling everybody being all up in her business. During the service, I'd drop my hand between me and Katrice then slid it up under her thigh. And she was accommodating by raising that ass up just enough for me to do it.

Katrice took me to see Prince while he was in town, and the concert was da bomb. Afterward, we hit our favorite spot, the Waffle House, and talked until they almost had to put us out. She didn't like the hoity-toity restaurants, and I wasn't feeling them either. So I ain't neva had to worry about trying to impress somebody who didn't want to be impressed.

After three months, it started to get to me. My little friend down *there* began to remind me that I hadn't hit it yet. Don't get me wrong. I sho as hell wanted to, but I didn't want to mess things up. Then one night while we was sitting at Fuddruckers—trying somethin' different—Katrice asked, "What you waitin' on, playa?"

"What you talkin' about?"

Taking a huge bite out of her burger, she tried to talk to me with a mouthful of food. "Um, you know," she said, licking her fingers.

"You talkin' 'bout sex?"

"Yep," she said while she bit off another mouthful. "You ain't asked for these draws."

I hastily dipped a French fry into the pool of ketchup on my plate. "You ain't said shit neitha."

"Don't be tryin' to turn it around. I think we should do that thang, so I can work yo' ass over with all this dick I got."

"Girl, you mad crazy. It should be more like you can't handle all this right here!"

We laughed about our silly-ass exchanges all night, and, when we got back to her place, that's where the story was told.

Katrice didn't have no dick. Her ass was straight-up pillow princess. I got up between her legs and planted myself right in the middle of her pussy. I knew from the first time I saw her that it was something about her. With her eyes rolling in the back of her head, I tapped that ass!. I rolled her nipples between my fingers as she pressed my body against hers. Her legs wrapped around my hips as I pounded her. The more I

sensed her carpet against mine, the more connected to her I
felt. When I came, I screamed, "Got-damn-muthafucka-oh-
yeah-this-my-pussy!"

My body jerked and shook and fell limp against her.
Katrice kissed me on the forehead as I lay there trying to
catch my breath. To me there was no better feeling than to
have my pussy pressed inside of another woman's—clit-to-
clit. It's like fucking magic.

A few minutes after that mind-blowing experience, Katrice
whispered, "Roll over."

I didn't want to tell her no because I still wanted more—
any way I could get it. I slid off her onto the bed and turned
over on my back. I was so accustomed to giving pleasure that
I'd forgot what it was like to receive it. Katrice kissed me
from the bottom of my chin to the tips of my toes and even
had the balls to lick the bottom of my feet. It drove me fucking crazy. Lying there body jerking every ten seconds, I was
ready for whatever came next. I felt something cold and
hard gliding up my legs, but I was too scared to peek and see
what it was. This thing made its way to my inner thighs and
the very tip of it entered my ass. It was for damn sure a different feeling for me. "Ooooh. Mmmm." Katrice consumed
my titties like apples as she moved this thing in and out of
every hole below my hairline. It was wild.

"What the hell is that, Trice?"

"A silver bullet. You like it?"

"Hell, yeah," I said, moaning. We went at it for hours. The
sex was so hot that I pulled out a blunt and smoked it; so did
she. Katrice got up and fixed us pancakes, eggs, and bacon
at four o'clock in the morning. I ate that shit and got right
back into it.

One afternoon Katrice pulled up to the gas station and sat
there. I was reading an issue of *Essence* with Gabrielle Union

on the front and wasn't trying to stop. That's a sexy-ass woman. Anyway, I'm sitting waiting on Katrice to get out and pump the gas, and I look over and see her staring at me. "What you waitin' on?"

Katrice questioned, "Well, ain't you gonna pump the gas?"

"Hell, naw. I thought you had it."

"Asia, you ain't gonna pump the gas for me?"

"Uh, I ain't planned on it." We sat there arguing like dumb and dumber trying to figure out who was going to be more gentlemanly and pump. She ended up getting her ass out and doing it. After all, it was her car.

After 'bout three months, Katrice asked me to move in with her, but I couldn't do that. My mama woulda had a damn fit. However, I did spend a lot of nights with her. Like I said, Mama didn't care where I spent the week just as long as I had my ass in church Sunday.

I ain't one to start no whole buncha shit, but I gotta tell you about Katrice and Peaches. First time I went to go get my hair done at Peaches's house, Katrice went with me and sat in the car. I ain't say nothin' at first because I knew she was tired and wanted to get a quick nap in before we went out that night. Me and Peaches was laughing about shit like we always do. She might rub my shoulder or sumthin' and then even reach down and kiss my forehead while she doin' my hair. When I got back to the car, Katrice was reclined in the seat lying on her side facing the window. You know, I'm drivin' and mindin' my business thinkin' that she was sleep. I turned on the CD player to play some Earth, Wind, and Fire because me and Peaches had been talkin' 'bout them while we were the porch. Next thing I know I look over and Katrice lookin' at me dead in the eye. I was like, "Damn, babe, I thought you was sleep."

"I can't tell you thought I was sleep by how loud you playin' that damn music."

It wasn't even loud. "I'm sorry. I ain't know it was that loud." I turned the volume down and kept on drivin'. A couple of minutes later, I felt like she was lookin' at me upside my head again. "What?"

"So. Why you get in here playin' EWF when you just got through talking to her?"

I didn't know where all this was coming from. "What you mean?"

"You know damn well what I mean. I heard y'all out there talkin' about Earth, Wind, and Fire, and then you get in here and start playin' the shit."

"Um, Katrice, I was looking for this song we was talkin' about. Why you trippin'?"

She ain't say nothin'. Katrice raised her seat back up and put her seat belt on. For a few minutes she was quiet, but then all of a sudden, she starts crankin' shit out. "Why she kissin' and touchin' all ova you like dat? She ain't gotta do all that to braid your hair."

"What?"

"Asia, don't be playin' dumb and shit. You know what I'm talkin' about."

I couldn't believe this. Katrice had the nerve to be jealous. "Gurl, that ain't nobody but Peaches, and she always playin' like that. That's my girl from way back. I told you that."

"Well, she don't need to be kissin' on you. Lemme find out she did it again."

From that day on, Katrice went with me to get my hair braided. Then finally one day Peaches went ova to the car and told her she needed to chill out and that it was rude for her to keep comin' ova to her house and sittin' in the car. So, Katrice still being a female no matter how hard she tried *not* to be, stopped goin' with me. Can't believe she just didn't get out and get to know Peaches. But Peaches, being like she always been, still kisses me on my forehead and rubs my shoulders. Her motto is, "I was here before the bitch came, and I'll still be here when the bitch gone." I ain't touch that, and neither did Katrice . . . *females.*

One night, after we had been ova to Mama's house, we was sittin' on the sofa 'bout to watch a movie, and what I thought was a mouse ran across my foot. "Was that a mouse?"

Snickering at my ass as I jumped up on the coffee table, Katrice said, "Yeah, it probably was." Her ass was calm as shit.

"Why you ain't scared?"

"Girl, they come in here all the time. Get one of the mouse traps out of the kitchen drawer."

"Uh, I don't do rodents," I snapped. "I'll do ants and maybe even a cockroach or two, but not no fuckin' rats."

Katrice acted like she was offended. "You kill me with this shit," she said as she got up and trucked her ass into the kitchen to get a trap.

Peeping around the sofa and end table, I climbed down from the coffee table to the ottoman and then jumped to the sofa in my socks and balled my legs under me. "Kill you with what shit?"

"This make-believe macho crap. One minute you all thugged out and the next minute you acting like a ol' bitch."

"Oh, see, you can't talk. You the same way."

"No, I'm not."

"Yeah, you are. What about the pumpin' gas thang?"

"Asia, I don't like pumpin' gas. I ain't never been with a woman that made me do it."

"I'm confused here. Who the fuck pumps the gas when you by yourself? You claim you don't get into labels, but yet,

you got shit you want me to do because I roll like that sometimes. You like runnin' a dick up in me, but you don't want
to pump a li'l bit o' gas. That's fucked up, Trice. "

Katrice plopped down on the couch next to me. "So what
the fuck are we supposed to do?"

I was hot. "At this point, I don't give a damn what we do. I
just know I ain't gonna be going through this bitch-ass shit
every time you want somebody to carry yo' bags, pump yo'
gas, or kill a rat. You can kiss my fuckin' ass with that." Still
fuming, I went to the refrigerator and got two forties, one
for each of us.

"Asia, I love you."

"I love your ass, too, but I ain't 'bout to be no fool." I
pecked her on the cheek. "Now can you fix me sumthin' to
eat?"

Weeks passed, and me and Katrice fell out a few more
times before we came to the agreement that neither of us
wanted to be with anyone else. My mama got cool with
Katrice after she came to church with me a coupla more
times. Soon Mama was alright with me movin' in with her
provided that we kept on comin' to church. We played ball
together and cruised the hunnies together. To hell with that
two doms can't be together. Katrice was the only woman I
wanted to watch WNBA games with, and she was the only
one I'd let stick a dick in me. I thought about the knowledge
Dad used to kick to me about broads, and I got to the point
where I carried Katrice's damn bags and pumped her gas. I
still wasn't killin' no fuckin' rats. But I love me some Katrice,
and, with the way Katrice lays it to me, I know she loves me,
too.

CAUGHT UP

(Part 2)

*W*hen Tammy told me she had a girlfriend, something inside of
me said, "So." They'd been together for many, many years
and were rock solid. They'd never had any interruptions or interfer-
ence. Quite boring to me, but I respected that. However, instead of
backing off, I came on even stronger. I called when it was normally
their quiet time together, and sometimes I'd let the phone ring and
ring until someone was forced to answer. I knew what made her
smile and made her feel like a queen. It was the things that her lover
didn't do. I could hear her smiles through the phone, and they energized me to no end. I wanted her.

My girlfriend, who I often conversed with throughout the day, appeared to do everything wrong. She wasn't giving me the attention I
wanted, and I tried everything I could to bring our relationship to
an end. I found every reason in the world to argue about the way she
washed my clothes, the way she talked to me, and the way she addressed my intimate needs. Whenever we made love, it wasn't her I
wanted kissing me and touching me. I didn't even want her talking
to me sometimes.

I couldn't take my mind off my new interest. If she told me her
lover never gave her chocolates, I went to Godiva and had two dozen
truffles sent to her. If she told me they never traveled, I'd plan a trip

*to the Caribbean for the two of us. I knew I was casting balls of fire
into a happy home, and I was determined to burn that bitch to the
ground.*

11:00 A.M., MST

I called because I wanted to talk to her. I wanted to hear her
voice. I didn't care she was with her family. The sound of her
voice rippled my mind with thoughts of ecstasy no one else
had ever given to me. During the week when I talked to
Tammy while she was at work, she made time for me, and I'd
finally managed to get her attention at night. Yeah, yeah, she
was taking time away from the kids and her girlfriend, but that
didn't matter to me. I needed her, and that's what did matter.

Talking to Tammy made me feel like the whole world re-
volved around me. Her musical talent energized me, and I
was completely blown away when she wrote a song for me. As
she read the words to me, I envisioned her planting warm
kisses on my neck. Then, I listened as she made love to the
saxophone and played every note like a symphony to my
soul. So many nights I fell asleep with the impression of
Tammy's spirit inside of me. I did this, night after night, with
Carlita by my side.

The morning I met Carlita, my girlfriend, I was at the gym
preparing to work out. I'd bought a one-year membership
with hopes of getting fit and fine. She was in the weight
room doing bench presses when I saw those sexy-ass legs of
hers hanging off the bench. I was headed to the back room
for my fitness assessment to see exactly how fat I was and how
much work I had to do to get the excess weight off. When I
came back out, she was standing at the water cooler talking
with one of the trainers. She looked at me and winked. From

that moment on, I knew she would be the one for me. Then I walked over to the cooler perpetrating like I was going to get some water and smiled right up in her face. Carlita snickered and passed me a cup from the top of the cooler.

"Thanks," I said.

Smiling, she replied, "You're welcome." And she kept on talking to the trainer. Later that same morning, I bumped into Carlita in the locker room where she was wringing wet with sweat from her workout. "Hey," she said as she turned to open her locker. The lockers were situated in a U-shape formation, and hers was across the way from me. It was only the two of us in the room.

"What's up?" I asked. I began undressing so I could get ready for work. As a freelance photographer, I worked my own hours, and, on this particular day, I had to do a shoot at a reception for some city dignitaries.

"Nothing much. About to get washed up and outta here. Today your first day?"

I'd gotten down to my bra and mulled over whether I should take it off in front of her. I didn't have a lot of time to waste, then I noticed that she wasn't hesitating about taking off her shit. "Yes, it is. I had my assessment and just got on the elliptical for a while."

"I see."

I caught her stealing a glimpse of my naked behind and smiled with flattery as I put on my earrings. "Do you ever shower in here?"

Putting on a dry shirt, she said, "Sometimes, but usually I take one at home. Oh, where are my manners? My name is Carlita. Yours?"

"I'm Liya." I'd gotten completely dressed and had opted to take my shower at home as well. "Well, it was nice talking with you. I've got to run home and get ready for work."

"Yeah, me, too. I'll see you around."

*   *   *

It took three weeks for Carlita to finally ask me out. I'd decided I wasn't stepping to her like that in the event she wasn't gay. After getting to know her, I discovered she was what I call, "T.P.," or the Total Package. She had her own car, she had at least two academic degrees, she was healthy, she didn't have any kids, and the best thing of all was that she didn't live with her momma. I could get down with her because she kept it real and obviously knew how to take care of business.

Five months passed before we had sex. I'd let her stick her fingers in my shit, and it drove me crazy watching her lick her fingers afterward. The kissing was OK. Nothing to really write home about. The sex was OK. All she ever wanted to do was eat my furburger. She did pretty well, but her way of doing it got boring after a while. As we talked sometimes, I couldn't help but notice that, despite those academic degrees, she was still . . . (forgive me, Lord) dumb. Her vocabulary wasn't as tight as it should have been for someone who had been in school for so long. I tried to ignore it, but I found myself always trying to correct her. Yes, it was insulting, but, hell, she needed to know how ignorant she sounded.

Something else that bothered me was that Carlita was always at work. She got up before dawn every morning and jogged five miles. After that, she went to the gym, then went home to change, and was off to work. We text-messaged each other and talked on the phone all day, and, although it took her a minute, Carlita spoiled me. She bought my clothes, my jewelry, my shoes, and got my hair done for me. I had my own sugar momma.

About a year into our relationship, I started feeling like I couldn't breathe. Before Carlita, I'd been in seven relationships, and none of them had lasted more than a year. I know that's not a good thing, but I have expectations, and I give you an opportunity to meet them. Carlita started spending even more time at work. I couldn't get her on the phone, and my text messages were answered with one-word responses after I'd been waiting for hours for them. We'd never moved in together, but she had a key to my apartment, and I had one to hers. When I was in the mood, I'd go to her place and clean up or cook for her and leave a nice note with my perfume sprayed on it. And when she had time, she did the same for me. Despite those deeds, I still didn't think it was enough.

One afternoon, my friend Fletcher invited me to go to Detroit with him to see this art exhibit. I hadn't been out of Phoenix in months and needed to get away, so I agreed to go. When I mentioned it to Carlita, she didn't even express an interest in going, no matter how many hints I dropped. So I was like, "Fuck it," and went on to Detroit with Fletch.

The night of the exhibit, I was determined to not let my anger with Carlita keep me from having a good time. While viewing an abstract piece by the artist, I heard a melody that my body instantly started to groove to. My hips swayed as I sipped the champagne that was so generously provided throughout the evening. The tune was "If I Kissed You" by Jonathan Butler off my favorite Richard Elliot CD, and it reminded me of this girl I used to date. She loved her some Jonathan Butler.

I walked through the thinning crowd and reached the stage to find a sistah playing the hell out of the saxophone. Her eyes closed as the instrument belted out this sensual tune, I felt her inside of me. Her fingering, each one performing trills up and down that brass dick, brought the house down. The power she had in that performance commanded the room, and with the sudden burst of applause at the end, I had to put my glass down on a nearby empty chair and give it up to the lady and her mad skills.

Standing in line to get her autograph, I studied her movements and her wit. She wore a plain white shirt that buttoned down the front. It was underneath a simple black pantsuit. Her nails were coated with clear nail polish, and her hands looked like they were the perfect size to handle my B cups. I couldn't find one piece of paper to get her autograph on, so I used the napkin that had been around my champagne glass. I knew it was tacky, but I had to have some reason to get close to her. When she shook my hand, I thought I'd melt. Her hands were as soft as cotton. Once I walked away, I didn't know what I wanted from her, but I did know that I didn't want her to forget who I was.

I was distracted the first couple of days after I got back from Detroit. I was trying to come up with ways to get Carlita out of my life and Tammy into it. Nothing about my girlfriend impressed me, so much so that I didn't even want her doing anything for me. I'd do mean shit like turning my cell phone off to keep her from getting through to me, or I'd go out with my friends and stay gone all night hoping she'd want to break up because I was never available for her. She could very easily be a man about things and just leave, but I knew she wouldn't do that.

I'll admit I schemed a little to get Tammy's email address, but what else was I supposed to do? I sent her an email, and it started from there. I have letters from her hidden all through the house and the car. Carlita couldn't find her way out of a paper bag let alone find her way through my belongings to call herself snooping. Now that I've gotten to know Tammy, though, I want her. I can fill that void she complains about, and I can be the only woman she desires. She's got this inner beauty I've yet to define. It's as if I looked up one morning and realized I was in love with her.

DRESS, RIGHT, DRESS

As we walked back into the room, I strolled in with Tweet and "Oops (Oh My)" on my mind. I hummed every damn word of that song until I felt like I wanted to take my own shit off. I watched her take off her shoes and toss them on the floor as she walked past the sofa. She took off her jacket, revealing her camisole and bra. As she reached for the light, I softly exclaimed, "No, leave it off."

"OK," she whispered. Her voice had a high-pitched tone to it, but there was a sexiness about it that made Daphne all the more appealing to me. "It's a little warm in here. That's why I took off my shirt," she said, laughing, turning on the air conditioner. "St. Louis is humid this time of year."

Stumbling across the hotel room trying to get closer to her, I agreed, "Yeah, it is a bit heated in here. I'm going to have a seat over by the air where it's cool." Reclining on the sofa, I put my keys in my purse and got comfortable. "That was a great concert. I love myself some Tweet."

Daphne came over to the sofa and sat next to me. Most of the evening she stayed a comfortable distance from me, and I had taken it upon myself to be accommodating and stay equally as far away from her. Positioning herself so that she could look me in the eyes, she said, "It's really wonderful being able to see you. We've been phone buddies for a couple of months now, and I couldn't wait to finally put a face with the voice. "

I never thought in a million years that I would talk to someone over the phone and fall hopelessly in love with her. Daphne and I met through my friend Cheryl who works at the library. I was going through a really bad time with an ex and felt as though I needed a change of scenery. I'd tried to find "something to do" pieces of pussy, but those bitches were crazy. After one orgasm, they wanted to move in. Then I met Justine, this White chick who had four kids. The kids weren't that bad, but Justine had issues. She would chain smoke three and four packs of cigarettes a day and wondered why I wouldn't kiss her. Then there were her crying spells that she'd have whenever she talked to her mother, the same woman who couldn't understand why her daughter had to date a Black woman. Oh, let's not forget . . . that bitch didn't want to work.

After telling Cheryl my horror stories month after month, she finally fessed up and told me she had a friend. Don't you hate that? Folks let you go down through there before they say, "Well, I got this friend." Anyway, I asked Cheryl about her, and all she would say was that her friend was cool and that I would really like her. Better yet, she wasn't full of drama, was kinda low-key, and might be someone I'd like to hang out with. To me, that meant the bitch was jacked in the face because not once did she mention how she looked. I didn't worry about it, though. I told her it didn't matter that her friend lived in St. Louis; give her my number anyway.

The first phone call I got from Daphne made me apprehensive about talking to someone I'd probably never meet in person. I lived in Portland, Oregon, and didn't foresee a need to ever be in St. Louis. While we were on the phone, this broad had the nerve to put me on hold four and five times. Every time we got a good conversation going she would say, "Hold on." By the sixth time this occurred, I finally told her she could call me back. When she did, I was prepared to relate that I was only looking for a friend. But then she apologized for the previous interruptions, confiding that there was a problem at work requiring her immediate attention; she and I would have to talk at another time. The date was September 11, 2001.

Three weeks later, Cheryl, after returning from vacation, pulled me into her office. Because she hadn't had an opportunity to talk to me since she'd given Daphne my number she was overflowing with curiosity.

"What happened? Did you like her? How'd it go?"

"Slow your roll, Cheryl," I said. I couldn't believe she was all giddy about this failed love connection. I closed the door. "There's really nothing to tell. We only talked for a little while, and then she had to go. I haven't spoken with her since."

A puzzled look crossed Cheryl's face. "Daphne was like that? Hmmm. That doesn't sound like her."

"It's no big deal. I've moved on anyway."

"No, what day did she call you?"

"September eleventh of all days."

"I see," she sighed. "Well, I'm sure you'll hear from her when things get back on track."

"Whatever." I returned to my office and shut everything down so I could go home.

Depressed about being alone, not lonely—there's a difference—I stopped by the liquor store and bought a bottle of Mondoro. Next on the list was a couple of CDs from Best Buy. Tonight I was going to spend my Friday evening mellowing out on the sofa. There wasn't shit on television, and none of the old booty-call numbers in my cell phone were worth the hassle. *Guess I'll call it a night.* Only two things could make this night a winner for me: a good nut and a hot shower. Lacking a partner and the motivation to self-induce the former, I resigned to settle for the latter.

As I lathered myself with body wash, I swore I heard the phone ring. I pulled back the curtain to see if I was imagining things. *Riiiinnnggggg!*

Hopping out the shower, I sloshed water with each step in my frantic dash to the bedroom to grab the receiver before whoever was on the other end hung up. "Hello?"

"Felicity?" a woman's voice asked.

"Yes. Who's speaking?"

"This is Daphne . . . Cheryl's friend."

I quietly smiled to myself but tried not to let my happiness show. "Oh, hi. How are you?"

She paused for a moment. "I know you're probably wondering what happened to me the other week."

My immediate reaction was to not care, but I had to hear her out since Cheryl claimed Daphne was all that and a bag of chips. "Well, I was shocked the call ended so quickly. I assumed you were busy."

"Girl, it was work. I'll have to tell you about it one day. What have you been up to?"

Monday morning came and found me still nude on the phone with Daphne—not from my shower on Friday, but preparing to go to work. I admit the conversation had been enthralling, entertaining, and very enticing. Once we stopped talking about one thing, we rolled right into something else. Before we knew it, the entire weekend had passed with each of us taking turns calling the other. I was laughing again, and I had her to thank for that. Daphne was captivating, and I knew this would be it for me. We talked every day like that up until the night we first met each other in person, the night of the concert.

I'd come to St. Louis to see Daphne. I'd waited long enough. We'd made plans to meet at the hotel so we wouldn't be out in public when we jumped each other's bones. What she didn't know was that I'd ordered room service and had had the suite decorated for dinner. When I opened the door, there she stood, a vision of extraordinary loveliness in a champagne suit embroidered with champagne-hued crystals around the hem of the jacket and skirt. Her legs shimmered with copper body glitter while her polished toes delicately rested in a pair of clear slip-on dress shoes.

"Am I what you expected?"

I was speechless. Was this ever an awkward moment? "Uh, hell, no. Get your fine ass in here," I teased. I gave her a hug, and while embracing her, I could smell every layer of her skin down to her Caress soap. "You smell wonderful," I smiled, rubbing her across her back as I showed her into the room.

"Well, thank you. We old ladies try." Looking around the room, Daphne gasped, "What's all this?" Tapered white candles set in brass candleholders adorned a dinner table set for two. A single red rose stood in a Waterford crystal vase that the manager allowed me to borrow.

"I figured we needed some face time alone so I arranged for us to have dinner here. You don't mind, do you?"

Daphne's long, black hair was grayed slightly at the roots. She didn't look anywhere near forty-five. As a matter of fact, with her hair pulled back into a ponytail, she looked twenty years younger. "No, I don't mind. I'm pleasantly surprised. I wasn't expecting this." She blushed.

The ambience of the room made everything perfect for

both of us. We went to the concert where Tweet rocked the house. I wanted to put my arm around her shoulder a couple of times, but I remembered she said she hated public displays of affection. While riding in the car back to the hotel, Daphne ran her fingers across the nape of my neck. I thought I was going to die. That shit felt so good. She kept doing it over and over like she was in a trance. I wondered what was on her mind as she ran her fingers across my curly white locks. I was looking forward to wherever this was headed.

Back at the hotel, I'd come to the conclusion that I was going to take things slow. At forty-three, I didn't need a lot of drama, and neither did she. We had all the time in the world. I returned her warm glances and continued to welcome her generous compliments. "Do you want me to massage your feet? I know they're tired."

Daphne smiled. "Sure, you can." She tossed her head back against the sofa and relaxed as I massaged her toes and the balls of her feet. "I have a confession."

"Oh, really?" I snickered anxiously.

"I want to make love with you."

"With me?" I'd never heard that before.

"Yeah, making love *to* you is comparable to being in charge, but making love *with* you is like sharing in the beauty of the whole experience because I believe you feel as strongly for me as I do for you."

Sitting in the dark, I contemplated what I was to say next. Her words were amazing. "You're right. I do feel very strongly for you, and I want to make love *with* you as well."

My massage moved from her feet to her calves, from her calves to her thighs, from her thighs to her hips, and from her hips to her waist. Slowly, my body moved in sync with hers as I made my way to her lips through the darkness.

With my breasts pressed against hers, I experienced a synergy I'd been looking for all of my life. I couldn't figure out what to do with my hands as I gently caressed every spot of her delicate skin. As we rolled from the sofa to the floor, they found a haven atop her plum-shaped ass. On our sides, we entangled ourselves, one leg wrapped around the other until our passions met. I embraced her as if to never let her go while she melted in my arms, having finally discovered a comfortable serenity within her. Within moments, we found ourselves insatiable.

Fully undressed, Daphne mounted me and made love with me, venturing into an ecstasy I never knew existed. As the tears streamed from the outer corners of my eyes, I knew love again and was determined to never lose it. Her slender body popped and jerked as the orgasms came one right after the other, for me and for her. This went on until the sun rose, and as I lay there on the floor watching her chest rise and fall, love consumed my entire body.

Her cell phone alarm went off at 7:00 A.M. She got up without hesitation. "I have to go to work. I brought my clothes with me. They're in the car."

"Oh, I'll go get them for you."

"No, that's OK. I'll do it," she said softly as she leaned over to kiss me on the lips. "Why don't you run down to the corner store and pick up some bottled water?"

"You can drink the water in here."

"Felicity, you're not paying four dollars and fifty cents for a bottle of water when it's only a buck at the corner store."

She had a point. "OK, I'll go. Anything else?"

"No, that's all."

There was a long line at the 7-Eleven, and I hoped I wasn't going to make Daphne late. I knew I'd finally found the one, and this was the first time in my life I could tell it was mutual.

I grinned all the way back to the hotel. Just as I was about to stick my card key into the slot, the door quickly open. I was traumatized by what I saw.

"I'd hoped to be gone before you got back, but it took a minute for the iron to heat up," Daphne said tenderly. She was standing in front of me in dress whites. Daphne was in the military. I panned her presence from head to toe. Not only was she in the military, she was also a lieutenant. Her loving countenance turned cold and emotionless right before my eyes. "I already know you have a lot of questions, and I guess now I'm going to have to answer them."

My initial shock was that Daphne was stunning in her uniform, but it was replaced by the fact that she was a lieutenant—someone who could lose everything if she and I were discovered. "Um, I don't know what to say right now," I said as people passed by staring at her. "I have your water."

"Thank you," she said, taking the bag from my hand and placing it on the table. "I wasn't expecting you to see me this way, so I need to gather my thoughts. I have to go right now before I'm late. Trust me. We will talk when I get back."

Nodding in agreement, I reached to give her a hug and a kiss, but she pulled away. "Good-bye."

Most of the day I sat in the room in a trance. I ordered a turkey burger from room service, but by the time it came, I couldn't find the strength to eat. Daphne's being in the military filled a lot of gaps for me, but I still had questions. The only thing I could do was wait for her to get back and, hopefully, provide answers. There was a knock at the door.

"Miss me?" she joked as she frantically brushed past me. "Oh, God, do I have to pee!"

Back in the bedroom, still in her uniform, she took a seat on the sofa as she placed her hat on the table and began unbuttoning her jacket. "First, let me apologize."

"OK."

"I'm sorry about this morning. I should've told you about my job a long time ago, but with my level of classification, it's not that easy."

"OK."

"And I couldn't hug you because, with this uniform on, I can't show any public displays of affection. I would've slipped and done it, but those people walked by."

"OK."

"You remember that first night I called you, and we kept getting interrupted?"

"Yes."

"The President was being flown to his secret location, and I was dispatched there as well. When the military calls, I have to stop whatever I'm doing and go."

"I understand."

"Well, that brings me to this bit of news that arose within the last two hours."

"What?"

Daphne sat there like she had a lump in her throat. Then she swallowed. "I've got orders to go to Afghanistan."

"What? When?"

"I have to leave by the end of the week."

My heart sunk to the floor. "For how long?"

"Six months, but—"

"Six months? Daphne, we just found each other, and now this?"

She tried to reach for my hand, but I pulled it away. "I know you're not trying to get soft on me, are you?"

I looked away.

"I can't afford a relationship right now, Felicity. Not while I'm in the military. I was planning to retire in six months anyway. This will be my last tour of duty. When I get back, you and I will have all the time in the world for each other."

I couldn't fight the tears. "What was all this then? A roll in the hay? A one-night stand?"

Daphne scooted over to me and took my face in her hands. "I love you, Felicity, and I'm too old to play games. I've searched my whole life for someone like you. This is my career we're talking about. If anybody catches wind of my involvement with you, then my over twenty years of service will be down the drain. I hope you can understand that."

This is where my age and eagerness to finally have it all came into play. "I do."

Smiling with a sparkling teardrop dangling from her eyelash, she said, "I did realize something, though, while I was away from you."

"What's that?"

"I'm in love with you."

There was no denying it for me either. "I'm in love with you, too."

Daphne and I never talked on the phone while she was away. When she wrote, she always addressed me as Felix. To make her life easier, I never addressed her in my letters. They always began with a simple "I love you." I never signed them. Once she wrote about wearing one's emotions on one's sleeve. "Man up!" she'd written. "Don't let everybody know what you're feeling all the time." It wouldn't be long before I understood what she meant by that.

One night, a little before midnight, I got a call from Cheryl. "You need to turn on your television."

"What for?"

"It's the war."

"Girl, you know I don't give a shit about that war."

"It's Daphne. Turn on the damn TV."

And there it was frozen on the screen. Her picture, looking much like she did the morning I first saw her in uniform, was plastered against the worn images of the American flag. She was gone.

At the funeral—after the last note of the trumpet was played, Cheryl, the only person mentioned in Daphne's will, was presented with the flag that was draped over Lieutenant Daphne Ritchie's coffin. As mourners filed past all the sprays and wreaths, I hung my head in agonizing pain. I couldn't fall upon my knees and kiss the mahogany that separated her from me, nor could I let out a cry that would ring through the heavens, shattering the marble headstones of the other slain soldiers. I had to stand there, without my anguish on my sleeve. I walked back to the limo with my soul in turmoil.

Watching the rolling hills of marble as we made our way out of the cemetery, I knew I'd never be at ease with what had happened. I pushed the button to close the privacy window, and my emotions exploded all over Cheryl.

"I have something to give to you," Cheryl whispered in my ear as I rested my head on her shoulder, drowning in my tears. "Daphne asked me to give it to you if it ever came down to this." It was a letter dated one week before her death.

Dear Felicity,

I knew this day would come, and I'm so very sorry to have to put you through this. After a career such as mine, my death while serving my country was inevitable. Despite our short time together, I feel as if I have loved you all of my life. Everything about you has made my entire life worth living. The morning you first saw me in my uniform, and I saw the shock on your face, I knew I had to do something to make it up to you. Although we only made love once, I experience it over and over whenever I think about you. I've never known love as I have with you. It's better to have loved at least once than to have never loved at all. Know that I love you with every fiber of my being.

*When I accepted this career, I knew I had to feel like the men,
I had to fight like the men, I had to love like the men, and, I
had to walk like the men. In the end, I will be honored for that.*

*I love you, Felicity, and I look forward to the day we will be
able to walk together again.*

*All my love,
Daphne*

As I sat there emotionally crushed, Cheryl compassion-
ately placed the folded flag in my lap while she was wiping
her own tears away. "She wanted me to give this to you."

Taken aback by the gesture, I lifted the flag and caressed
it. Then I rested it next to my heart.

TASTES LIKE CHICKEN

"It's finger-licking good."

After five Choc-latinis and two apple martinis, I was too through with myself and knew I was going to have sex with Lilah. I'm not gay, and I'd convinced myself of that all the way over to her apartment. But instead of me coming back there and going to my bedroom, I followed Lilah to her room and insisted we talk.

"Iris, I need to take a shower to get this L.A. humidity off me. I'll be right out, and we can talk as long as you want."

When Lilah got out of the shower, though, talking was the furthest thing from my mind. I'd undressed and was lying butt-ass naked on her bed with my leg cocked up against her pillow. "Fuck me."

Lilah and I had been friends since college. We'd dated best friends and brothers, but Lilah confided in me three years ago that she was gay. I was shocked because I had seen her fuck this brother's brains out so tough that he actually had tears in his eyes when she got up off him. She was gorgeous; there were even times when I envied her beauty. Lilah could've had any man she wanted, but I guess that wasn't enough for her. With her new lifestyle choice, I was bound to see some changes.

Once with shoulder-length platinum-blond hair, Lilah now sported pale yellow dreds that touched the middle of her back, and cowry shells dangled from a few locks in the back. They were perfect with her olive complexion. When she picked me up from the airport, she was dressed in a pair of gray men's slacks with the cuffs tailored to touch the top of what appeared to be Stacy Adams. Cufflinks bearing the initial "L" on them pulled together the sleeves of the crisp, brilliant white man's dress shirt that coordinated perfectly with her necktie. I knew somewhere underneath that ensemble was a pair of titties. I was puzzled to see my best friend like this, but I never questioned her. As I reached to hug her, I smelled Vera Wang for men, the fragrance my brother wore, all over her and damn near creamed on myself.

Smiling at me with still-beautiful white teeth, Lilah surprised me with six red roses and baby's breath wrapped in pink cellophane. I felt slightly uncomfortable because people were beginning to stare, but Lilah didn't care. She picked up my carry-on bag and walked me to the baggage claim area with her arm around my shoulders. Just like everyone else, I even did a double take when Lilah wasn't looking. She asked me what my bags looked like. When the carousel brought them around, she retrieved them and carried everything to the car. I couldn't believe what she had done to herself. Hell, I couldn't believe that I actually liked it.

Dinner was at Morton's where the steaks were thirty dollars apiece, and a baked potato cost seven dollars. I remembered times when Lilah and I pinched and scrimped to find fifty cents for the vending machines in the dorm, and now we're ordering thirty-dollar steaks. Lilah told me to order whatever I wanted, but to keep in mind she wasn't paying for a salad, so not to even ask for one. I obliged and requested the grilled salmon, creamed spinach, and my first Choclatini. I don't know what she ordered because I was too busy concentrating on how fine she looked. I would've never thought that about her when we were in college. I mean, Lilah was my girl. Maybe three days out of the week, she wore stilettos to class . . . *to class.* Tight-ass miniskirts and revealing blouses completed her ensembles, and you couldn't do nothing but envy style like that. Now I'm sitting here with her, and she looks like a dude straight out of *Ebony Man.*

After my fourth drink, I sprung it on her. "What's going on, Lilah, with this new look of yours? I mean, the only things that make you not be a man right now are your titties and the pu-tang that I hope you still have between your legs. You still got a pussy, right?"

Lilah chuckled to herself as she wiped her mouth with her napkin and took a sip from her beer—a beverage she would've never touched while we were younger. "I was wondering how much longer it was going to take. You've been staring at me all afternoon."

"I'm sorry. I didn't mean to stare. It's just that . . . you've changed."

Taking another sip from her beer, she smiled at me and said, "I haven't changed. I've always been this way. It's just the first time I've ever let you see it."

"I don't understand."

"Iris, you and I have been best friends since our freshman year, and I feel like I've misled you all these years. I don't care for fucking men. I know you've seen me do it, but I didn't like it. I was performing for an audience—you and the guy I was with . . . whatever his name was. One afternoon I met this girl in the dressing room of Hecht's at Metro Center in downtown D.C. I'd bumped into her by accident, but she smelled wonderful." Lilah's brown eyes lit up when she started talking about this woman. I'd never seen her like that. "When I came out of my dressing room, she was standing there. Next thing I knew, she had me sitting on the ledge in the handicap dressing area and was licking my kat. After that she asked me out. We went to dinner and talked for hours in her dorm room. Later in the evening we were kissing and sticking our fingers in each other's shit. I was expecting my mouth to say *ewww,* but my mind and body were responding, 'Oh, yeah! Hell, yeah!' And I've been into putang, as you say, every since."

"I see."

Lilah leaned in closer to me and whispered, "I don't want you to be diggin' on me because you think I look like your dream guy. Underneath all this, I am a woman. I'm still Lilah."

"I know," I said, squirming in my seat. "It's just that you look so different. You got rid of your perm, your bling, your nail polish, and your perfume and came back with locks, cowry shells, natural nails, and men's cologne. You're wearing men's clothing, and God forbid you have on . . . *arrgghhh.*"

"Men's boxers?" Lilah laughed.

"Yes."

"Well, I do, and they are more comfortable than those damn thongs I used to wear. Look, I don't want to spend a lot of time talking about me and my life. It is what it is, and if somebody doesn't like it, then to hell with them, and that *can* include you."

"No need to get defensive. I'm curious. That's all."

Lilah chuckled. "That's a dangerous thing to say to a lesbian. Curiosity can get you into a lot of trouble."

"I don't get it."

With one hand, Lilah pulled my chair around to hers and whispered in my ear, "I can feel you looking at me . . . wondering what I'm like. Wondering what I could do for you.

That's what straight women do. I'm the image that makes you masturbate when you don't got a man around. C'mon, tell me what's on that crazy mind of yours."

I felt myself turning red and took the last gulp of my drink. Had she peeped my cards? Did Lilah know I wanted to have sex with her? Was it that obvious? Clearing my throat, I replied, "You don't want to know what I'm thinking, and I do respect who you are and who you've become. I'm cool with it."

I couldn't debate the issue with Lilah because I was, indeed, curious. I wanted her in the worst way and was ashamed to admit it to her or anyone else. It was something about her that made me forget right and wrong. I'd always admired and loved Lilah but never like this. I watched the masculine ways about her: the way she held her fork, the way she cupped her beer bottle, the way she chewed her food, the way she sat in her chair, the way she signaled for the waiter, the way she glanced at me when she thought I didn't see her.

I was in love. I could love her if she'd let me. I knew her strengths and weaknesses, her idiosyncrasies, her humor . . . I knew how to love her. The hard part for me was that I wasn't gay. Or was I? Had I suppressed these feelings all these years? Had I always loved her but wouldn't because she was a girl and now that she was almost like a guy it was OK? I inched my chair back around to my side of the table and summoned the waiter. "I need another drink, and this time, make it a double."

After dinner, Lilah announced that she was taking me to an L.A. hot spot called The Abbey. Riding down Santa Monica Avenue with her, I felt like I was with my man. We grooved to Heather Headley's "He Is," a cut that was definitely on point with the way shit was going. While stopping at red lights, I felt folks checking out Lilah's serious gangster lean in her Mercedes S500. Her license plate read, WHO AM I. I wondered the same thing. By now I was three sheets in the wind and could really use another drink. What was wrong with me? Hell, I didn't know. All I understood was that I never drank like this.

When we reached the club, I discovered it was also a restaurant that served the most delectable desserts.

"I'll have a slice of chocolate cake," I requested from the waitress, "and can you add a scoop of vanilla ice cream?" The place was full of men whom I knew had to be gay by the way they were touching each other. They were clean cut, smelling and looking absolutely fabulous. The few women there also appeared to be quite chummy with their female companions. "I can't believe you brought me here!," I yelled through the thumping music, an awesome combination of house music and club mixes.

Lilah laughed as if the joke were on me. "I knew you'd freak out."

"No, I'm fine with it. I've never been to a gay club before."

"Actually, it's not a gay club. Gay people just happen to hang out here. A lot of celebrities do, too. This is West Hollywood, baby."

"OK," I responded. The waitress brought my cake and ice cream, which I devoured as if I hadn't eaten in days. With every bite, I bopped my head to the beat of the music.

"Damn, girl, are you hungry? It hasn't been an hour since we had dinner."

"I know. I have a sweet tooth," I lied. The problem was that I ate sweets whenever I was nervous. I kept looking around like I was paranoid. "I need to go to the bathroom."

"It's straight to the back. Do you want me to come with you?"

"No, I can make it alone." I know she saw me almost fall off my stool, but I pulled myself together enough to make it to the line for the ladies' room. Waiting there, I rested my head on the wall and drifted off into a daydream where Lilah was fucking me. And, oh my God, was she working shit out! Before I knew it, someone was tapping me on the shoulder telling me the line was moving. I had to shake this shit off.

When I returned to the table, I asked Lilah, "Do you go to the men's restroom or the ladies' room?"

"I could punch you dead in your face for asking me some dumb shit like that. I use the ladies' room, fool."

"I was just wondering." I don't know what I was thinking.

Lilah looked around and signaled for the waitress. "We need to get out of here before you order anything else to drink. I've never seen anyone down seven martinis in one evening. I'm surprised you're not somewhere puking your guts out."

"I can hold liquor pretty good, but I am ready to go now that you mention it."

I was lying on my best friend's bed with my shit dripping wet. It had never been that way with a man. My nipples stuck up like mountain peaks and the thought of Lilah touching me made me shiver. The hair on my arms and neck stood at attention as I heard the water in the shower stop. The door opened.

"Fuck me," I demanded, trying my best to give her this look of sensuality.

"Iris, what are you doing?" Lilah asked as she reached for her robe. "I know you ain't got your butt on my pillow. That is gross. Been across two-thirds of the damn country and God knows what else, and you got your funky ass on my pillow." She could talk to me like that and not hurt my feelings because we were friends like that. "And why are you naked?" She walked to the CD player and put on the Maxwell's

Embrya album she brought from the car. We used to jam to that whenever we took road trips, and I always joked that it was good fucking music.

"Didn't you hear what I said?"

"I heard you, and you have lost your damn mind. Girl, put your clothes on."

I lay there and waited. I knew she'd give in. A wet pussy staring her smack dab in the face. "You know you want me."

"Iris, you're drunk," she said, picking up my garments as she walked toward the bed. "Here, put your clothes on."

I had to be honest with her. "Here's the deal. I've been watching you since I first saw you at the airport, and my mind and body have been telling me some weird shit. I want you, Lilah."

"No, you don't. You want someone who reminds you of a man . . . to make it easier for you. Now put your damn clothes on."

"You're wrong. I want you to make love to me, and I don't want you to hold back."

I've loved Iris since college, and I've never been able to tell her. The first time I ever saw her I couldn't believe my eyes. She had long beautiful legs like Tina Turner and the prettiest smile I'd ever seen. With her wit and glowing personality, we instantly became friends. That night she watched me fuck a guy's brains out, I was really thinking about her—fucking her—and, now here she was lying in front of me with all of her ass at my disposal to do what I want, how I want, and how many times I want. If this happens, things may never be the same. But damn, I haven't had any pussy in almost a year, and, if anybody even blew on my shit, I'd cum. I know if I make another move, our friendship will never be the same, and do I really want that? Iris is my girl, and . . . well, if this happens, there won't be any turning back—for either one of us.

Before I knew it, Lilah had dropped her robe and pounced on me like a beast from the wild.

I sat astride Lilah like I was a cowgirl. I rubbed myself against her, spreading my passion like hot oil. She pulled herself to me and took hold of my titties with her mouth and massaged each one of them over and over. I rode her like a prize rodeo bull while she entered me with her fingers, which were just beneath my ass. Every part of my body was at her mercy.

"I wanna try something," she whispered. "I want you to eat me while I'm eating you."

"You want me to put my mouth on your pussy? That's nasty, Lilah."

Lilah, with me sitting in her lap, gasped. "You've done all this freaky-deaky shit and now you got the nerve to tell me you don't eat pussy?"

"Well, yeah. I never intended to go *that* far. Putting my mouth on the same thing that . . . well, you know, we have our periods out of is just too much for me."

"Iris, I'm not on my period. I know you're not going to come all this way to get scurred right before it's about to really get good."

"I just can't, Lilah. You can do me, but I'm not doing you."

"That's not fair. Shit, you told me to fuck you, and I haven't even gotten to that part yet."

I climbed off her lap and sat next to her. "Lilah, so far this has been great. You've done some shit that no man has ever done to me, but I can't have oral sex with you."

"Tell you what. Go take a shower and think about it. Even if I were to do you, your pussy's got some miles on it."

"What?" I was appalled.

"Don't be acting like you don't know. Your shit ain't fresh. Since you want to insult me by not eating my pussy, I'm taking it there about your own. I don't put my mouth on rank ass. You got that not-so-fresh odor about you." After that, she got up, put on her robe, and went onto the patio and closed the sliding door.

Embarrassed, I sat on the edge of the bed and rested my head in the palms of my hands. I'd never had anyone tell me my vagina was smelly. I thought I kept it pretty clean. In any case, I got up and took a bath. I couldn't go wrong soaking it.

The water was scalding with steam rising from the tub. I poured some of my orange ginger oil in it and watched the drops dissolve. Reclined against the back of the tub, I rested my arms beside me and dropped my thighs open. It felt like my pussy was going to fucking explode every time I thought about Lilah. The memory of when I saw her at the airport constantly danced through my brain. Damn, she looked good. You know how Denzel has that stance you can recognize even if he had a paper bag on his head? That's how Lilah looked to me. She'd always had broad shoulders, and ol' girl must have been working out or something because she was more buff than any man I'd known. *Shit, what I am doing?*

The patio door slid open and closed again. I cleansed myself *thoroughly,* stroking the washcloth against my face one last time. I rose from the water, stepped onto the bath mat, and didn't bother drying myself off. I walked back into the bedroom and found Lilah lying across the bed . . . nude. Her body shimmered with candlelight as her skin glistened with sweat and oil. I sat next to her because I had another important question. "What does it taste like?"

"It tastes like whatever you want it to taste like," she whispered as she got up, mounted the bed on her knees, and lavished kisses along my spine. "You smell good."

I closed my eyes in ecstasy, drifting deeper with each

touch of her lips. I felt the hair on my back rise to attention. It was becoming increasingly harder to resist Lilah's request. "My pussy smells even better," I murmured.

"We'll see."

"You still didn't tell me what it tastes like."

"Iris, it's not as bad as you think. Once you're into it, it actually tastes . . . like chicken," Lilah laughed as she sat back on the bed.

"You're too funny," Iris cackled. "Chicken? Ain't no way your pussy tastes like the barnyard pimp!" We both laughed, and there it went again. I was intrigued by her, and, with that beautiful smile, Lilah had me.

"It's all in the imagination. Just trust me." That was the one thing I'd always done in our friendship. I trusted Lilah with my life.

I'd engaged in 69 with two guys, and both times it sucked, no pun intended. One time the guy's balls were funky, and the other time the brother's feet were so stinky that I spent more time holding my nose and gagging than I did with his dick in my mouth. Lilah knew about each of those times and how horrible they had been. Knowing my friend the way that I do, she wasn't going to let this be a repeat.

Sitting on Lilah's face backward was how we started. Resting on my knees, I rocked and bounced, trying hard to not smother her. That shit felt so good that my toes curled. My pussy vibrated like a massage chair, and before I knew it, I'd leaned forward and pushed my face into Lilah's bush. I was drawn to the smell . . . the aroma of mandarin oranges and sex. I was captivated as I took the plunge into cunnilingus.

Her hair tickled my nose at first, but my tongue made its own path; I simply followed. Wet with sweat and passion, I tasted her, rolling my tongue around the lips of her pussy, finding my way to a pleasure I'd never known. At the same time, Lilah entered me with her liquid finger as she pressed her bottom lip against my clit, and I, without warning but certainly with great cause, poured into her like running water. Patiently, I waited for my own thirst to be quenched. Stroking my tongue against every piece of her love, I palmed Lilah's buttocks and found myself drowning in her. Maxwell was now playing for the fourth time.

Stretched out, upside down, on top of Lilah, wiggling my bottom in and out of her mouth, I realized Lilah was satisfying my request. She was fucking me, and I absolutely loved it. I shrieked, I moaned, I grunted, I felt like testifying actually. My elongated spine slithered over Lilah's body as I moved to a groove that satisfied me. Pleasure for me had never *come* in this form, and to think, it had been right in front of me the whole time.

Lying there between her legs, I took a moment to taste it . . . to taste her. I didn't smell anything foreign as I'd imagined, nor did I see anything that would have made me choke. I wet my lips and licked them, savoring the delight. I chewed and sucked on her clit like it was a piece of soft caramel. Gently, I ran my fingers around the edges of her lips, spread widely enough for me to enter her tunnel. Slowly, I massaged her walls like they were made of liquid gold, and intrigued by her movement and light moans, I tasted her again. My fingers, wet with pleasure, made their way to my lips. I couldn't help but think about partaking in my favorite meal prepared by my grandmother down south—collard greens, macaroni and cheese, candied yams, and fried chicken.

It was far from unpleasant . . . actually, it was anything but. My imagery baffled me because, for a moment, she really did taste like chicken, and it was finger-licking good.

Two months after my trip to L.A., Lilah and I took a break from each other—or should I say, I took a break from her.

Where she and I used to talk every other day on the phone, I now tried my best to avoid her—I *was* avoiding her. Jerrard, my boyfriend of two years, kept telling me that the trip must have rejuvenated me because our sex was better than it had ever been, and I told him that we'd talk about what happened during the trip one day. During sex, I was uninhibited and found myself wanting to explore every sexual detail about him. I wanted to discover if there was a reason why Lilah could make my toes curl, but he could not. I wanted, at least, to give him the chance to satisfy me like Lilah did.

Late one night while Jerrard and I were making love, there was a knock at the door. I ignored it and begged Jerrard not to stop. I didn't need him to lose his concentration because he'd found that spot, and I knew I was about to cum. Then the house phone rang. Normally, I would've peeped over his shoulder to check the caller ID, but this time I didn't. Next, my cell phone rang. "Damn," he yelled. He yanked himself out of me and ordered me to answer the phone.

"Hello?" I quietly took long breaths to calm myself down.

"Iris?" It was Lilah.

"Yes?" That was all I could say.

"Open the door," she requested softly.

Fuck. "Are you outside as in like not in L.A.?"

"Yes, I am. Would you open the door, please?"

I didn't know what to say as I searched for some shorts and a T-shirt to put on. "Um, I'll be there in a second." After I hung up the phone, I told Jerrard that Lilah was outside and she needed to talk to me.

"She came all the way from California to talk?" He was a bit agitated with his dick still at attention.

Scrambling for Jerrard's clothes, I said, "Yes, she did, so something must be wrong, and I might need you to make yourself scarce."

Jerrard, pissed as all get out, snatched his clothes from me
and went into the bathroom to relieve himself. I couldn't get
the smell of dick and wet pussy out of the bedroom, and as I
made my way into the living room to open the front door,
I noticed that the odor had drifted to the front of the house.
I sprayed some ginger peach room spray and lit three candles of the same fragrance. With the way things had been left
in L.A., I instantly realized what I was about to do. Before I
opened the door, I took a deep breath and assured myself
everything was going to be alright.

"Hey, you," I said, peeping through a crack in the door.

"Hey, you, back," Lilah responded. She looked pleased to
see me, but her aura gave off this vibe that all hell was about
to break loose. Swiftly brushing past me, she made her way
into the living room and placed the car key from Hertz on
the breakfast bar. And then, that feeling went through me
again. Lilah was fine, and had things been different, she
could've been all the man I'd ever need. She stood there,
staring at me as if she were wondering what she was going to
say next. "Well, I guess it's safe to say that your phone isn't
out of service or that you aren't dead. I mean, I haven't
heard from you since you left L.A."

Watching for any movement from the bathroom, I walked
over to her and kissed her on the cheek. "I've been busy."
Her face was stern, and at that moment, Lilah looked more
like a guy than Jerrard did. I wanted to get the discussion
over with before that light went off in the bathroom. "You
know how things get."

"Iris, I've known you most of your life, and you've always
had time for me, so don't pull that shit with me." I watched
her peruse the room. She glanced at the burning candles
and recognized that the bathroom door was closed. For a
minute, Lilah didn't say anything. Then as she walked to the

other side of the breakfast bar, she asked, "Do you mind if I use the bathroom? I came straight here from the airport."

My girl was smooth. The light was still on in the bathroom, and I wasn't sure if Jerrard had fallen in or what. "Uh, look, I might as well be honest. I have a guest, and he's in there right now."

"I see."

"Lilah, I'm sorry for dropping things after the trip, but all kinds of things have been going through my head." Still watching the bathroom door, I continued, "That whole experience was different for me, and I've needed time to sort things out."

"So, you're having these all-out fuck fests with your man to make sure that you're not gay, right?"

She was right. That's what I'd been doing. "Lilah, it's not like that. I truly enjoyed myself, and believe it or not, I don't regret one moment of it."

There was never any mistaking Lilah's facial expressions, and I knew she'd grown upset with me. "You don't get it, do you?"

"Lilah, what do you want me to say? We had sex, we made love, we fucked, we . . ."

Now, as she was watching the bathroom door, she walked over to me and took me in her arms. "This isn't about what happened during your trip. This is about our friendship." Tears started to fill the wells of her eyes, but I knew Lilah like I knew the back of my hand, and she wasn't going to let a single tear drop. "I didn't come all the way out here to catch you in the middle of a late-night booty call. I came out here because I thought something was wrong with you, that something had happened to you."

"Lilah, I . . ." The light went off in the bathroom, and then the door slowly opened. Jerrard came out and had this furious look on his face. He walked over to the sofa and got his overnight bag from underneath the coffee table. I know he heard us, but Jerrard wasn't the type man to make a big fuss about stuff. Instead, he let his actions speak for him. He glanced at Lilah, shook his head, and sighed.

Lilah, always pleasant, took the initiative to introduce herself. "What's up, man? I'm Lilah, Iris's . . ."

Jerrard interrupted, "Yeah, her best friend she always talks about. How you doing?"

"I'm good. Just in town to check on Miss Lady here since she seems to not want to answer her phone. Shit, I thought something was wrong."

They started this shucking and jiving shit that men do. Then Jerrard, after he realized he had all of his belongings, said, "Look, it was nice to finally meet you, but, um, it seems like you and your girl have some things you need to work out, so I'm going to give you two some privacy. I need to get out of here." The look Jerrard gave me was enough to know that I'd never see him again because he was a religious man and wasn't with the gay thing at all.

Lilah extended her hand and said, "Nice meeting you, man."

Reaching for his coat and completely disregarding her gesture, Jerrard replied, "Same here."

When Jerrard closed the door, my tears finally came, and my heart opened up. "Lilah, do you know what you've done by coming here? Now, I don't have anyone."

Lilah looked at me in disbelief. Then she asked, "Do you not know that I've lived vicariously through our friendship? It's been the reason I've wanted to get out of bed some days. Damn, Iris, you're my best friend, and I've never needed anybody else in my life because of that."

I was speechless as I watched her maintain her composure. Yes, I'd taken her for granted, and, yes, I'd denied her access to me and our friendship. I knew that we'd never return to the way things used to be. The only memory I'd have was that she tasted like chicken. Anything before that didn't matter.

Shocked at my silence, Lilah asked, "Do you even realize that fucking you was the last thing in the world I ever wanted from you? You might've lost him, but you could've always had me." Before she said another word, she wiped her eyes then reached for the car key. "Iris, I loved you as my friend. The sex just... happened." Heading for the door, she stopped and turned toward me and said, "I'd rather be your friend for life than a fuck for a night."

CAUGHT UP

(Part 3)

When you've been with someone for as long as I've been with Tammy, you know when something's wrong. I first noticed she was spending an enormous amount of time on the phone . . . more than what was normal for her. When she came in from work, she had nothing to say about her day. She'd walk into the kitchen, drop her bags, check the mail, and then go upstairs to either get on the phone or on the computer. Whenever I tried to ask her a question about her day, it was like I was bothering her because she snapped and frowned at me every time. I never said anything and went on about my way.

Her attention toward the kids was strange. She made sure they ate and had what they needed, but she didn't make time for anything else. On the weekends during our family outings, Tammy was always in a constant daydream, and when she wasn't doing that, she was trying to rush through everything we did so she could get back home . . . to the computer and the phone.

Then she stopped eating and sleeping. I thought maybe she was coming down with something. When your girl is sick, you're going to do whatever it takes to make her feel better.

She stopped welcoming hugs and kisses from me since that was my way of reassuring her everything would be alright. Before, she wrapped herself within me so tightly that nothing or no one could come between us. Where she used to curl up with me when it was time for us to sleep, she now rolled to the edge of the bed on her side and stayed there the whole night. Each time I wanted to make love, there was an excuse, or even worse, she'd go to bed before me to avoid my request.

No, I'm not making the kind of money I used to. With age, money isn't as important as a peace of mind. Instead of being the provider, I'd learned to be someone who enjoyed being taken care of and relished in the comfort of stability and being home with the kids. I do the laundry now and make sure our home is a showplace that is inviting and entertaining when need be. I never thought I'd be the one wearing the apron, but I am and wouldn't exchange it for anything.

And the kids? My life would be shit without them. In retrospect, I can somewhat understand Tammy's boredom with this arrangement. I never have much to talk about other than cooking and the kids. A woman like Tammy needs more than that.

At first I was fine with this new friend of hers. It gave her a break from us and our routine. Tammy, although she's an extraordinary woman, is a bit habitual herself, and any deterrence from that is a sure sign that something somewhere is wrong. This woman wasn't like Tammy's other friends. Every once in a while she mentioned Liya but kept much of their conversation guarded. If I walked in the room while she was on the phone, her voice would suddenly drop just below a whisper, or she'd stopped talking altogether. If she was on the computer, she closed the IM screens and pretended she was playing a game or something. Then one night I observed her deleting emails like crazy before shutting down the computer.

I've never pried into her personal business because that's not fair, but one night, after she'd gone to bed, I couldn't help myself. In the very back of the closet, Tammy kept a box of letters and other mail she wanted to keep for whatever reason. She never talked about it, nor did she ever let anyone go in it. I discovered the clear box covered with clothes and coats that weren't even in season and saw that it was full of colorful envelopes. Opening the box, I exhaled and then the overdue tears filled my heart and eyes. The return address on most of the envelopes was from Phoenix, and I knew I'd come too far to not open them. After hours of reading through love letters and greeting cards, I was faced with making a decision about revealing my discovery. Then I found a song she'd written Liya, and that hurt the most because the words said it all. They were in love.

I thought about the day I met her and where her troubled heart and mind had taken her, and then I thought about the good times we'd had. There'd been a trial or two, but for the most part during our nearly twelve years, things could have never been better. As the sun peeked through the blinds in the bedroom, I quietly folded the letters and placed them and the cards back in their respective envelopes. I cleaned up the mess I'd made and put the clothes and coats back on top of the box and closed the door. I undressed and got in on my cold side of the bed and faked sleep. In my mind, I couldn't help but wonder if Tammy had responded to any of those letters, but now that I think about it, I'm sure she did.

Accusing my wife of something that may or may not be wouldn't be right. Honestly, I'd only seen proof of one half of the story. I wanted so badly to ask her what's going on because, in those letters, there's something between them. I'm sure nothing physical has ever transpired, but emotionally, my girl is got. Every time I've asked her about Liya's obsession with her she insists that it's nothing. Whatever.

I'd almost rather Tammy fucked her—do a one-night stand even—than stand by and watch Liya have a piece of my baby's heart.

1:00 P.M., EST

There that damn phone goes again. I wish I could I snatch it out the fucking wall. I feel her cut her eyes at me to see if I'm listening to her conversation. Most times if it's a good buddy of hers, she'll take the call in front of everybody. But, if it's *her,* she'll talk for a minutes in code before leaving the room. It makes me so angry with her that she's doing this right underneath my nose without any regard for my feelings.

Tammy and I weren't lovers at first sight. Like most lesbian relationships, ours began because I knew somebody who knew somebody who knew her. From what I'd heard, she'd been through her share of bullshit and drama, but was salvageable. The first time we talked I could tell she was extremely intelligent. She didn't know that I knew she'd attended Dartmouth, nor did she know I knew she'd been stealing from her mother. I was told about the kids, but I felt like it might not make that much difference if Tammy were all I was told she could be. I'd been alone for nearly two years and was ready to give love one last try.

Tammy moved in with me practically right after we met. I can't say that I was in love with her right off, but I had some feelings for her. She and that ex of hers seemed like they wanted to be the death of each other, and somebody needed to save Tammy before she self-destructed. With all that Ivy

League education, she didn't have a job and wasn't trying too hard to find one. I was making good money at my job as the director of a local nonprofit and could afford to take care of her and the children.

Hell, even if I couldn't afford to take of her, I was going to because she had a pussy that wouldn't wait. Following two nights of sex with her, I was ready to give her all my damn money. Yes, I was pussy-whupped, but I'd never tell Tammy that. The first time we had sex I know I startled her when I stretched out across the bed. I mean, I like to get done and don't care much for being the doer. When she spread out over me, my heart raced and almost sent me into convulsions. The tiny tips of her breasts matched spaces with mine, and as she moaned and worked her body like a belly dancer on top of me, I knew I wasn't going to be fit for any other woman. After a few minutes of gently mashing her lips into mine, she arose from me, sliding off the foot of bed. Kissing the tips of my toes, which I never got manicured, she grabbed me around me ankles and pulled me toward her. I was slightly ashamed because, when I did start cumming, I couldn't stop. My cream ran from me like hot lotion. The thought of her doing that for somebody else absolutely drove me nuts.

The fact that I've never been a shit starter may very well be the reason why Tammy and I have been together for so long. There was only one other time I considered walking away, which was after I'd received a phone call that Tammy had "entertained" her ex in our home. I never confronted her about it because I was afraid of what she'd tell me. Sometimes she could be brutally honest, and I couldn't handle that. This time, though, it was different. To me, an emotional affair is just as bad as, if not worse than, a physical affair. Liya had gotten Tammy in the head, and from what I could surmise, Tammy had done the same to Liya. Tammy was draining every ounce of emotion from our relationship and was pouring it into this "thing" she had created with this other woman. At times, I felt like there was nothing left. One morning before she left for work and after the kids had gone off to school, I asked, "Baby, can you come home for lunch so we can talk?"

Tammy never broke her stride. It was like she was trying her best to get away from me. She went searching through the cabinets and drawers and was completely ignoring me. "What are you looking for?"

She never answered me and continued slamming doors and drawers. Then she grunted, "What for?"

Her tone was emotionless. "We don't talk anymore. I just wanted to spend a little time alone with you. I can set aside time, and—"

"You need to go to work. We can't afford you to be off right now. I don't know why you won't look for something."

This wasn't my Tammy. "We've talked about this. You wanted me to be here with the kids in the afternoons."

"Look, I don't want to argue this morning. Do what you want. I'll try to make it."

I sat at the dining room table waiting for her to come home, but she never did. I called her office, but kept getting her voicemail. When she got home that evening, she had this huge box in her arms. *A gift?* The kids ran to her and showered her with hugs and kisses. She glanced up at me and winked. Then she took her ass straight upstairs and got on the computer. As I walked up the stairs to try to get a peep at what was in the box, I heard all of this commotion. A lot of bumping and thumping was going on. Then I heard her go into the closet. I turned and headed back downstairs.

Later that evening when I'd gone upstairs, Tammy made no mention of the box, but I refused to let it go. "What was in that box you brought home?"

As she slid her nightgown over her head, she replied as if she was anticipating the inquisition, "Nothing. Something I got from work."

"Well, can I see what it was? That was a pretty big box."

Tammy sat on the edge of the bed and peered at me as I leaned against the computer armoire. Her eyes burned a hole through me—and my heart. "Morgan, don't do this."

"Don't do what?"

"Start something you can't finish."

"What the fuck is that supposed to mean?" I'd never heard her talk to me like that.

"Just let it be. I'm tired." Tammy pulled the bedcovers back and got in.

"Tammy, you must think I'm some kind of fool. I've been through the closet and your little secret box, and I've noticed your behavior around here. All I want to know is are you in love with her."

Rolling over on her side, turning away from me, she mumbled, "I don't know."

With that, I stormed toward the closet and was startled by the Indian porcelain doll that stood on Tammy's side of the tiny room. She collected dolls and had seen this particular one in a magazine a while back. I couldn't afford to get it at the time, but offered to get it once I'd saved the money. Apparently, she couldn't wait. "I see I was moving too slow for you."

"It was a gift."

AN INDECENT PROPOSAL

I can't believe I asked my brother to let me fuck his girl-friend. I caught his ass, standing there with his tongue in his cheek and this big-ass smirk on this face. To most men, the thought of watching two women snatch the panties was the ultimate fantasy. I wasn't giving him any money to do it, I wasn't buying him shit, and I hadn't decided if I was going to let him watch. He'd been complaining about her from day one. "Man, I can't get her to suck my dick, and she won't even let me stick it all the way in. Shit, sometimes she won't even look down there. I think she's scared of it. She can't handle all of this big, black—"

"Alright," I yelled. "I don't need to know all of that."

Listening to him and how frustrated he was that this woman wasn't setting it out told me right off the bat she was gay. It was either that or she had some other issues. I will say this: I know my folks when I see them and when I hear about them.

Roderick told me that he was bringing her to our family reunion picnic so everybody could meet her. He said he met her at a friend's house and immediately knew she would be his wife. Anyway, when they stepped out the car, everybody was justa looking. "Who dat pretty-ass woman Rod got with him?" everybody asked. I looked at her and concluded she looked a'ight, but she wasn't for my brother. For my girl, Reesie? Yeah, but not my brother. They came over to the table where I was sitting with my uncle and some of his boys playing a game of Tonk.

"Everybody, this is Maria. Maria, this is my uncle Peanut, his boys, Jordan and Stanley, and they cousins Marven and Marcel."

"Nice to meet you," Maria said.

Rod looked over at me checking out his lady. "Oh, and this is my sister, Rita."

"Nice to meet you, too." Maria smiled.

Now, Rod ain't said shit about his girl being Filipino. She had long, black hair and slightly sun-baked skin. I know the reason he wants her to be his wife is so that they can have pretty-ass kids with good hair. Everybody in my family got nappy hair . . . hair so nappy that a super relaxer barely works. I just cut my shit off and wear a natural. I'm still a young lady now, but I like to keep it real. My family knows I'm gay, and they don't like it. But I don't give a shit. Out of all the women who come around my family calling themselves liking somebody, I bring the best-looking ones, and they know it. My oldest brother, Wade, married this Ching-Chong girl from Chinatown in D.C. Seems like the only things they got in common are fucking and eating because she don't speak English or Ebonics, and he ain't been trying to learn no damn Chinese. Um, but when it's time to eat, she hooks up some Egg Foo Young and fried rice. Both they asses big as two houses, though. Then there's my brother, Duane. His wife is a doctor and ugly as sin. I don't mean no harm, but she couldn't be in the bed with me. Next, there's

Sinny—short for Sinbad. Yes, my mother named him Sinbad. He's married to this broad who swears she's White. She uses White girl makeup even though her skin is the color of a Hershey bar, and she wears these blue contacts and talks like she's from the backwoods of Arkansas.

My brother, Rod, is the last to get married—if he gets married. He can be a tough Negro to please. The previous girls he's brought around were all sistahs, but they couldn't hang with this long-ass dick he claims to have. I saw it once when we went swimming at the community pool because it fell away from underneath his trunks. But that was when we were kids. I sure as hell don't know what he has now, and I don't want to know. What I'm sure of, at this very moment, is that this chick that he's brought to this picnic? She don't like dick, and I'm going to prove it.

Rod and I met over at the grill where Aunt Peggy was flipping burgers. She'd dropped a couple of them, and you could tell she had because grass was sticking out some of them. She claimed it was seasoning, but we knew better. Actually, those were the best ones on the grill. I got two burgers and two ears of corn and waited for Rod to get his food. As we walked toward the table with the drinks and beer, I nudged Rod on his arm. "Dude, is this the chick you been telling me won't let you hit it the way you want to?"

Rod smirked. "Yeah, that's her. What you think? Fine, ain't she?"

"I guess so if that's what you want."

Rod stopped dead in his tracks. "What you mean?"

"Man, that girl is playing you. I don't think she's into men. As a matter of fact, she looks like this broad who rolls through the club every now and again."

"Is that right?" Rod was acting like he was pissed with me about calling his girl out like that. "Well, you know, Rita, you don't know the ladies as well as you think you do because right before we came over here, we had sex, and she let me hit however I wanted."

Rod's ass was lying. One thing he bragged about more than any of us was his ability to keep a woman cumming all day long. He boasted about this endless sex drive he had that gave him the appetite of a giant. So if that were the case, he would've had a plate full of food, but all he had was a hamburger and a piece of watermelon. "A'ight, Rod, whatever you say."

When we got back to the table, I recognized that Maria didn't have a plate. *If the pussy was so good, then why didn't he fix her a plate?* I sat down across from her and caught a glimpse of her ring, which had the colors of the rainbow stretched over the band. "Oh, my bad, Maria, did Rod get you a plate?"

"No, he didn't. I'm not really hungry. My mother cooks all the time, and I was over there before I went to Rod's. She made me eat a plate of food and some cake."

"Oh," I said. *That lying bastard.* "Nice ring."

Maria looked at me like I'd busted her balls or something. She turned blood red in the face. "Thank you," she said, pulling her hand from the table and resting it in her lap. She knew her ass had just got caught. "Is there any beer over there?"

I looked over in the direction of the Igloos and saw Rod. "I'll go get you one."

"Thank you."

Rod's punk ass was standing over in the sun drinking a beer. "Rod, niggah, why ain't you taking care of your woman? You didn't bring her no plate, and you didn't bring her nothing to drink."

"Oh, shit. I forgot."

I started laughing. "And your ass is trying to marry her? I don't think the problem is her. It's your ass. You don't know how to look after no woman's needs."

Rod tried to man up and got loud with me. "Rita, you know what? If you think you can do a better job than me at treating my lady right, then you go right the fuck ahead. I get tired of you telling me you know *your* folks."

Fortunately, Rod's voice was drowned out by the speakers that were fifty yards from where we were standing. "You know what, Rod? You're a liar. You ain't fuck that girl before you came here. She told me herself she was at her momma's house. So, like I told you before I laid eyes on her, you need to let me fuck her. I promise it'll save you a trip down the aisle."

I know the thought of me having his girl fucked with him, but I knew what I was talking about. I'd already seen the ring. Rod turned away from Maria's sight. "Do what you gotta do."

"I tell you what, Rod, since we family and all, if you let me fuck her, then I'll let you watch. I'll set a little something up at the crib, and you be in the next room. She won't even know you're there."

"And you think you got game like that . . . to make her get down with you like that after only knowing her for a few hours."

"Shit, ain't that what you guys do? Fuck 'em before you know 'em?"

"That's different. It's a man thing."

"What the fuck ever. You down or not?"

Rod hesitated before giving in. "And you'll let me watch?"

"Yeah, you freaky fucker, you can watch."

I walked back to the table and gave Maria her beer. "Maria, Rod had to leave to take my drunk-ass uncle home. He'll be back in a minute."

"OK," she smiled. No one in the family had come over to welcome her to the family, and it's a good thing they hadn't because my family had a tendency to come off all fucked up sometimes. Prolly would've scared the girl away or maybe even told her that Rod didn't really go to take Peanut home.

"Uh, so, you and Rod going to do that thang? *Dum-dum-de-dum. Dum-dum-de-dum.*"

Rolling her eyes, she said, "I don't know. He's a great guy and everything, but . . ."

"But what?"

She turned her face away from me and said, "I don't know."

"Well, he's been telling everybody that, um, he's going to marry you."

Sheepishly, she said, tapping her fingers against the bench, "I wish he wouldn't do that. I don't know what I want right now."

I knew how to get her. "So, where'd you get your ring?"

Maria stared me straight in the eye then asked, "Why?"

I chuckled, "Because I have one, and I know where I got mine from."

"Then why are you asking all of these dumb questions if you supposedly know it all?"

"Hey, you're the one who came here with my brother."

Maria leered at me and nodded. "You're observant."

"Very. Especially when it comes to women." I looked around at the tables and didn't see Rod anywhere. "You feel like taking a walk with me?" I was going to take her onto the trail, so we could really talk.

"Sure, but you're going to protect me from the lions, tigers, and bears, right?"

"Girl, ain't no damn animals out here. We're in Hampton, Virginia. The most you'll see is a rabbit or a squirrel."

"I know. I was just checking to see if you were a chicken shit like your brother."

"Not hardly."

Once we got on the trail, we both realized there were more people than what we expected. I didn't have a problem with it. I kept on talking. She, on the other hand, wasn't offering up much. Ten minutes passed, and we found ourselves pretty deep into the park. I saw a bench alongside the trail and took a seat. Maria sat next to me. Her thighs were wet with sweat, and little gnats had started sticking to her skin. "Well, I guess it's safe to say you're into girls, right?"

Maria leaned in front of me and glanced up and down the trail. "Yes," she blushed.

"Then why you with Rod?"

Leaning back on the bench, she replied, "A last-ditch effort to satisfy my family."

"I see."

"They swear there's a man out there for me, and maybe Rod is the right one."

I broke out into this hearty cackle. "Rod knows you ain't been giving up the ghost for him, and he's just a little bit frustrated by it."

"I know."

"Just by the way he's been describing your sex life, I knew you weren't into dick. I've been trying to persuade him into letting me fuck you, and before he left today, he told me I could."

"You are lying." Maria was pissed.

"No, I ain't. Good thing for you I don't fuck on the first date. Maybe tomorrow, though." I could be a cocky bitch when I wanted to be.

"You think I'm easy like that?"

"No, I just know I'm the shit like that." Then I leaned over and gave her a quick peck on the cheek.

"Well, that was nice, but I sure as hell don't like the way you come off."

"Look, why don't you tell my brother you like girls?"

"Because I don't want to just yet. Rod really likes me, and my family really likes him."

"Girl, fuck that shit. You do what you need to do for you. That's what I say."

Maria didn't say much more after that, so we started walking back to the picnic site. Sitting on the bench next to the beer, we found Rod, and Maria ran to him and jumped in his lap like she hadn't seen him in days.

"Hey, baby!" she yelled.

I was too through. This bitch was a fucking trip! Rod stood there with her hanging all over him, grinning from ear to ear. I think he was faking it. "So, Rita," he began to ask, "you gonna do that thang or what?"

"It's on you, bruh. It's on you."

Putting Maria down to the ground like she was a toddler or something, he yelled, "I'll be through there about ten tonight."

"A'ight. I'll be at the house."

I must've gotten home around 9:30. I smelled like charcoal and sweat. I jumped in the shower to wash off all the dirt and ran some shampoo through my do. As I turned off the water, I heard the phone ringing. I dashed down the hallway and answered. "Hello?"

"Yeah, what's up?" I knew my brother's voice anywhere.

"Nothing, dude. What's going on?"

"That's what I'm asking you."

"I just finished taking a shower. Y'all still coming?"

"Yeah, we on our way. Now how we going to do this?"

"You still got your key, right?"

"Uh-huh."

"You bring her here, and we sit and chill for a minute. After a little while, you can say you want some chips or something . . . I don't know. Then say you going to run to the store. I'm pretty sure she's not going to want to go with you."

"You sure about that?"

"Trust me."

Maria and Rod showed up a little after eleven. His ass was always late. He had a bag full of shit from Taco Bell, and nothing to drink. I assumed that would be his way of getting out of the house. "Damn, man, you didn't bring nothing to drink?" I asked, playing into this part of the plan he'd come up with on his own.

"You know I don't drink sodas, and they don't sell bottled water. You got some water here?"

"Nope." As Maria sat there going through the bag of burritos and tacos, Rod gave me this nod, acknowledging that it was cool to go through with our plan. "Niggah, you better take your ass right on back out the door and go get something to drink."

Playing this shit to the hilt, he asked, "What's close by?"

"Well, you know the Kmart around the corner closed at ten. You can go to the Wal-Mart up on 17, and get something from there." My ass was dead wrong because there was a Wal-Mart on Mercury, which was about five minutes from my house.

"A'ight. I'll be back."

Maria was wearing this pink mini-dress that actually looked like some shit that Barbie would wear. "I can't believe that niggah didn't bring nothing to drink," I said, waiting to get a response from her. While sitting next to her on the sofa with my arm across the back of it, I leaned over and looked out the window to see if Rod's car was gone. And it was.

"Rod thinks with his dick and nothing else. Want some nachos?"

I took a nacho from her container and dipped into her cheese sauce. "I know you don't like getting into this, but why you with Rod? I know you told me that shit about your family, but what about you and what you want?" As a rule, I don't have sex with a girl the same day I meet her, but, this was for my brother and the security of his future. It's all about blood, baby.

Maria eased away from me and into the corner of the sofa. Licking the cheese from her fingers and from underneath her nails, she answered, "Rita, woman to woman, dyke to dyke, I come from a family that doesn't understand how we live and love. They don't want to hear it. We came here from San Francisco because my father found a job at the shipyard. We've been here about six years. The first time I brought a girl home and said she was my girlfriend, my father spit in her face. The next one I brought home, both my parents got up and left the room after I introduced her. And the final straw was my brother. He cornered Raquel in the kitchen and tried to rape her while everyone was out in the backyard. When she returned to me, I saw it in her eyes. Then my brother came outside, mouth bleeding from where she'd popped his ass. She and I got our purses and left. It was months before I stepped foot back in that house. Despite their issues with my lifestyle, I love them dearly. When I'm not with a woman, I turn to my family for comfort and security. Without them, I'm nothing."

I couldn't believe my ears, and my blood was boiling. "That's some shit."

"Yes, it is. Rod is a man with great integrity, and he loves me better than any guy ever has. The first time my family met him they all but rolled out the red carpet for him. My father, who has a tendency to be somewhat racist, loves him to death. If you want me to say it, then, yes, I love pussy, but I don't love it enough to lose my family."

"Excuse me, Maria, for saying this, but I think you're full of shit. The right woman at the right time, can make you do thangs you never thought you would." Betrayal of blood is one thing, but the defense of womanhood is something else. "So, you been thinking about letting me get those panties?"

She sat there in disbelief, acting like she had amnesia. "What?"

"He recognizes that you ain't giving up the draws, and I told him you'd be more into me than into him."

"Did he believe you?"

"Um, I don't really know. I can say that he intentionally forgot the drinks."

Maria folded her arms and was on the verge of pouting. "Oh, he did? I figured something was up with us coming over here this late, and then you sent him to the Wal-Mart on 17 when there's one right around the corner."

Pissed was an understatement. Now, I didn't know what to do. "I apologize."

"You know what? Don't. If he wants you to fuck me, then I say give him what he wants."

My bedroom wasn't as junky as it normally was. I'd picked up the dirty laundry and the beer bottles. I wasn't sure how she wanted to do this, so, unlike other times, I asked Maria what she wanted me to do. "I'm open to everything. I wouldn't want to disappoint him," she said snidely. Having said that, she raised up her dress and threw it on the floor. Underneath, she had on a thong and nothing else. Not skipping a beat, she took it off and jumped onto my gigantic bean bag sitting in the corner. She was closely shaven around the lips of her punany, leaving only a small patch of hair at the tip of it. "Do you have a strap-on?"

Still trying to get out of my tennis shoes, I nodded. "Yes," I shamefully but proudly admitted, "but it's a double-ended one."

"Oooh, goody," she exclaimed. "Get it!"

I went over to my nightstand and pulled open the drawer. Digging through all the "toys"—vibrators, whips, KY Jelly, condoms, and whatever else you could want—I stumbled across the dildo I was looking for. "Uh, I haven't washed it in a while."

"Girl, slap a condom on it and call it a day. But, hey, let me be on top first."

I was blushing. Somebody wanted to do me? She got up from the bean bag and gestured for me to lie down. I was getting ready to recline when she said, "Unh-unh, on your stomach."

Dayum. Rod had messed around and got a woman in the streets and a freak in the sheets, and I wasn't mad at him. I kindly turned my happy ass over, on all fours, and stuck it in the air. My dildo wasn't that long, maybe about eleven inches total. Before sticking it in, Maria stroked her fingers across my clit, and she immediately realized she wouldn't need any of that KY Jelly. *Mmph.* I gasped. It slid right in. I heard her fumbling with her end and felt the tension when she'd gotten it in there. Maria pumped my ass something fierce, and I couldn't complain.

"Does it feel good? Huh? Does it feel good?"

"Awwww, yeah. It feels so good."

"Who's your daddy?"

"What?" I panted.

"Who's . . . your . . . daddy?" she asked, yowling.

"Oh, shyttttt. You are." I nutted all down my leg.

Maria withdrew but didn't remove her end. "OK, my turn, but first I want you to suck it."

I jerked the condom off and began gently licking the ebony-colored dick. You know those red, white, and blue bomb pops you get off the Popsicle truck that are cherry, lemon, and blue raspberry, the ones that you can only suck by moving it in and out your mouth? Well, I had my own personal one, except mine was black cherry. "Oooh, this is good dick, baby."

Maria delicately pushed my mouth away and plunged backward into the bean bag. She widened her body, sinking deeper into the seat and stuck her legs up in the air with the black cherry dong protruding from her. Falling helplessly into her web, I rested upon her and attached my body to hers. I didn't even think about not having a condom. We were moaning and kissing so loudly I never heard Rod enter the apartment. With my tongue twisted against hers, I opened my eyes and saw that Maria was enjoying herself more than I thought she would. Eyes rolled in the back of her head, she didn't see me staring at her and watching her facial expressions. In my movement, I thought I was hearing her charm bracelet jingle, but as I turned my head to look down at her wrist, I saw feet in my peripheral vision, next to the keys that had hit the floor. My brother's feet were in the doorway of my bedroom.

I guess men's egos aren't all they're cracked up to be because my brother hasn't spoken to me since. As a matter of fact, when Maria and I had our going-away party, he didn't even come.

Punk.

P.I.M.P.

Big booties. I love them. I'd take a ho with a big ass over a girl with brains any day. Have you ever seen a ho who's well endowed in the back work a pole? After a blunt and a couple of shots of Hennessy, that's some shit for you. When I go to the club, I try to take a ho who's not going to be all up under me the whole night. The minute we hit the door, she goes her way and I go mine. I need my space so that, in case I see another ho I want to step to, I can do my thang without any distractions. I remember one time I met this ho named Lisa at a house party. She was fine as hell with a body shaped liked a guitar—I mean this bitch had a bangin' ass. From the back, that shit looked like a damn cherry if you ask me. Anyway, I was watching her ass all night long, and it took me a minute to get my rap together. As soon as "Lately" by Tyrese came on, I walked over to her and extended my hand. "I know you want to dance with me. I've been watching you watch me all night."

"What?" she said, giggling.

I threw that Mack Daddy pose on her and pulled her to her feet. We danced until they shut the party down, and afterward, I went back to her crib. Before we could get in the door good, she was tearing off my clothes. "Dayum, girl, hold on a minute. You gonna tear up my shit," I said as I planted kisses on her lips, one right after the other. Hell, she was about to fuck up my seventy-five-dollar Sean John shirt.

"I'm sorry," she whispered, "but you smell so muthafucking good. Whatever it is got me horny as hell."

"Giorgio Armani for Men."

"Oh my gosh, that really smells good," she said, sniffing around my neck and behind my ears.

Lisa took me out of my clothes and was kissing me all over my nipples and chest. I liked that shit, too. Then she fucked up and started kissing me around my pussy, trying to give me head, I guess. You know, that kinda shit don't get me off. She tried to put her fingers in between my shit, but I pushed her hand away and held it. "I don't roll like that. Don't nothing go up there."

Still returning my kisses, she replied, "I was," *smack, smack*, "just gonna," *smack, smack* "stick . . ."

"I said no." Lisa respected my demands and went on with her seduction of me. I ain't never liked nothing going up in my pussy. When somebody told me that the gynecologist stuck shit up there, I vowed to never go. When I die and the coroner does the autopsy, bats and cobwebs and shit gonna be flying out from down there. I ain't never had no dick, no fingers, no tampons, nada. In spite of everything she was doing to turn me on, I wasn't truly fazed until she took off her clothes and I saw that ass.

Dayum. "Bend over and touch your toes," I demanded.

"What?" she chuckled.

I swear I thought she had blond roots beneath that weave. "I said touch your toes." I didn't yell. I just said it with force.

Lisa bent over and bam! My clit got rock hard. I scampered over to her with my pants down around my ankles and stuck it right in the crack of her ass. As her cheeks pounded against my groin, my thrusts became more powerful. I didn't need to massage her titties or her pussy. I was fine with resting one of my hands around the back of her neck while the other planted stinging palm prints on her butt cheeks. That nut shot spasms through my back so tough that I slumped over her back, and we both fell asleep, right there, in that very position, on the chair that sat by her front door.

Later that morning while trying to put on my shoes, I noticed my cell phone was missing. I checked in all of my pockets and couldn't find it. The last time I'd had it was when I was at the party. Lisa was in the kitchen eating a boiled egg and sipping on juice.

"You seen my phone?"

She looked up at me and replied, "No, I didn't even know you had one."

"Yeah, I do, but I can't find it." That bothered me because all my bitches' phone numbers was in it. "Can I use your phone?" I figured maybe I'd call it and see if I'd dropped it somewhere in her house.

"Sure."

The phone rang and rang, but I didn't hear anything. "Look, it was nice meeting you, but I need to run back over to where they had the party last night and see if my phone is over there."

Lisa, nonchalantly replied, "And you gonna leave just like that so you can find your damn phone? You could at least . . ."

"Look, I don't mean no disrespect, but I gotta find that phone. I need it for work. Maybe we can hook up later today and I can take you shopping or something. Dinner, maybe?"

That was the lie I always used, and it never failed. "OK. Call me later."

"A'ight then," I said, knowing full well I wasn't going to call because I'd never asked for her phone number.

When I arrived at the house where the party had been, I

knocked and this old broad came to the door. "May I help you?"

"Uh, excuse me, but I was at a party here last night and wanted to know if anyone found a cell phone."

The woman glanced over her shoulder then looked back at me. "Nope, no one found a cell phone in here," she said and closed the door. The bitch didn't even look.

I stood on the porch retracing my tracks from the night before. It was like once I met Lisa, everything else after that became a blur.

I went home and fixed me a bowl of Trix before taking a shower. Lying in the bed half wet, I closed my eyes and focused on where I'd been. No matter how much I thought about it, I kept ending up with Lisa. That's why I hate fucking around with bitches sometimes. They like playing too many games. About an hour later, my home phone rang. It was Shelly, this trick I met a while back. "Um, Brianna, why you got your bitch calling here playing on my phone?"

Shocked, I replied, "I ain't got nobody calling you. What you talking about?"

Shelly didn't play games. "Look, the caller ID's got your cell number on it, and you know I don't get down like this." She was a crazy bitch, and I didn't fuck with her too much.

"Shelly, baby, some ho must've creeped my phone last night at the party. I swear."

"There you go, calling women hos again. It's bad enough the men disrespect us with that terminology. It's even worse when another woman calls us that."

"Mayne, whatever. I didn't call your house. Now get off my phone." Shelly was a bag of her tricks her own damn self. We met at the car wash over on Main Street while she was getting her grandmomma's Benz washed. I was there with one of my boys when I saw her. Damn, she had legs like Amerie and long, flowing hair that I eventually found out wasn't hers. I hate that in a ho. All that fake-ass hair and nails and shit. Just be yourself is what I say. But that day, the fake stuff didn't stop me from getting the booty. She slid me her digits, and that night I called her and met her at Denny's. I paid for her dinner, and then she insisted I follow her back to her place.

Shelly had a nice little crib in the projects on the lower end of Main Street. I mean, I didn't have no problem fucking a project ho from over there if that's what you're wondering. It wasn't my style, but I dealt with it. Besides, I heard they were uninhibited—would do anything you asked them to. One thing you have to know about me. If a ho got a big booty and a smile, she could have ten kids and live in the bottom of the ghetto; I'd still fuck her. A big booty and a smile . . . that's all it takes. Anyway, once in the apartment, Shelly started lighting candles and shit. When she started for the bedroom, I grabbed her by the arm and pulled her close to me. I kissed her in every available spot and then pushed her to the couch. Through the candlelight, I saw that smile of hers and was determined to go to work on that ass.

But then, she says, "Hold on a minute. I'll be right back."

She got up and went into the bathroom and stayed in there for like ten minutes. I was hoping she hadn't gone in there to shit or something because that would've been just nasty. As she was making her way back to the couch, I was trying to make out what was heading in my direction. "OK, now, I'm ready," she said. I'm looking at her like, damn, this ho done took off her wig. I was quietly pissed off, but it didn't stop me from hitting it. Having those Amerie-like legs wrapped around me was enough to make me come. I worked it all night, and, through it all, I knew I had no intentions of seeing her again.

The next morning Shelly had gotten up to make break-

fast, and the smell of fresh cooked sausage was seeping underneath the bathroom door while I was washing up. I couldn't
resist that. She'd made eggs, grits, and toast. It appeared she'd
gone out of her way to cook for me, so I did stop and eat. While
we were sitting at the table, I couldn't help but glance up at
her hair while I was eating my grits. "Can I ask you a question?"

Smiling, she responded, "Sure you can."

I cleared my throat and took a sip of orange juice first.
Then I continued, "Why do you wear a wig?" I stared at the
hair sticking from under her stocking cap.

By the way Shelly looked at me before answering, I knew
she was offended. "What do you mean?"

"What do I mean? Shit, the question is just what I said.
Why you wearing wigs and shit?" It was then that I noticed
she had on fake nails, too. "Why not simply be yourself?"

Shelly didn't trip or anything. She said, "I wear them
'cause I want to, and that's that. You got a problem with it?"

"Sort of, but I don't even know you like that to be all up in
your business."

"Yeah, you're right. You don't. I think you should leave."

Well, since it seemed that she was putting me out, I went
ahead and spilled all the beans. "So, you wear fake nails,
too?" That generated a smack upside the back of my head
and almost across my face. I shielded myself and jetted for
the door. As I stood in the threshold, I tried to calm her by
asking if I could see her again. Surprisingly, she said yes. We
went out two more times, and I even took her shopping—
bought her all kinds of stuff, most of it fake. Pussy was good,
but I'd made up my mind that I didn't want nothing else
from her counterfeit ass.

Stretched out across my bed, I couldn't, for the life of me,
figure out what happened to my cell phone. *Riiinnggg!* My
house phone rang again.

"Yeah."

"Don't be no damn 'yeah' with me. Who the fuck y'all think y'all playin' with?"

It was Danyele, the drama queen of the year. "What's up?"

"Don't you and your bitch fuck around and get cut, hear?"

"What the hell are you talking about?"

Danyele took in one deep breath then let it all out full of nothing but lip. "Some stank-ass ho done called over here talking shit about you and her are an item now and I'd better back the hell off. If she knew like I knew, she . . ."

"Don't you even go there, Danyele. You know you my one and only." I'd met Danyele at the library of all places. I was in there checking to see if they had a copy of the latest *Metro Weekly* so I could see if there were any parties that weekend. On my way out, I felt the urge to pee and whisked my ass into the ladies' room. You know, if they had a restroom for female playas I'd sure as hell use it. It gets on my nerves when females be looking at me all crazy and shit when I come out the stall. Anyway, this time when I came out the stall, there she was . . . Danyele. She gave me a different kind of look—the kind I get at the club.

"'Sup?" I asked.

"Nothing," she said in a soft voice, looking at me like a piece of cold watermelon in the summertime. "So, did you shake it all off?"

Blushing as I washed and dried my hands, I replied, "Yeah, I handled it."

Danyele giggled and went on to ask me my name. She had on this long, black sleeveless dress that hugged her ass like a glove. I walked up behind her and pressed my groin against her ass, bracing each side of the sink with my hands. I looked at her in the mirror as she rested her ass against my lap. "My name is Brianna, and I want you to be my date tonight."

Danyele, trying to slowly remove herself from my entrap-
ment, said, "I don't date girls."

Laughing as I rested my head on her shoulder still ex-
changing glares through the mirror, I said, "Oh my bad, I
made a mistake. I'm sorry." I moved my hands from the sink
and headed for the door.

"Wait," she exclaimed. "What time you gonna pick me
up?"

Later that night, Danyele and I fucked in the car something fierce. The only thing that bothered me was she had a
little odor to her. It was enough of one to keep me from
putting my mouth on her. She kept begging, kept pleading
for me to eat her, but I wasn't in the mood for rank pussy
that would make me sick for weeks on end. Danyele was mad
as hell with me, but I wasn't taking no chances. I kicked it
with her one other time thinking she'd washed it a little
more thoroughly, but, nope, that ass was still fonkyfunky.

"What she doing with yo' cell phone, then, Brianna?"

"I don't know what the hell is going on." I was trying to
conjure up sympathy without telling Danyele I'd met somebody at the party. "I lost my cell phone last night, so ain't no
telling who that was calling you."

"Well, whoever she is know you like she know the back of
her hand. Got all your business out in the street."

"A'ight, Danyele. I need to go." I slammed the phone
down and put on some clothes. I lit a cigarette and paced
through the bedroom. Some bitch had my phone. My house
phone rang yet again.

"Hello."

"Brie?"

"Yeah, this me."

"What's wrong with you, dude?" It was Chalon, a niggah I hung out with at the job.

"What you mean?"

"Word out that you quit today."

"What?"

"Man, they said you called in and cussed Mr. Perkins out and told him to kiss your ass."

I couldn't believe that. "Look, somebody lifted my phone last night and has been calling everybody in my contact list. The damn house phone has been ringing all day with bitches pissed at me. They say it's some girl."

"Whoa, dude, you got some fatal attraction shit going here. If I were you, I'd handle the job thing right away because they pissed as a muthafucker around here."

"OK, I'm doing that right now." I jumped off the phone and called my boss to clean that shit up. Although it sounded unbelievable, Mr. Perkins actually listened to me and gave me another chance. I told him I'd bring in proof if I needed to, but he said not to worry about it.

By the end of the day, every ho in my contact list had called me and cussed me out talking about me being a playa and a pimp. I wouldn't admit to none of them that I was either of those things, but I secretly thanked them for giving me my props. At this point, though, nobody was even speaking to me. I couldn't get nobody to cook me dinner or go to dinner with me. Hell, Shelly's greedy ass was always ready to get something to eat, but she'd blocked my number out of her phone.

The only person I could speak to was Lisa. That ass of hers could make me do things I'd be ashamed to admit. But I couldn't give her a call because I didn't ask her for her phone number. I didn't even remember how to get back to her house. Shit, I knew I wouldn't be going back over there anyway. I wanted to know where my cell phone was, and for the second time, I decided to dial the number. I was blown the fuck away when somebody answered it.

"Uh, hello? Who the fuck is this with my phone? Hello?"

"Hello, Brianna."

"Who the fuck is this?"

"How has your day been? Busy, I bet."

I wanted to get Chuck Norris on whoever was on the other end of the phone. "Look, bitch, I ain't the one to fuck with. Who is this?"

"Do you miss me?"

I was going to explode. I was so damn mad that I punched a hole in the wall. "Who is this?"

"Don't you know it's not nice to fuck someone and then leave them without even telling them your name?"

"What?"

"How were you going to call me when you didn't even ask me for my number?"

Lisa. I couldn't say shit because I knew I was dead wrong when I hit it and quit it. "Lisa . . ."

"Yes, Brianna?" she said softly.

"Why are you doing this? Why have you been destroying my life all day long calling all of my friends and trying to fuck up my job?"

Lisa sat silent for a moment before she said anything else. "I have power in my pussy. If you hadn't come here and fucked me like some gutter-rat ho then left like the pimp you claim to be, then I might not have taken your phone. But you treated me like a ho, Brianna, so I used the power in my pussy to bring your ass back down to earth."

STRAPPED

My moms didn't know I was packing heat. I got it from my boy, Jamal, when I was at the teenage runaway shelter. His ass had two of them because he'd run away from his stepdad who had been molesting him and beating his mother. I couldn't blame him for that because I was living proof that muthafuckers is crazy. Once I told him what happened to me out in the field that day, he told me he'd heard that the candy man had been in the hospital for a few days and that he had reopened for business. That bastard had a limp, but he was going to live. If that son of a bitch Mr. Luther even looked like he was stepping my way, it was really going to be all over. The nightmares would stop, and I'd be free to dream again.

The counselors called Moms within forty-eight hours of my arrival and told her what happened. The first time she came to visit she had problems looking at me, especially with the way I'd cut my hair and all. She hated the way I was carrying myself, and she detested the name Mo.

"Where did you get this Mo crap from? Your name is Monique."

I sat at the table carving my initials in the table with my fingernails. I was more into that than I was her visit. "I know they told you why my name is that."

"Why couldn't you come to me with this?"

I wanted to gouge her eyes out. "I did try to tell you, but you chose to ignore me."

Moms seemed like she was getting annoyed with me and started rushing me with my answers. "Why did you cut all your hair off, and why are you wearing your clothes like that?"

I wasn't liking Moms too much right then. "I . . ."

"Don't you hear me talking to you?" The counselors were watching her and decided they'd had enough. One of them came from the back office and asked her to leave. "I'm trying to talk to my daughter or whatever the hell she is."

"Ma'am, she needs her rest. Maybe you should come back when you've had some time to gather your thoughts. Your behavior isn't helping the situation."

Moms sat there, shaking her head. "Lawd Jesus. Help me, Father," she cried. She collected her things and got up from the table and stared at me like I was the villain. "Well, call me if you need me."

I didn't need her. I hated her, and instead of rising with her to embrace her, I tearfully turned and departed for my room.

To prevent further humiliation, I dropped out of school and spent my days and nights at the shelter. In the evenings, some of the boys and me would hang out on the corner by the Kitty Kat Club and watch the perverted folks go in and out. I wondered if Mr. Luther's ass ever went up in there. If I saw him, I would kill him, and my partners would back me up, too. He wouldn't even know it was me. I'd been gone for almost two years, and Moms was still too ashamed to tell folks how I was doing. What was she gonna say, "Oh,

Monique, she doing alright down there in that juvie home for crazy runaways?" She was too proud for that. I'd found a barber who cut my hair for me exactly the way I liked it. I'd actually let him cut me bald one time, but the fellas said it didn't look right on me because my face was too round.

The shelter had an arrangement with the deli next door to hire kids who were old enough to work. That's where I got my first job as a stock boy. They paid us under the table, so there was no papers to fill out and shit. As I requested, everybody called me Mo. One day while I was stocking the canned collard greens, this young lady approached me and asked me if we carried Glory food products. She was a nice-looking woman wearing Baby Phat denim capris with a tight yellow shirt to match. Other than that I didn't pay no more attention to her than I would have anybody else. "Naw, we don't carry Glory stuff. We got Sylvia's, though."

"Oh, well, that's OK. I was looking for Glory." She turned to walk away but kept looking over her shoulder at me.

Later that evening, my partners and I was hanging out in front of the Kitty Kat Club when a group of ladies walked past us. Bringing up the rear was the same girl I'd seen at the store that day. When she got up closer to where I was standing, she stopped in front of me, leaned in, and asked, "So, this is your night job?" She had to have felt my piece tucked inside of my jeans.

I cracked a smile and said, "Nope. Just hangin' with the fellas." I looked over to where they were standing because they knew what was up. I was pretty sure they'd have jokes when we got back to the shelter.

"Oh."

"You cook dem greens?" I laughed.

Blushing, she responded, "Yeah, I did actually. Found some Glory greens at Mr. Habib's store." Her friends had stopped and gave her that bring-yo'-ass-on look. "I have to go."

Jamal was standing there chuckling when the girls finally went into the club. "Uh, you gonna handle that, Mo?"

"What you mean, playa? It's all good."

"A'ight, it's all good. You better watch yo'self."

That Friday, which was also payday, I was walking down past the club and found this novelty shop that sold rubber dicks and other freaky shit for the bedroom. Jamal had gotten me a fake ID, so I strolled in like I knew what I was looking for and was prepared to flash that bitch if I needed to. The dicks were in all shapes and sizes, colors and varieties. There were some that could squirt shit in you and some that vibrated. I merely wanted one that would look real beneath my zipper. The salesperson, who'd been busy when I first came in, approached me and asked if there was anything in particular I was looking for.

"I want something simple that I can wear all day long and be comfortable in." The people who worked in those kinds of stores had to be some all-time freaks because her ass knew exactly what would work for me. She reminded me of those ladies who work in the fancy department stores who help women get fitted for bras.

"Now for the first few days you're probably going to look like you got your hands on some Viagra, but the way you fix that is to buy you some men's bikinis. Boxers might even work for you."

I tried it on, and I looked great. "I'll take it." I bought the harness and shit to wear with it, too. When I got back to the shelter, I locked myself in the bathroom so I could put on this new part of me that, as far as I was concerned, was permanent. I was sure I could wear it even while I was on my period, wearing it over my panties. My transformation was complete.

On the corner that same night, Miss Gurl and her friends walked by going to the club. I was looking pretty fresh with some new Timbs, new jeans, and a flannel plaid shirt. I'd thinned out quite a bit since high school, so everything hung off me. "What's up, Martha Stewart?"

The whole group busted out laughing because they knew she liked to cook, and, although she appeared slightly embarrassed, she started laughing herself.

"You know you wrong," she said as she pressed her body against mine. She had to feel that bulge in my pants. "My name is LaQuita."

"My bad. LaQuita Stewart then."

"You're funny."

"I try." I felt like I had much game that night, and despite Jamal's evil looks every now and again, I was determined to holla at LaQuita.

"Look, I'm late for work. Can I come by and talk to you at the store tomorrow?"

"Yeah, you can do that. I get off at three."

"OK, I'll see you then."

As soon as I walked out of the store, I saw LaQuita standing across the street smoking a cigarette and holding a brown paper bag. I'd developed this trot like my partners and had even learned how to hold my dick while I was doing it. "'Sup witcha?"

"Nothing much," she smiled. She smelled like vanilla and sugar.

"What's in the bag?" It had a big grease spot on the bottom, so it had to be food.

"Something for you. Compliments of LaQuita Stewart."

I opened the bag and saw a plastic container full of greens. On top of it was a piece of corn bread wrapped in Saran Wrap. I hadn't had any greens and corn bread since I was at home with Moms. "Dayum, baby girl, you hooked a niggah up, didn't cha?"

"And they ain't from the can either. I made 'em this morning. I figured you don't get stuff like that in the shelter."

"How you know I'm at the shelter?" I was defensive.

"Everybody knows you guys are from the shelter. Calm down. It's not a big deal."

If she knew that, then I wondered what else she knew. "A'ight then, since you know sumthin' 'bout me, tell me sumthin' 'bout you."

"What do you wanna know?"

"You work at the Kitty Kat Club?"

"Yeah, I do," she said, taking a drag from her cigarette.

"What, you a dancer or sumthin'?"

Hesitating before she answered, LaQuita flicked her cigarette to the ground and replied, "Yeah, I'm a dancer. You got a problem with that?"

"Naw, do ya thang. You let dem men feel all over you?"

"Unh-unh. They not allowed to touch."

For some reason, I was relieved. LaQuita and me walked a few blocks to the basketball courts and sat there and talked until it got dark. She seemed cool but not cool enough to know my secret yet. I walked her to her apartment and told her I'd see her later. Couldn't define when later was, but I knew it would be soon.

Jamal was sitting on the steps of the shelter when I came in. "You been with that girl, Mo?"

I wasn't ashamed about it. "Yeah, why?"

Jamal had been like a big brother to me. He knew about the shit with Moms, he knew about my pain, and he knew my secret. "Look, if that girl ever finds out that you walking around with a plastic dick on, she's gonna have your business all out in the streets. Are you ready for that?"

"Mayne, I don't know. We just talkin'. Ain't nobody tryin' to get wit' nobody. I ain't never said nothin' 'bout likin' chicks no way."

Jamal was an intelligent brother who could have had a lot of shit going for him if he ever got his head on right. Word had gotten back to him that when his mom tried to divorce his stepdad, the punk-ass bitch beat her into a coma. Jamal slipped into the hospital one night to see her, and it took everything in him to keep from going to bust a cap in his stepdad's ass. He cried like a baby on his mom's bed until the morning came. "You know why that niggah beat my mom?"

"No, why?" I asked, taking a seat on the step below him.

"I had this aunt named Yvonne that wasn't really my aunt. She used to be my mom's girlfriend. I was crazy about her because she could cook and shit. I ain't never seen my mom so happy. Then, one day, out of nowhere, Yvonne just up and left. No phone calls, no letters, no nothing. Next thing you know I came home one day, and my mom was laying up with that fool. He was alright for a minute. 'Bout two months after he'd been living with us, Aunt Yvonne called and wanted to come back home. Mom tried to put Stanley out. She even 'fessed up and told him why she wanted him to go. That's when the beatings started. He grabbed me by the neck in front of her and made me suck his dick while he held a knife at my throat. That shit didn't have to happen to me but once before I knew I needed to leave. He told me if I ever told anybody he'd kill her."

"What about your aunt?"

"You remember that body they found in the river a while back?"

"Yeah, the woman who had been shot in the head."

"That was Yvonne." Jamal, the hardest fool in the shelter, was crying. Wiping his eyes, he whimpered, "I don't want you to end up like her. I know he did it because he said he'd kill her if she ever came around again. Mayne, you couldn't stop the bond she and my mom had." He looked off into the distance, shaking his head. "He caught them one night sitting in my mom's car. Soon after that was when Yvonne disappeared. That almost killed my mom, and to look at her in pain and in fear all the time, I couldn't take it, so I came here."

There was a time when I felt that no one could possibly hurt as badly as I did, and after hearing Jamal's story, I still felt that way. I understood why he packed heat. He was waiting for the perfect time to catch Stanley alone. I could tell, though, Jamal had worked through his anger because, when I first met him, he was spending every day running streets looking for Stanley. Now, he'd found better, more productive ways to occupy his time.

"Jamal?" I said.

"Yeah?"

"What do I do if I'm gay?"

He started laughing. "Don't do shit. But you need to tell that girl you ain't no niggah. If she cool wit' it, then work your magic and pop that coochie. It's 'bout time you did that anyway."

"I mean, how am I supposed to know what to do?"

"Oh, you'll know. Trust me."

LaQuita and I chilled a lot after that. I'd saved up enough money to get me a little apartment that the counselors helped me find. They asked me if I wanted Moms to have the address, and I told them it was OK. I hadn't seen her in months so I knew she would never come to visit anyway.

The place wasn't much, but it was mine. Outside of Jamal, I didn't have many friends. That made me enjoy LaQuita's company even more. As a housewarming gift, she bought me a leather loveseat and a television. One evening while we was watching TV, somebody knocked at the door like they was the po-po. *Who the fuck?* I'd been in the apartment for two months, and the only visitors I'd had were Jamal, LaQuita, and one of the counselors. With each knock, my heart raced and the thought pounded through my head that Mr. Luther had finally come to seek his revenge. "You invite somebody over here, Quita?"

"No." She sat up on the loveseat, just as startled as I was.

I pulled out my nine-millimeter, released the safety, and walked slowly toward the door. Whoever it was had become impatient and was trying to turn the knob with one hand while pounding fiercely with the other. I was ready to blast his ass. "Who is it?" I yelled.

"It's your momma. Now open this door."

I stood there contemplating what to do. Moms wasn't going away, especially since she knew I was in there. "A'ight, hold on."

LaQuita, still sitting on the loveseat, was all geeked and excited. "You ain't never said nothin' 'bout your momma. I can't believe I finally get to meet her."

There wasn't another room for me to send LaQuita into, and the closet had too much junk in it. Besides, Moms was going to come in and look through the place anyway. "Before I open that door, I need you to know I love you . . . no matter what."

"OK," she smiled curiously.

Shoving the gun back in my pants, I opened the door, and Moms barged in spitting fire like she was on the warpath. "What the hell took you so long to open the door?"

"I thought it was somebody for the folks across the hall."

"You a damn lie. Who is this?" she asked, glaring at Quita as she took a seat next to her.

"Uh, this is my friend LaQuita."

Moms rolled her eyes and continued her tirade. "Monique, why couldn't you bring your ass back home to stay instead of moving into a dump like this?"

I was fucked. She'd called me Monique. LaQuita's gaze turned toward me, but she didn't move or say a word. Since motor mouth was telling everything, I saw no reason to hold back. "I'm more comfortable here."

"Monique, Moesha, Mo . . . whatever you calling yourself, you too young to be living on your own."

I had to stop her. "What don't you get? I don't want to live with you. You want to blame somebody for me being like this then blame yourself. I tried time and time again to tell you that bastard was doing some awful shit to me, and you ignored me. Yeah, I tried to slice his dick off, and every day I wish I had. Because of that, I don't want shit to do with no man. I don't want no man touching me or kissing me or even looking at me. That's why I look like this."

Moms sat there conspiring against me. I didn't know what she had for Mr. Luther because she never tried to protect me from him. It was all about what I had done. She mean-mugged LaQuita again. "So I guess you dyking now?"

"What?" I cried.

"This tramp you got here."

I pulled my nine from the back of my pants. I'd had enough. "Get out." Her eyes were like tiny balls of fire. Through them, I saw the woman I used to get pickles for—the one who I wore the dresses, hairbows, and Mary Janes for. And I hated her.

"Oh, so now you bad 'cuz you call yourself being strapped?

Well, lemme tell you something. You going to hell. All this shit you dun brought on yourself ain't gonna do nothing but get you a first-class ticket to hell," she screamed at me.

By now, LaQuita had gotten up from the loveseat and was standing by my side with her hand resting on my arm. "Give me the gun, baby. Don't do this."

Pulling a gun on Moms was something I never thought I'd do. But as I looked at her, I felt nothing—no love, no compassion, no connection to her at all. If the gun had accidentally gone off, I probably would have dragged her body into the bathroom, cut it up Tony Soprano style, and put all the pieces into a big trunk and tossed her in the river. There wouldn't be no love lost either.

"I hate her, Quita," I wept as I knocked her hand away from my arm.

"I know, baby, but give me the gun."

Moms was like a pit bull. She just wouldn't stop. She kept at me, hurting me more with every word. "You must still have some girl in you 'cuz you standing over there crying like a ol' bitch." With that said, she stormed past LaQuita toward the door, slamming it when she left.

"You should've let me kill her," I said, handing my girl the gun.

"No, I wasn't going to let you do that. No matter what she says or how she acts, she's still your mother." LaQuita took me by the arm and guided me back to the sofa. Then she went into the kitchen and brought me back a glass of water. "So, when were you going to tell me about Monique?" she asked as she plopped down in the seat next to me.

"Never. As far as I'm concerned, she's dead." LaQuita felt my pain. My tone had changed, and it was clear that we'd never talk about Monique again. "I'm sure you want to get out of here, considering you know the truth now."

Sitting there kissing my muscles, LaQuita took me by the

hand and said, "Actually, I thought I might hang around to get to know you better." With those words, LaQuita, the twenty-one-year-old dancer who'd never let any man at the club touch her and who could cook greens better than Moms ever could, and who'd kept me from ruining the rest of my life (because I was going to kill Moms's ass), made love to Mo that night and rescued me from my nightmare.

THE GREATEST LOVE STORY NEVER TOLD

There was nothing special about her that created a spark. I can honestly say that about the first time I saw her and the last time I saw her. It was those things in between that made my heart of no use to anyone else.

I met her at the Starbucks in the Jacob Javits Center in New York City. She and I were reaching for a straw at the same time. As I pulled my hand away, I bumped her arm, causing her to spill her latte on the front of her white suit. "Damn."

"Oh, my gosh. I am so sorry."

"Damn. I can't believe this." Her outburst caused everybody to stop. Some of the employees came over and tried to help her clean up the mess. "All over my white suit. The ceremony starts in an hour, and I . . . Damn."

I assumed that she was headed to the same event as I and the other hundreds of women dressed in white. We were on our way to the opening ceremony of our sorority's national convention. "Let me help you, soror," I offered.

"Help me do what? This suit is ruined, and there's no way I'm going into the main hall looking like this. Shit!"

As I wiped off her bag and tried to pick up her things that had dropped to the floor, I realized there was nothing I could do. "Look, I really am sorry." Reaching into my purse, I pulled out my wallet. "Here's my card and a hundred dollars to buy you another suit. If you find one that costs more than that, then call me, and I'll send you the difference."

Snatching the card from my hand, she replied, "Oh, yeah, you better believe I'm going to call you."

One of the ceremony attendants was also buying coffee and had seen the whole thing. "Excuse me, soror. You'll be fine. No one is going to care about the stain on your clothes. If you're still worried, then come down to the west end of the hall, and I'll let you in myself. Once you're in, you're in."

Rolling her eyes at me, the woman snarled, "Thank you, but I think I'm going to head back to the hotel."

Standing there with her belongings in my hand, I asked, "Can I have your name, so in case you call, I'll remember you?"

Yanking her things from me, she snapped, "It's Karen." And she stomped off to hail a taxi.

I stood in the bathroom mirror looking at my edges and wondered if I should've followed my intuition and gotten a perm. "Damn, this is nappy." I rubbed Ampro gel onto my fingertips and massaged it into my hairline. Then I tugged at it, pulling it taut, and brushed the new growth until it was smooth. Despite my efforts, I ended up putting on a wig that I'd been saving for a bad hair day. "This is going to have to do for today. I'm already running behind."

Stepping over newspapers strewn about Nadia's side of the bedroom, I stretched over the bed, pulled my skirt above my knees, climbed in the bed, and kissed Nadia on the forehead as she slept. I set back on my knees in amazement while I watched her sleep. Her breasts were a perfect D cup, a 34 actually, and they were firm. Not a stretch mark or blemish in sight. Nadia's titties looked like a work of art. In previous relationships, I had never been a mountee, but over the years, I had grown accustomed to making love to Nadia with a strap-on, and she loved it. It finally became the only way we had sex. I couldn't bear to tell her that I hated it that way. I once asked her if our sex was all about penetration then why not just be with a man. She took my comment in jest and never elaborated on it. I loved Nadia; therefore, I refused to admit that I was bored with her.

I was always ready for vacation after Nationals. Running from here to there the entire week and partying until all hours of the night had worn me out. As the owner of Two Men and Hoe Landscaping Service, I could take one when-ever I wanted, but there was work to be done, and I had to make sure that it was.

"Hey," Nadia whispered. "You're back?"

"Yes," I said softly. "I got in late last night, and I didn't want to wake you."

"You should have. I missed you," she smiled, stretching her arms upward toward my neck. Morning breath and all, she pulled me close to her and kissed me on the cheek. "You're about to leave already?" she asked, glancing over at the clock. "You've got appointments this early?"

"Yeah, there's this city contract I'm trying to land, and I have to meet with the city manager at nine."

"Oh, OK," she said, reaching for my neck to give me an-other hug and a kiss. "You want some coffee?"

When I met Nadia, she was an avid coffee drinker, but I wasn't. But then, after smelling the fresh-brewed coffee morning after morning, I started drinking it, too. "No, thanks. I'll get some at the office."

"I bought Hawaiian Kona," she flirted.

That coffee was forty dollars a pound. "I'll have some after dinner tonight, OK?"

"I can't believe you're turning that down. How was the convention?" she asked as she got up to put on her robe.

I caught a glimpse of her naked ass while I was smoothing out the wrinkles in my skirt, and just as she crept up on me, I smacked her on the butt cheeks when she passed by. Ain't nothing like the crack of woman's naked ass against the palm of my hand. *Shit!* "It was nice as usual," I answered.

"Meet any sexy women you want to have a baby with?"

There it went. An accusation without an accusation. "No, Nadia I didn't meet any *family* members if that's what you're asking. I don't go there to look for women, especially when I've got one at home."

"Puh-leeze. There's no way you can tell me that you didn't get a number or two while you were there. All those fine-ass women?"

Nadia, although she went to college, never pledged a sorority and automatically believed that sorority meetings were like wild-game nights. "It's not like that, Nadia, and why do you keep trying to push me into stuff? I'm with you, and you know that. We go through this every time I have to do something with a bunch of women. I wish you weren't so insecure."

"I'm not insecure. All I'm saying is you know you ain't bad to look at, and you should be flattered if all the women are throwin' their panties at you."

"For what? For me to have to deal with you and this drama? No thank you."

Wiping her face with her washcloth, Nadia came out of the bathroom. As I watched her walk toward me with a body that reminded me of my favorite dancer, Oohzee, I was tempted to call and cancel my meeting. My baby knew how to give me a show whenever I wanted one, and although I felt her to be a bit limited with her skills, I was content and had even been tempted a few times to put a pole in the shower for my own personal entertainment. I told her I'd pay her twice what I'd drop for Oohzee if she could move like her just once. Nadia's response was always, "I'm not into that." A Harvard grad, she had the tendency to be quite prudish. "Whatever, Frankie," she said, rolling her eyes as she switched past me. "It won't be long before some hooch calls here."

"OK, baby, whatever you say. I'm out."

I was ready to leave. I loved Nadia, but she could get on my fucking nerves sometimes. When we first met, she began the conversation with, "Don't even look this way if you ain't trying to have a kept woman." Business was profitable so I had the extra cash to spend on someone special. Besides, Nadia's game was always tight. She knew the right people in the right circles and helped me to pull in some pretty heavy-duty clients. Nadia's all femme, and so am I, but in the bed-room, I was the one doing all the penetration—the fucking. In the very beginning, she asked me to humor her and wear men's cologne. My response was, "Hell, no. If you want that shit, go get you a niggah." She said she was just kidding, but I didn't believe her. Even though I wear my pearls, skirts, and four-inch heels, Nadia keeps trying to make me into . . . a man. Around the house, she does all the girlie shit like the cooking, the cleaning, the entertaining, and the shopping. I take out the trash, kill the bugs, lift the heavy things, and un-clog the backed-up toilets. The man shit. Oh, and I let's not forget the lawn. At first I was mowing my own lawn because I liked the exercise. Then one day she came home from the nursery with a carload of flowers and wanted me to plant them since I owned a landscaping business. I planted the shit while she sat on the patio drinking lemonade, but I quickly gave one of my employees a side contract of doing my lawn. Hell, I wanted to sit on my ass and sip lemonade, too.

Around our house, money was never limited. I could easily pay all my bills—and hers—without any help, but Nadia wanted to continue "working" as an educational consultant. I never asked her for a penny of her money, and she never offered it either. I often showered her with small gifts, but I rarely got anything from her in return. On my birthday, she cooked for me and gave me a card, but that was it. The first year it didn't matter, nor the second, the third, or the fourth year either. I just wanted Nadia's love, and I would love only her in return.

"Good morning. My name is Francesca Wyatt. I have an appointment with the city manager." I'd made it with three minutes to spare.

The receptionist scanned her list. "I see your name. It's right here. Have . . ." she paused. "Hold on for a moment." She looked puzzled.

"Is there something wrong?"

She picked up the phone and started asking questions about the information next to my name. I couldn't see what it was because she'd covered it up with a folder. "Ma'am, I'm going to send you to the procurement department."

"What?"

"They'll explain everything to you there."

Following her directions, I rode the elevator down to the next floor and approached the receptionist's desk. "Hi, my name is Francesca Wyatt."

"Good morning," she smiled as she extended her right hand. "Ms. Davenport will be with you in a moment. Help yourself to some coffee and muffins."

"Thank you." I walked over to the table and picked up a banana nut muffin and poured myself a cup of coffee. I glanced at my left hand and realized I'd left my ring at home. I'm sure Nadia was having a fit by now.

My hands were full with my purse and my briefcase, so I

placed the muffin and coffee on the table while I carried my belongings to a nearby empty chair. I returned to take a bite out of the muffin while I sorted through the condiment basket for a packet of Splenda. Then I poured some cream into my cup and mixed in the packet. Just as I was about to take a sip, I felt eyes on me, staring hard.

"Careful not to spill it," a voice said.

I looked up and . . . *Awww, dayum.*

"I'm Karen Davenport, Director of Procurement."

Protocol was that I give her hug. She was my soror, so I put my cup down and reached to embrace her. "Well, hi. How are you?"

She seemed more pleasant than the last time I saw her when I accidentally spilled coffee on her. "I'm fine. And you?"

"I'm good." This felt strange.

"Come on back to my office. Do you need any help?"

Fumbling with my purse and briefcase, I said, "No, I can manage." I was trying to figure out what the hell was going on.

Her office was at the end of a very long hallway. It was so big that you could put a basketball court in it. On each wall, intermingled with all of her degrees in walnut frames were pictures of her with every city official imaginable. "Have a seat."

I sat in the chair directly across from her desk and prepared myself to conduct business. "I suppose you're going to tell me what's going on here."

Karen chuckled. "Are you nervous, soror?"

Clearing my throat, I said, "A little."

"You shouldn't be. The city manager and I have decided we're going to award the landscaping contract to your company. The name is definitely a lot different than most, but I think it's cute."

"May I ask how my company was chosen?"

"Well, it certainly wasn't because you ruined my Dolce and Gabbana suit."

Shit, and I only gave her a hundred dollars. I was too embarrassed. "Um, OK."

"Seriously, though, we haven't awarded any minority landscaping contracts in several months, and we needed to in order to meet government funding guidelines. Don't get me wrong. We were quite impressed with your portfolio. You do awesome work."

"Thank you."

"The other factor in your favor was that I remembered your name from your business card, and I wanted to help a soror out. I've been pulling for you from the beginning."

Beaming with pride, I thanked her again. Karen walked me through the contract process, pointing out all the places I needed to sign.

"Now, explain to me what my company is to do for you," I said when we were done.

"Well, for starters, you'll have city hall and the federal courthouse. Those get attention before anything else. You'll also have all the city-owned and county buildings. The convention center and city college are included along with all of the street medians, city-owned parks, bus stops, and the zoo. This beautification project is high on the mayor's agenda, so there'll be plenty for you to do."

I wasn't expecting all of that, but I was very pleased with the outcome. "I assure you that you've made an outstanding choice."

"You know, it was the city manager's intention to simply be on your client roster, but . . ." She got up from her desk and came around to take a seat in the chair next to me, "I wanted to have your services exclusively."

"Exclusively?" I asked as I watched her crossing her sexy

thighs. She had on a pair of black Stuart Weitzman pumps just like the ones I'd bought for Nadia, and she was working a black suit to match. "I don't think I could do that. Most of my clients have been with me for years. Don't worry, though. We can handle the job."

"I'm quite sure you can," Karen agreed, looking at her watch. "Wow, it's lunchtime. Would you like to grab a bite with me at Applebee's? It's just across the street."

I wasn't a big fan of the place, but I was hungry. "Sure, I'll join you."

I was a little uneasy about being seen in public with another woman. Nadia knew everybody, and the last thing I needed was my cell phone blowing up in the middle of lunch. But this was business, so I didn't care what she might think. When the waitress brought our drinks, I seized the opportunity to ask Karen the easy questions. "So, Karen, when did you pledge?"

Licking the soda from her cherry, she replied, "Undergrad. Fall '92. What about you?"

"Undergrad. Spring '92."

Karen rested her soda on the table and folded her arms. "Well, I'm going to skip all the bullshit and jump right into it. Are you gay or merely in a gay-friendly business?"

"Why?" That was a strange question coming from a city employee unless . . .

"I was just wondering. I saw your ad in the gay yellow pages."

"If you must know, I'm gay. Is there a problem?"

"No, there's no problem."

"In all fairness, I should ask why were you looking through the gay yellow pages."

Karen's face turned a light shade of red as she began to fidget. Finally she flashed a heartfelt smile. "OK, you got me. I'm in the life."

With that admission, we began a conversation that lasted way beyond both our lunch hours and, for the first time in a long while, I was fulfilled.

When I got home that evening, Nadia met me at the door in a red negligee. Did I tell you she looks like Vanessa L. Williams's twin sister? She'd prepared dinner, set the table, and had decorated it with Hershey's Hugs and two cards. I was beside myself because she'd actually tried to do something special for me. I was still full from lunch, but I opened the cards and forced myself to eat anyway. Then I told her about the city official I'd met. Nadia was so overjoyed with the news of the contract that she didn't go off on her usual tangent about the woman . . . maybe because I didn't tell her Karen was gay.

In the master bath, I found she'd drawn an aromatherapy bath for me. While she cleaned the kitchen, I relaxed in the tub and reflected on the good fortune that had come my way. With this contract, Nadia and I would be set for a very long time. I reclined against the back of the tub until I heard Nadia's footsteps come up the stairs. "Honey?" she said sweetly, peeking around the corner of the bathroom.

"Yes, baby?"

"Can I get in the tub with you?"

She must've been reading my mind. "You sure can." Nadia hurried back into the bedroom. I thought she'd gone to take off her negligee or to turn on some music. Instead, I looked up, and there she stood with that damn strap-on. "Babe, can't we do this without that for a change?"

"Well, what else are we supposed to do?"

I was too tired for an extensive discussion so I helped her into the tub and made love to her the way she wanted until the water got cold.

The next morning when I arrived at work, there was a

beautiful bouquet of lilies on my secretary Rose's desk. "Oh, what gorgeous flowers," I exclaimed as I leaned over to smell them. "What did you do to Pedro last night?"

"Not a damn thing. Those are for you."

"Me?" Maybe Nadia was trying to come correct. I opened the card.

Welcome to the family.
Karen

"That was sweet of them. These are from the city."

"They smell wonderful. Oh, by the way, the procurement office called and wants to meet with you this afternoon to go over some more information pertaining to the contract."

"OK. Thanks, Rose."

I arrived at the meeting to find only Karen in the conference room holding one final document that required my signature. As I pulled my pen from my purse, my three-carat diamond caught Karen's eye. "That's a nice ring."

"Thank you."

"Married?"

"Yes."

"Happily?"

I was uncomfortable. "You need me to sign on the first line, right?"

She knew I was being evasive. "Yes, the first line on both pages. You didn't answer the question."

"I know," I said with a bit of hesitation. I signed the papers and stole a moment to check out what Karen had on. A sharp-dressed woman was my weakness. "How are you doing today? You look nice."

"I'm fine and thank you. Want something to—"

I had to cut her off. "Karen, I need to get back to work because we have to start going through applications. Thank you for the flowers."

"Not a problem."

As soon as I got in the car, my cell phone rang. "Where are you?"

"Uh, hello?"

"What the hell you mean, 'uh'?"

"Nadia, what's up, baby?"

"Nothing. Why are you back at city hall?"

"They had more papers for me to sign. Look, I'll call you when I get back to the office. I left my earpiece there." She hung up without even saying good-bye.

When I pulled up to my building, the delivery guy from the florist was getting back in his van. I walked into the office and found an arrangement of lilies, roses, and birds of paradise. Rose was already gone for the day, thank God, so I took the flowers back to my office to read the card in private.

Just something for you to think about on your way home.
Have a good night.

Karen

It was after 5:00 P.M. A woman like her worked late. "Ms. Davenport, please."

"This is Karen Davenport. How may I help you?"

"Why don't you tell me how you can help since you seem to have all the answers?"

"What do you mean?" I knew the call was flattering to her.

"I mean the flowers. How did you know I like this kind of attention?"

"I didn't. I was hoping they'd make you smile."

As bad as I hated to, I needed to tell her about Nadia. "Look, I have a wife. A beautiful wife. And well—"

"You know what? You never answered my question about whether or not you're happy."

"Why is that so important to you?"

"Actually it's important for you to answer that question. I already know the answer."

"Is that right?"

"Francesca, if you were happy, you would have told me about your wife yesterday. That's what happily married people do. They talk about their spouses."

She was right. "I don't like discussing my relationship with other gay women, especially cute ones. They always try to find a spot of vulnerability and harp on it. Next thing you know they're trying to do for me whatever my woman isn't."

"You're probably right."

Karen and I ended up talking for hours. I knew I would catch hell from Nadia, but I didn't care. For as long as I had been with her, I hadn't had the opportunity to talk to other gay women. Knowing Karen gave me that chance. We conversed about business, women, the sorority, but I refused to discuss Nadia.

It was 11:00 P.M. when I finally pulled into the driveway, and for a minute, I sat in the car and contemplated what I was going to say. I'd never been this late before. God knows I knew I was wrong. My dinner plate was sitting on the stove covered neatly with aluminum foil. Nadia usually did that for me when I'd had a long day, but the more I thought about Karen, the less hungry I became. When I got upstairs, I knew the angels must have been watching over me because Nadia was sound asleep.

Every day my arrivals at work were met with a dozen or two of fresh flowers. It was like I had my own floral shop. Karen didn't hide her identity, signing each card with a sweet saying and her name. I was intrigued with her because, although we were both very successful businesswomen, her world was new to me. Though every conversation was different, it was amazing how much we were alike. With the mountain of extra work on my hands, it was easy for me to be away from home; I spent several evenings having drinks with Karen or on the phone with her. If asked, I wouldn't have known how to explain what I was feeling. All I knew was that I liked it.

One afternoon I was surprised to come in from a job site and find Nadia waiting for me in my office. In all of our four years together she had never visited me at work. If I hadn't felt before that moment like I was doing anything wrong, that sentiment was about to change.

Nadia, sitting on the sofa with her ankles crossed and every one of the note cards spread out on her lap, asked the question any wife would, "What's this?"

My initial reaction was to lie and remember how I told that lie so that if I had to repeat it I wouldn't get caught. But she, as my wife—the woman who wore a ring that would make even Whitney Houston jealous—deserved the truth. "They're from a friend."

Nadia was astonishingly calm. "Are you sure about that?"

"Yes."

"Frankie, I think you owe me more of an explanation than that. You haven't been getting home until long after I've gone to bed, and you never have time for me. Here I am thinking that you're working, and—"

"Nadia, I am working."

"That's bullshit, and you know it."

It was time to ante up. "Baby, I met her at nationals."

"What?" She threw the cards into the air, and, for the first time since I'd known her, she called me a bitch—a lying one at that.

"Nadia, will you please let me explain? It's not what you're thinking."

"And how do you know what I'm thinking, Frankie?" Even through her rage, she managed to find tears.

I confessed to her how first I bumped into Karen at Starbucks and then how I met her again in the city manager's office. I was surprised . . . she believed me. "I promise you, Nadia. We're just friends."

"Do you love her?"

"What?"

"You heard me. Do you love her?"

"It's not like that. If nothing else, she's been great conversation."

"I see." Nadia pulled herself together. "Does she know about me?"

"Yes, but you know I don't discuss us with other people. She respects that."

"She needs to stop sending you flowers. Tell that bitch your wife knows, so she needs to cut this shit out."

I hated Nadia referring to Karen, my soror, that way. But given Nadia's style from time to time, I expected it. Not wanting to start an entirely new argument, I simply replied, "I will."

I finally persuaded Nadia to go home. Convinced that she needed time away, she decided to leave the next morning for a visit with her mother. No sooner than she was out the door, my office phone rang. Nadia had sent Rose home, so I took the call. "Yes, this is Frankie."

"Hello, Ms. Wyatt."

From out of nowhere, I got butterflies. "Hey, you."

"Busy?"

"Not really. What's up?"

"You crossed my mind, so I figured I'd call. Are you OK? You don't sound like yourself."

What the hell. "Nadia just left, and she saw the flowers."

There was silence. Then, somberly, Karen responded, "I'm sorry. I'm so, so sorry." Her voice was trembling. "I hope you believe that."

I had no reason not to believe her. My next move surprised even me. "I want to see you." I needed to see her was more accurate.

"OK."

Karen and I met at the Embassy Suites in downtown. She got the room, and when I was close by, I called her to find out the room number. Like I said, Nadia knew everybody, so Karen arranged for me to have access through the delivery entrance. For the first hour, I simply sat on the bed and stared at her; she did the same. We smiled and shared silly giggles high school kids sometimes exchange. "Are you hungry?" she asked.

"No, I'm not."

"Frankie, what are we doing?"

I was about to cheat. That's what I was doing. "I don't know. I do know that we're sorors, so we need to think first."

"I've been thinking about that, and, with the way I feel about you, I don't care." She leaned over and lightly kissed me on the cheek. Then she stood and walked over in front of me. Karen climbed on my lap and began unbuttoning her blouse, exposing her breasts. The soft yet perky masses of intoxicating flesh pointed toward my face, begging to be touched, caressed, savored, and enjoyed. I leaned forward and gently nestled my head between them. They smelled faintly of J'Adore. Suddenly Karen became irresistible.

Her breasts tasted like Popsicles, dripping with cherry flavor. Karen wrapped her arms around my neck and rested her head upon my shoulder. I sprayed her neck with soft kisses that traveled northward to her delectably luscious lips. I savored every inch of her. This moment would never happen again. "I can't do this." Passionately returning my kisses, Karen seemed to not hear me. I hesitantly pushed her away. "Karen, I can't." Deep down inside, I trusted that Karen could and would treat me like the woman I knew I was, but letting her do it this way, while I was married, was not right.

Disappointed, she arose from my lap and posed in front of me with her hands on her hips. I thought she would be pissed. But instead of laying me out, she moved in closer, cupped my chin, and kissed me on the cheek. "I understand, baby. You're a good lady." She put her blouse back on and picked up the room service menu. "I'm going to order something to eat. Sure, you don't want anything?"

I needed to take my ass home. "Are you going to be here all night?"

"Yeah, I am. I like the quiet." Karen dialed room service and placed her order, acting as if I was no longer in the room.

"I need to go home and take care of something," I said as I headed toward the door. She waved me off and continued talking on the phone.

Riding in the car, I realized that I had some major soul-searching to do. While holding Karen close to me earlier, I realized that I was no longer in love with Nadia. I couldn't give her what she needed. I could, however, provide her with what-ever finances she required to make it without me, but I could no longer offer her my heart. Karen, however, was a gem, and I wanted to be closer to her. I wanted to be free to take it slow. It was still early, and we didn't know each other well enough for me to say, "Hey, you want to move in together?" I'd made that mistake with Nadia and wasn't about to go there again.

Before reaching home, I concluded that I needed to make two important phone calls. The first one was to Nadia to make things easier.

"What's up?" I asked after she answered the phone.

"Nothing." She sighed.

"Can we talk a minute?"

"Yes."

Although my heart believed I was doing the right thing, my mind was telling me something different. Did I really know what I was about to do? "It's time."

"Time for what?" she asked.

"Time for us to call it quits. I'm not into it anymore, and it's not fair to keep pulling you along like this."

"Well, Frankie, I agree with you. I've been unhappy, too. I was just waiting for you to say it's over." End of conversation. I looked at the receiver and listened to the dial tone. I couldn't understand why Nadia was so casual and calm. We never really argued because I always let her have her way.

Before returning to the hotel to tell Karen how much I enjoyed her company and revealing that I wouldn't mind spending the rest of my life getting to know her, I wanted to talk face to face with Nadia. I needed to be certain that she understood that I wasn't leaving to be with someone else. I was, in fact, leaving because I was no longer happy. Now for call number two. This time I voice-dialed Karen. "You still awake?"

Cheerfully, she answered, "Yes, sweetie, I am."

"Did you eat?"

"Actually, I did, but it wasn't all that. What are you up to?"

"I just pulled up in the garage and am about to go into the house and pick up some clothes." I was bursting at the seams with things I wanted to tell her. "I've got a story to tell you when I see you in about an hour or so."

"Oh, really?"

"Yeah, it's a love story, and . . ."

In what seemed like slow motion, Nadia appeared in front of me as I sat in the car. Suddenly, I heard what sounded like a M-80 firecracker going off . . . an explosion of light . . . a ball of smoke . . . a shattered windshield . . . a hole in my chest the size of the Grand Canyon.

CAUGHT UP

(Part 4)

She thinks I'm stupid. I've been looking at the cell phone bill for over a month now, and this same number keeps popping up. Twenty minutes here, fifty minutes there. She said it's a client. I think she's lying. Every other day she's trying to pick a fight with me about the things that used to be OK with her. I found a letter in her glove compartment that said it all. Something was definitely going on. My girl wasn't even setting out the cookies like she used to, and whenever we did do something, she just laid there like a fucking knot on a log. What she doesn't know is that I was looking for a girlfriend when I found her, so I wouldn't be fucked up about it if she wanted to leave.

She'd made this "client" fall in love with her and had no qualms with breaking up somebody else's home. Did she want her, or did she want me? Just be honest is all I say. If you want somebody else, then say so. Come to think of it, if she decides she wants to try to leave, then I'm going to make the shit fun. I ain't going no damn where.

Liya's ass is full of games, and I ain't about to get played. She's mentioned this musician a few times to me, and it

seems like she's obsessed with her. Tammy this and Tammy
that. Enough already. I can't be around Liya 24/7 because I
have to hold it down with the job and things. I buy her whatever I can to make sure she ain't got no need to go to somebody else. I went in her glove compartment the other day to
make sure she had the car registration in there because the
cops had set up road blocks all around our neighborhood. I
came across this envelope from Tammy—the musician. Hell,
I had to read it. It was thick like a credit report or something, and I wondered what all she had to say to my girl
when she supposedly got a woman of her own. I opened that
shit and read every last word of it. Then I knew why Liya had
been so distant with me. When I read that letter, my heart,
like, stopped beating for a minute. I couldn't understand
what the fuck I was reading. Were they lovers? Had they
kissed? A million and one questions popped into my head,
and the main one was "Why?"

Lord knows I ain't trying to hurt nobody, and I, for damn
sure, ain't trying to be the bitch who gets hurt. But she's
doing this shit behind my back. I do everything I can for her,
and this is how she repays me?

I'm almost fifty years old, and Liya's in her thirties.
There's a problem right there. I was hesitant to start fucking
around with her because she was so young. I saw some of the
immature shit she'd do like wink and smile at a bitch while I
was sitting right next to her. Let's not mention the text mes-
saging me every five minutes to see what I was doing. If I didn't
respond quick enough, then she'd call. Shit, I was working
and didn't have time to keep answering her calls and shit. I
wasn't talking to nobody else and wasn't thinking about nobody else. I give all I can to her, but she never seems satisfied.

I'm not going to sit here and complain about the things

that are wrong in our relationship because it's only going to piss me off. I just wanted to have some young pussy that didn't have no whole bunch of miles on it. When she told me she'd had seven other girlfriends, I thought, *Damn, is she a ho or what?* But you see, she was slick. She didn't tell me about them other hoochies until after we had done the do and *after* I'd spent a whole paycheck on some clothes and shoes for her. What crossed my mind was the fact that these were her girlfriends. What about the one-night stands or the something to dos? Anyway, I love her, but not as much as she thinks. I'm a lonely ol' broad with nothing else to do but work out, go to the job, and get in all the fucking I can before I die.

It pisses me off to no end that she's lying. It's one thing to lie by omission, but she's telling them one right after the other. Just the other day, the phone rang at four in the morning, and I felt her get up and look at the caller ID. She laid back down for a minute, waiting for the answering machine to click on. Whoso-never it was didn't leave a message. Later that morning while she was in the shower, I took it upon my feeble old self to check the caller ID box, and Tammy's name was on there. When I heard the water stop, I ran into the spare bedroom and pretended as if I was looking for something. I went back into the bedroom and gave her a hug while she was standing there dripping wet with her towel wrapped tightly around her body. I kissed her neck, right beneath her ear, and proceeded to run my tongue around the outside of her ear. She loved it. Reaching under her towel, I took a huge handful of her pussy and tenderly stroked it. I pushed her up against the wall and kissed her from the middle of her breastbone to the top of her hairline. I then lifted her, like I was bench-pressing for my life, and propped her up on my shoulders. I stuck my pink magic wand into her and turned her into my trick. I licked her and tasted her until she screamed and filled my mouth with satisfaction. While I had her there, now flaccid from her excitement, I laid my head between her legs. I rested in the comfort of her womanhood. I was sure I was going to work with the smell of pussy in my hair. As she ran her fingers through the back of my head, I kissed her clit and asked, "Who was that on the phone this morning?"

Her fingers came to a complete halt, and then she said, "I don't know. I think it was a wrong number."

Now what kind of fool did she think I was? I slowly removed her legs from around my neck and slid her body toward the floor. "You sure about that?"

"Well, yeah, Carlita."

From that moment on, I ain't trusted nothing that's come out of that bitch's mouth.

PENIS ENVY

O K.
I met this chick named Geena, and I was immediately attracted to her. She was about five-four with shoulder-length hair and pretty teeth. Geena smelled like a dream with Michael Kors drenched into her supple skin. I didn't approach her because I've never been one to pursue a woman. I have, however, on occasion, allowed myself to be pursued. I've always liked to just let things happen. When you try to force something that doesn't fit, it pisses every-body involved off, and, instead of making a friend, you've made an enemy for life. Let me tell you about me and Geena.

On the night we met, I saw her from across the room while I sat at the bar, and for some reason, our eyes met. I turned to the bartender and asked for another glass of wine. The wall behind the bar was made of glass, and I managed to find her reflection making its way across the crowded room. Before I knew it, she was standing right next to me.

"Can I have a glass of champagne, please?" she asked the bartender. "Actually, can you make it a whole bottle?"

The bartender brought back a bottle of Korbel and placed

it on the counter. "You want just the bottle, or you need some glasses?"

I looked up into the mirror and saw her looking at me with a gorgeous smile. I smiled back then sheepishly turned away.

"I need some glasses. My girl got a promotion at work and is being relocated to Chicago," she said as she continued to look me over.

"Wow, that's a long way from South Beach. Tell her I said congrats. How many glasses you need?"

"Five. Well, six including my friend here," she said, looking at me. "No need to leave her out of the celebration."

The bartender winked at me and proceeded to set a champagne flute next to my half-empty wineglass. He opened the bubbly and poured until its froth reached the rim of the glass, and I signaled to him that was enough. "Thank you," I said to her as she reached in her purse for her money.

Handing the bartender the cash, she beamed at me and said, "No problem." Then she turned away and rejoined her party of friends on the other side of the room.

Maybe an hour later, she returned to the bar to find me still sitting in the same spot nursing the glass of champagne. She brushed up against my shoulder as if to apprize me of her presence, but I knew she was there. I could smell her. Just as I was about to say something—what I don't know— the bartender reappeared and asked, "Back for another bottle?"

Taking a seat on the stool, she replied, "No, they've left. I came up here to get a cup of coffee to try and sober up before I drive home."

"Black?"

"Yeah, black with a couple of packets of Equal."

"Sure thing." The bartender disappeared through the swinging metal doors, and I took another sip of my wine.

"I see you didn't drink any of your champagne."

Wiping the inside corners of my lips with a napkin, I answered, "I don't like mixing my liquors, but thanks again for the drink. It's nothing against the gesture."

"Oh, OK. My name is Geena, by the way."

Extending my hand, I replied, "Nice to meet you, Geena. I'm Stacy."

Shaking my hand, she said, "Nice to meet you, too."

The next couple of moments were awkward because I never knew what to say to a woman. I always let her talk to me, and I limited myself to merely answering questions and making intelligent comments. The bartender arrived with her coffee and Equal. I glanced down at my watch and noticed that it was after midnight. "So, your friends left you here by yourself?"

As she stirred her coffee, Geena looked around the room as if to see if all was clear. "Yeah, they had to go. My girlfriend has an early flight out and needed to get home to finish packing. Everybody else has to work in the morning."

"Oh, and you don't?" That wasn't an intelligent comment.

"Well, when you're the boss, you can go in and take off when you want."

"Oh, I see. I'm sorry I didn't mean to suggest—"

"Girl, it's no big deal. Why are you here all by yourself? You're very pretty."

"Thanks," I said. "I chose to be alone tonight. I needed some me time."

"Oh, I understand. I do that from time to time, but I run away to the spa instead."

"Go, girl. I feel you." It was getting late, and I was ready to go home. The humane side of me didn't want to leave her there, intoxicated, relying on only herself to get home. "Look, um, can I give you a ride home? That coffee may take all night to work."

I actually was expecting her to say no because, let's get real, I was some strange woman offering to take her home. "You know, I'd really appreciate that. I can come back and get my car in the morning."

We pulled up to her place, and I got out to open her door and help her out. Geena lived in a high-rise condominium right next to the ocean, and I wasn't mad at her. "I can make it from here," she said.

"OK," I said. "Will you need a ride to pick up your car in the morning?"

"Damn," she said, stumbling onto the curb. "Yes, I will. My girlfriend's flight leaves at six A.M., and I'm supposed to take her to the airport."

"Well, here's my number. Call me when you get up, and I'll come right over to take you there."

"You don't have to do that."

"It's no problem. I only live a few blocks from here. I don't mind at all." I knew the more time I spent with her, the more likely I'd be to get to know her without chasing her.

"OK. If you insist. Come to think of it, just be here about four-fifteen."

A bit groggy, I was on time, but Geena wasn't. She was fifteen minutes late. When she got in the car, she thanked me again for my kindness. Her eyes were a little bloodshot, but her beauty was still apparent. Nodding off from time to time, she spoke only when spoken to, and with me being me, that wasn't very often. We arrived at the parking lot, and she directed me to the spot where her car was. Before she got out, she paused for a moment. It was obvious she had something to say and had been thinking about it for a minute. "Um, once I drop Rhianna off, you want to meet me back at my place for some coffee?"

That was odd, but hell, I wasn't going to turn her down. "Sure. I'd love to."

"Cool. Meet me there in about an hour." Geena got out, closed the door, and waved good-bye through the window.

Before going to Geena's, I went back home to freshen up . . . nothing major. I put on a little makeup and lipstick. I stopped by the grocery store and picked up a small bouquet of flowers to give to her. I walked through every aisle trying to find something else to bring and ended up settling for just me. While sitting in the parking lot waiting for Geena to arrive, I watched people come out of the building, heading off to work or whatever their destination. Geena must've been doing pretty well for herself because nearly everybody who came out of that building drove some type of sports car, luxury car, or luxury SUV. Hell, Geena was wheeling one of those big-boy Escalades. Maybe after a couple of cups of coffee, I'd ask her what line of work she was in.

My body was still limp from the lack of sleep, and I dozed off for a second only to be awakened by the bass thumping in somebody's car. The closer the distraction got, my keys jingled in the ignition. I looked through the rearview mirror and saw a black Escalade coming toward me. It was Geena. She pulled into the spot next to me, smiling through the window like this burden had finally been lifted. "Hey, lady," she screamed through D'Angelo's "Brown Sugar."

Embarrassed as hell because everyone was looking, I waved, closed my roof, and then turned off the car. I opened my door and pulled the flowers from the backseat of my SC430. "Damn, you think your music is loud enough at six in the morning?"

As she slammed her car door and made her way to the

trunk, Geena said, "Oh, I'm not bothered by what other people think. They asses drive around here blasting music at three A.M., and nobody says a word to them." She reached for three grocery bags sitting in the cargo area. "Sorry about being late, but I needed to stop at the market."

"No problem. Let me help you. By the way, these are for you," I said, handing her the flowers.

Geena didn't seem too fazed by the gesture, but she thanked me anyway. I took one of the bags in one hand and used the other hand to activate my car alarm.

"Nice ride," she said.

"Thanks."

Walking to the entrance, Geena mumbled on and on about being tired and needing some rest. I listened as I tried to keep up with her because she walked faster than most women I knew. "So what kind of work do you do? A ride like that doesn't come cheap."

"I'm an attorney for the WNBA. I help negotiate contracts with sponsors, arenas, and occasionally players," I said.

"Damn."

"What?"

"Seems pretty high profile."

"It's OK. Pays the bills."

"And then some." She laughed.

As we stepped into the elevator, I took the opportunity to ask her a little bit about herself. "Which floor?" I asked. Instead of telling me, Geena pushed the penthouse button. "If you don't mind me asking, what do you do?" I noticed as people were getting on and off the elevator everyone was speaking to her.

"I'm a real estate developer."

"I see. How'd you get into that?"

"Girl, that's a long, boring story for another time." The elevator stopped, and the doors opened at the end of a long hallway. "I own this building, and life's been very good to me. We can talk about the rest later."

She unlocked the door to what I would call a piece of heaven. Everywhere you looked there was a picture of the ocean. Every room was clad in white, and the floors were made of red oak. There was a white baby grand sitting in the middle of the floor with silk red rose petals thrown against the keys and the stool. Despite all of this grandeur, my concern rested on the walls, on the tables, and on the bookshelves. Upon these fixtures were pictures of Geena and one of the women I saw in her party from the night before. There were boxes strewn about the room packed with shipping tape, marked for Chicago.

"Geena?"

"Yes, sweetie?" She was pouring coffee beans into the grinder.

"Who's the woman in these pictures with you?"

Silence, but then she continued preparing the coffee. "That's my girlfriend, Rhianna. The one I had to take to the airport this morning."

"Your girlfriend?"

"Yes, my girlfriend. Well, she *was* my girlfriend. We decided we didn't want to carry on a long-distance relationship, so we broke up amicably. No hard feelings. She did what she needed to do for her, and I'm doing what I need to do for me. And that means moving on."

"And you can do it just like that? How long were you two together?"

"Fifteen years. We met as freshmen in college. You like cream and sugar in your coffee?"

"Uh, yeah, that's fine." I had no desire to pry and silently chose to change the subject. "You play the piano?" I asked, walking toward the balcony door.

"No. She did. The movers will be here later today to get it along with her other things." Geena, with a cup of coffee in each hand, made her way around the boxes and over to where I was standing. "Here you go. Hope it's OK."

"Thank you. This is really beautiful . . . this view."

"Yeah, it is. You want to sit inside or outside?"

"Outside is fine." We walked out onto the balcony, which extended around the entire residence and took a seat. I didn't have many women in my life because I hated the confusion. I made a little money, lived well, and had certain ways I liked to do things. I was too old to get involved with somebody who wanted to change me. On the outside, I was this timid kitten who enjoyed being chased, being romanced, but on the inside, I was the baddest bitch with the biggest dick. Quietly, I was searching for a lady who would woo me into her bedroom and allow me to take advantage of her. I couldn't tell yet what to expect from Geena. There were an awful lot of pictures still on the wall for a relationship to be over. "What kind of work does your friend do?"

Geena never seemed annoyed by my questions because she offered up answers so quickly. "She's in pharmaceuticals, and she's also a concert pianist. She got offered a spot with the Chicago Symphony—an offer she couldn't refuse. So she left. It's too damn cold up there for me, and deep down inside, I think we both knew it was time for us to be over."

I stared out into the horizon at a passing cruise ship and took in her words. "I know you're going to miss her."

"Stacy, you have to understand that Rhianna and I have been together most of our lives. I started fiending for other women, but she started partaking of other women. Our actions were comprehensible. It's like having crabmeat all you life until someone let's you taste lobster. Want more coffee?"

"No, I'm good." I wanted to move on to a more selfish

conversation. "Why did you share your champagne with me?" I asked, turning my head away from the ship that now looked like a speck against the sky.

Glancing over at me with a devilish smile, Geena said, "You were the best-looking woman in the room—besides me, of course. You were alone, so I figured you'd enjoy the attention."

Women can be funny at times. They always think that because you're alone you're lonely. I personally find it alright to be alone sometimes. "Well, I was fine just hanging out. Wasn't looking for any sympathy."

"To be honest, I did think you were very pretty, and I still do."

I was flattered. It had been a while since someone told me I looked good to them. "Thank you, Geena. That was sweet of you."

"I was being truthful. Let's talk about you. We've discussed me enough."

"Fair enough. What do you want to know?"

"Oh, I don't know. Um, what law school did you go to?"

"Columbia."

"Ohhh, you go, girl. What made you choose this job, and why are you here in South Beach?"

"The job was offered to me about four years ago. The salary was attractive, and I was working at a law firm in Montgomery County, Maryland, that wasn't suiting my needs. It was mostly bankruptcy law, and I didn't care for it. One weekend while in the skybox at a Mystics game, the president of the league stopped through, and she and I talked for hours. A job offer came out of it, and I left the firm two weeks later. The reason I'm here is because I'm on vacation and needed to unwind. I bought a condo actually around the corner from here about two years ago, and this is the first time I've had a chance to stay in it."

"So you don't have any family here?"

"No. My family is in Buffalo, New York. I go home once or twice a year before it gets too cold."

"I feel you on that. I hate the cold air. Fucks with my skin."

"You have family here?"

"My mother lives in Tampa. She comes to visit every once in a while. My dad and his wife live in Utah. I have two sisters. One is a college president, and the other is a doctor."

"Damn, talk about ambitious. I don't have any siblings. I'm really close to a couple of my cousins, but that's it." I was enjoying my discussion with Geena. It was the best conversation with another woman I'd had in long time, but then she took it there.

"Do you have a girlfriend?"

"No, I don't. There isn't enough time in my life right now for a girlfriend. My schedule is too demanding, and I hate the drama."

"Pardon me for saying this, but you don't look too busy to me."

See, see, that's why I don't want to be with anyone. "Look, Geena, so many times in relationships women are looking for sponsors or whatever you call it. I've worked hard for what I have, and I'm not trying to give someone a free ride."

"Now, I take slight offense to that because I have just as much as you have. I don't need anyone to take care of me. Rhianna had her own money, and now that she's gone, I'm not sitting back worrying about how the bills are going to get paid. How old are you, Stacy, if you don't mind me asking?"

"Almost thirty-five."

"How many relationships have you had?"

"Two. One died, and the other decided after five years that she wasn't gay."

"I see. You should give love a try because I think you have a lot to offer."

"Thanks, Dr. Ruth. I'll give it some thought in the next

year or two." I don't know why Geena went there with me. I had started fantasizing about sticking it to her.

I ended up chatting with Geena up until the movers came. Although she insisted I stay, I left to avoid being in the way but agreed to meet her for cocktails later that evening. We talked some more, and I found myself taken by her. She was a little edgy at times, but I could handle it. Every so often, she'd run her hand across my thigh or whisper something dirty in my ear. I found her to be just as cocky as me, and I didn't know if I was going to like that.

Geena kept saying she had a dildo in her purse and wondered what it'd be like to stick it between my legs while we were at the table. I thwarted her advances and settled for her hand in my crotch. In spite of the fact that I hated public displays of affection, I let her kiss me, and I politely kissed her back with tongue and all. It was hard to know what to expect from her because she was so spontaneous. After two glasses of wine, I realized that my pleasure—my dick—was hard, and it was time to take this to the next level. I was never one for sex within the first week, but Geena had pushed all the right buttons.

"You want to go back to my place?"

"So we can do what?" Geena asked.

"I don't know. A nightcap maybe?"

Geena didn't skip a beat. "No, I think we should call it a night. We've talked damn near all day and night, and I haven't heard from Rhianna yet."

Rhianna? "OK, I understand." I paid my bill and told her good night.

After she saw that I was only going to pay for my drinks, Geena cleared her tab with the waitress, never commenting on my actions. "Well, we'll talk soon. I've got to get home and get ready for work in the morning."

I went home and did something I'd never done before. I masturbated and gently rubbed my pussy and me to sleep.

A month after I returned to D.C., I called Geena a few times and got her voicemail. She was doing exactly what I thought she'd do. I'd exposed myself to her, and she didn't react. My car was just as expensive as hers, my job was just as good as hers, and my crib was just as lavish as hers. I often thought about our conversation over that day and a half and wondered where I'd gone wrong. When I got home one evening after a stressful day of arrogant female wanna-be pro basketball players, I saw there were twenty messages on my answering machine. Puzzled because no one I knew would call me like that within a day's time without calling my cell phone or calling me at work, I started playing the messages back.

"Hi, Stacy. This is Geena. I was calling to see how you were and to let you know I was in town. I'm staying at the Four Seasons. Room 531." As each subsequent message began, I got the same thing: "Hi, Stacy. This is Geena." *Damn, is she sweatin' me?*

"Good evening, thank you for calling the Four Seasons Hotel. This is Margaret. How may I be of service to you tonight?"

"May I have Geena Austin's room, please?"

"Sure, hold please."

I didn't have much to say to Geena, but what the hell? It wasn't going to hurt to see what she had to say for herself. We didn't owe each other anything.

"Hello?"

"Ms. Austin, this is Ms. Samuels. I'm returning your call."

"Oh, hey. I was starting to think I wasn't going to hear from you."

"I had a long day at the office and I'm just getting in. I saw your messages and wanted to give you a call before going to bed."

"Sorry about the messages. I was getting a little over-anxious I guess. What have you been up to?"

I was tired as shit. My feet were hurting, and I had a headache that was driving me crazy. I didn't have the energy to get into a long, drawn-out conversation. "Not much. Work mostly. Look, I don't mean to be rude, but I'm beat. How long are you going to be in town?"

"Well, that depends on you."

"On me?"

"Yeah. I came to town to talk and spend some time with you."

"How's Rhianna?" I figured that would jolt the discussion and abruptly bring it to an end.

"I'm not sure. I haven't spoken to her in a while. Why do you ask?"

"No reason. I have your number and promise to call you in the morning as soon as I get up." You could cut the tension on the other end of the phone with a knife, but I didn't care.

"I guess I have no choice but to wait, huh?"

"Basically. I'll talk to you in the morning." I hung up the phone, undressed, and crawled into bed. Deep down, I'd wanted to talk to her, but I was going to do it on my terms this time.

The next morning I didn't call her as I promised. Instead, I went in to work to finish up some files and took off the rest of the afternoon. I went back home and saw that my answering machine had four calls on it. I pushed the message button before walking to the bedroom to change clothes. All of the calls were from Geena. After changing into a pair of jeans and a shirt, I made me a cup of tea and found some loose change for the metro.

I'd remembered Geena's room number from the night before, and as I stood at her door, I thought about where I wanted this to go. I gave a deep sigh then knocked.

"Who is it?"

"It's Stacy, Geena. I . . ." The door opened so fast I didn't have a chance to get the rest of my sentence out.

"Damn, is this how you return calls? Come on in."

"No. I had to go to work this morning to finish up some things and figured it'd be easier to come over here than to keep going back and forth over the phone."

Closing the door behind me, Geena commented, "You're looking good. You've lost some weight, haven't you?"

"A little. You're not looking bad yourself." She was wearing an orange sarong with a bright yellow tank underneath and was barefoot. "You want to step out and take a walk with me around Georgetown?"

Geena stretched out across the bed and rested her on a pillow. "Not really. I was hoping we could talk in here."

I wasn't entirely comfortable with that, but I didn't want any drama. "OK, whatever you want." Watching Geena's demeanor, I grasped why I hesitated with her. Everything was always on her time, and I was like that, too. I sat on the edge of the bed next to her and took her hand in mine. "Geena, why are you here?"

"I came to see you and hopefully pick up where we left off."

I perused the room and wondered what I'd have to lose if we had sex. We had nothing, so what the hell? I leaned over and kissed her. For the first time in my gay life, I was repulsed by a woman's kiss, but I didn't stop. She pulled me in closer to her, but I felt myself trying to pull away. Geena's energy was one of control—she pulled me, rubbed me, stroked me, did everything she could to get me to give in to her. I climbed on top of her and felt this bulge between her legs. It was that damn dildo we'd talked about before.

"I can't do this, Geena."

"What's wrong?" she asked, looking into my eyes. "Am I too rough?"

Maybe. I had no control here. She was trying to show me what she had without giving any consideration to what I had to bring to the table. She was trying to hold me, and I was used to being the one doing the holding. She was trying to fuck me, but I was used to being the one doing the fucking. "This isn't going to work. Maybe we should stick to being friends."

Geena was ticked. "Friends? I have enough friends." Reaching for my hand, she asked, "I thought you liked me."

"I do . . . I mean, I did like you like that, but I'm used to things being a certain way."

"Where do you get this ego from, Stacy? You act like you're some goddess or somebody."

"My ego is no bigger than yours." I stood and straightened my clothes. "We want two different things out of this. Sexually, I want to show a woman what I got down here by making love to her until she screams my name in ten different languages. I want to give pleasure. I'm not caught up in receiving it. I want to be the provider. I want to be in charge. And you? You want the same things. I'm not turned on by dildos unless it's my own, and I'm giving it up the ass."

"I see. Well, you're right. This won't work because I like to run the bedroom, and I ain't taking nothing up the ass."

I left the Four Seasons Hotel that afternoon and never looked back. Like I said earlier, when you try to force something that doesn't fit, it pisses everybody involved off, and, instead of making a friend, you've made an enemy for life.

CAUGHT UP

(Part 5—The Redemption)

For the first time in my life, I wanted to kill somebody—not Tammy but *her*. I felt this woman breathing down the steadily crumbling walls of my relationship. She seemed to know my weaknesses, which meant Tammy was telling her things that she wouldn't tell me, and to me, that was unacceptable.

The day following the doll incident, I woke up in the guest room to find the kids lying in the bed next to me. I could only imagine what they were feeling. Tammy had shut and locked the door to the bedroom, and there wasn't a sound coming from that part of the house. I walked downstairs and helped the girls make themselves bowls of cereal and made myself some tea. Then I heard footsteps in the room above the kitchen and realized she must've been awake. I went upstairs and knocked on the door, but she didn't answer. I removed the skeleton key from atop the doorframe and unlocked the door. Tammy, still in her nightgown, was sitting on the floor in the closet when she looked up and saw me standing there. She was looking through a box of letters that I'd written to her over the years.

"You were so busy in here trying to find my secrets that

you failed to notice I have a box of letters from you, too."
She was crying.

I didn't want to hear it. "You know, in all our years together, I've never slept in the guest room, and I don't plan
on doing it again."

"OK, I—"

"I made a decision last night."

"And what's that?"

"I'm leaving. I'm not going to stand by and let you allow
someone to come between us and the home we've built."

"Home?"

"Yes, home."

Putting the envelopes and pictures back in the box,
Tammy said, "This is far from a home. It's an institution if
you ask me. We do the same shit day in and day out. The
newness is gone."

"And your way of dealing with it is by having an affair?"

"Girl, I'm not doing anything. So what she's sent me a few
cards and a couple of gifts? It's more than you've done
lately."

"Tammy, I shouldn't have to buy you things for you to
know I love you."

"You don't get it, do you? Liya appreciates me for who I
am and does these things for me from the heart."

I sat down on the bed. "Well, then, that's who you need to
be with. All I've ever tried to do is be here for you and your
children, and now you're showing and telling me it's no
longer enough. You consider me security and have always
believed I'd never leave."

"And you won't."

"Watch me." I hadn't planned on packing right at that
moment, but her callousness made me change my mind. I
climbed over her piles in the closet and started taking down
my clothes from the racks and flung them to the bed. I

grabbed my suitcase from underneath the bed and started laying my clothes in it. Any and everything of mine, I threw in the luggage. Next thing I knew, Tammy was helping me. Then, without cause, she abruptly stopped and left the room.

By the time I came downstairs with my bags, the kids had finished breakfast and were watching television in the den. I loved those kids like they were my own, and I needed to leave the house before they discovered this travesty between their mother and me. I opened the door leading to the garage and saw Tammy sitting on the passenger side of my truck. I walked around to the trunk, unlocked the bed of the vehicle, and gently slid my bags inside.

As I moved alongside the truck, I heard music softly playing inside. The tune was unmistakable. It was Celine Dion's "Because You Loved Me." From time to time, Tammy would tell me the song reminded her of the love I had for her. When I opened the door of the truck, she was sitting there, still in her bedclothes, reclined in the seat. "You know, I love you, Morgan, and I didn't realize how much until I saw you packing your clothes," she said, wiping her eyes.

"I love you, too, Tammy."

"I know I've fucked up. There's nothing special about Liya, but I know you think that there is. I mean, those cards don't mean nearly as much to me as the ones you've given to me. I don't know why I've been keeping them."

"Tammy, you haven't been just keeping them. You've been hiding them. We promised to never keep secrets."

Looking down at her ashen legs, she answered, "OK, then, what do you want to know?"

"Have you slept with her?"

"No, I haven't. I met her that one time in Detroit, and that's it."

"Do you think about sleeping with her?"

Like I said, Tammy can be brutally honest. "Yes, but not

enough to fly to Phoenix to do it. I haven't been intimate with you because I felt strange trying to have sex with you when my mind was with someone else. All I know is that I feel safe with you and will admit that the promise of security made me take advantage of you and our love. I'm sorry, Morgan. But the more Liya came at me, the more I responded. You have to believe me."

"I'm trying to."

"Baby, I got caught up, OK?" The tears cascaded from her eyes. The words of those letters and cards kept fluttering through my mind, but I also reminisced about the cards and letters Tammy and I had given to each other over the years. I hadn't been all that I'd promised I'd be to her. Not excusing her for allowing someone to come between us, my level of trust had been jeopardized. All of those times I thought that such shit would never happen to us began rushing through my mind. It had happened, and neither of us had been prepared. Tammy told me that, through all of the emotional feelings she had for Liya, she never stopped loving me.

Simply put, I believed her.

After hours of sitting in the truck talking about where we'd gone wrong and what we were willing to do to fix it, I wanted Tammy in the worst way. In all of our years together, I was always on the bottom when we made love, and I let her do whatever the hell she wanted with and to me. But, while sitting out there in the garage, it came over me that I needed to let her know that I could love her, too. I leaned my five-three frame over and kissed Tammy in her mouth. My lips and tongue gripped her in a way never done between us before.

I owned her passion and desired to give back to her what she'd given to me over the years. Grasping the back of my neck, Tammy pulled me in to her and squeezed my shoulders and back into her body. I couldn't help myself. No matter the time of day her skin smelled of jasmine and vanilla, and one whiff was all it took for my nipples to harden. She was enticing, and her magnetism brought my body to the same side of the truck as hers where I straddled her tiny lap. I slipped my hand beneath her gown and reached for her warm inner beauty, making a temporary home for my fingers. Tammy whimpered from my movement and embraced my actions with juices that streamed from within. With my other hand, I held on to the top of her seat and pumped into her until the muscles in my legs went numb. My body relaxed against hers, and as I stole a look into the back of the cab, I saw a bagful of what appeared to be confetti.

"What's this?" I asked, sticking my hand in the sack.

Tammy, looking at my hand in the bag, said, "Oh, some things I need to take to the Dumpster."

"But what is it?" I asked again as I stuck my hand farther into the sack. Then I felt hair. "What the fuck?" I yanked my hand from the bag.

She moved from beneath me and picked up the bag. Careful as to not spill its contents, she sorted through the pieces of paper until she came across a piece with writing on it. The strip of paper was from one of the envelopes I'd flipped through the other night. I recognized the handwriting. Tammy had, at some point, shredded all of the cards and letters, and at the bottom of the bag was the head of the Indian doll she'd once wanted so badly.

"I don't need these things as much as I need you."

To me, Tammy had redeemed herself. Sure, throwing away the letters and the doll were gestures of respect that I'll always admire, but emotionally, I don't expect a change overnight. I just pray that wherever her mind takes her that her heart isn't too quick to follow.

SO BLACK, IT'S BLUE

Icouldn't understand why Alisha never had dinner ready when I got home. I made sure she had everything she needed to cook—a food processor, blender, cookbooks, knives, mixers, all that shit—but my dinner was never ready. I expected my shit smoking hot and sitting on the table when I walked through the door. She did OK for a minute, but then she started slipping. Meat would be burnt, greens cold, macaroni and cheese runny, and I don't have to go on because it gets worse.

The first blow I threw made her hit the floor. I didn't even look at her to see if she was hurt or bleeding. I popped that ass and kept on going. Alisha's a pretty red girl with blond extensions, rosy red lips, and green eyes. She ain't never had an ass about nothing, but her pussy, in my opinion, was lined in gold. I'm her first love, and, if she could, she'd move the pearly gates from Heaven for me and sit them in the front room. That's why I know she can fix my dinner the way I want it.

In my previous relationship, I beat her ass, too. The thing with her, though, was that she hit me back. We got to fighting so tough one night at the club that the bouncers had to pull me off her, and, if it hadn't been for the fact I knew the security guard, we would've gotten locked up for it. And that couldn't happen . . . a paper trail. Everybody would know that I was an abuser—of women; everybody would know I was a dyke.

My name is Lorraine, and I'm a ten-year veteran of the Milwaukee Police Force. My partner is Eric Laeden, and he is the biggest homophobe I know. We went through the academy together right after I got out of junior college. I was with him when he first met his wife, Leanna, and was even at their wedding. He and I go to the bar, Loodie's, every Friday night after work and shoot pool until somebody gives in. I've never been a drinker, but he can toss back a keg if you don't watch him. There have been many times I've wanted to tell him about my sexuality, but I hesitated because I knew he'd try to kill me.

One night, after we'd been on the job maybe five or six months, we were called to The Shell, a gay club downtown where two cross dresssers were being beaten in the alley next to the building. Just as I was about to grab my Billy club and jump out of the car, Eric grabbed my arm and told me to wait. I said, "What do you mean, wait? They're about to get killed." He'd turned off the radio and the lights.

His reply was, "That's what those fucking faggots get. That'll be two less freaks in the world."

I let the beating continue for another minute or so before I shoved the door open and rushed out of the car. Fortunately, I had because one of the guys ended up with a cracked skull. Had I been a second or two later, another blow would have killed him. Eric hesitated before arresting the perps, saying we should reduce the paperwork by letting them go with only a warning. The guy with the messed-up head was going to be brain damaged for life because he'd lost so much blood. I broke ranks with Eric and arrested the bums. Eric fucked me over when he didn't show for the hearing. He blamed it on a spastic colon that, in my opinion, acts up because he drinks so much beer. The suspects got off, and the victim? He died a month after the incident from swelling on the brain. I attended the funeral and watched his mother bury her only child.

Lorraine bought me this big, old pretty house with all the bells and whistles—with things I'm not used to. She was the first person to buy me my first pair of jeans—I'll explain in a minute. My sister and I were raised by my grandmother, sleeping in the back room of a three-room house. There was a hole in the roof that created a horrible draft in the winter. When it rained, Grandmomma would put a pail right next to our bed to catch the dirty raindrops. Our room was only big enough to hold a full-size mattress. That's it. The folks at the church got it for us from the Salvation Army. It smelled moldy, mildewy, funky, and had lumps all through it. Grandmomma did what she could to get the odors out, spraying so much Lysol that it made us choke.

Gloria, my older sister, got all the new clothes, and, when she outgrew them, they were passed down to me. Panties, bras, jeans, shirts—everything. I never knew my mother; I was two when she died and can only vaguely recall her face. She was always in and out of the hospital from what I was told and died from AIDS before anybody ever knew what the disease was. She died a painful death and had made no provisions for me and Gloria. I met my father once when he stopped by on Gloria's tenth birthday. I was seven at the time, and damn, I fell in love with that man because he was neat, clean-shaven, and smelled so wonderfully masculine.

The first couple of hours that he was at the house he talked to Grandmomma about my mother, and they reminisced about his younger days. From what I gathered, he was hell on wheels back in the day, and my family loved his dirty draws. Somewhere along the line, he and my mother drifted apart, and he went away to make a

*better life for himself. He's a stockbroker now or something like that
and lives in Secaucus right outside of New York City. When Grandmomma asked him to take us with him so we could have a better life
than what she could offer, he said he needed to go back and prepare
a place for Gloria and me. It's been eighteen years, and I'm still
waiting.*

*Gloria went to college for a couple of months but dropped out after
the first semester. She'd gotten financial aid or something to pay for
it and talked about it like it was the worst thing she could've done
for herself. When it was my turn to go, I got financial aid and opted
to go through the nurse's assistant program. I finished all but three
courses and know how to wipe asses and clean up shit. I'll go back
and finish one day after Lorraine completes her degree.*

*One day Gloria got up and just left. She didn't tell me or
Grandmomma anything. All of her clothes were in their usual place.
I think she might've had her purse since we couldn't find it anywhere in the house. Grandmomma didn't bother with filing a police
report because she said that they never took looking for black folks seriously. A couple of months after that, I was sitting on the couch
watching television with the only person to ever give me the time of
day. I was missing my sister.* The Color Purple *came on, and
Grandmomma and I both just fell to pieces when Nettie and Celie
were separated. She was crying on my shoulder, tears that were long
overdue from years of dissatisfied contentment and loneliness. I understood her crying, and instead of shedding my own tears of pain and
disappointment, I held it together for her. After the movie went off, I
got up, put on my clothes, and set out on a search to find either my
sister or maybe . . . a Shug Avery for myself. That was three years
ago.*

*I've dated off and on, but I never seem to be enough for anybody.
I don't care who loves me, man or woman, so long as somebody does.
Loodie's was a club for everybody—Black, White, Puerto Rican, you
name it. I went in there and, damnit, I found me a Shug Avery, a
woman who bought me a whole new wardrobe, including my first*

*pair of jeans, a new mattress, a car, a beautiful ring. But now that
I've been this punching bag, this doormat, I sometimes think I
fucked up and got me a Mister instead.*

I'm not sure if I need any help for this problem I have
since I readily admit that there is a problem. Sometimes I
feel bad about it, but most times I don't. She oughta do what
I tell her to do. I know she's not going to ever leave because
she doesn't have anywhere to go. I've been to her grandmother's house, and it's rat-infested and smells like old people and piss. Alisha's got this palatial estate here or something
similar. Anything's better that what she had. I told her that
her grandmother could move in with us if she wanted her to,
but she said no. That old biddy is set in her ways, and there's
no need to have grown women butting heads, especially if
they don't have to. Besides, it wasn't going to stop me from
smacking that ass if I had to. Dealing with Eric at work was
frustrating because I felt like I was always hiding something
from him. I suppose that's why I beat Alisha so bad, trying to
get all of that confusion out.

I came in one evening earlier than usual and found Alisha
sitting on the couch watching television. The house was a
mess, as far as I was concerned, and dinner wasn't ready.

"Hey, baby," she said. "You're home early." She jumped up
from the couch to hug me, but I pushed her away. "I'm
going to go ahead and start dinner."

No sooner than she took a step from me I grabbed her by
her extensions and yanked her to me. I pulled her back, almost snapping her neck, and snarled, "You've had all day to
have dinner ready, but you got your ass sitting up here in this
filth." I pushed her away from me, and it was like she trying
to run away from me. "Oh, you gonna try to run?" I swung at
her and missed. I hated when I missed. I trapped her against
the wall and punched her in her jaw. Something moved out

of place, but I kept hitting her. Alisha struggled with what strength she had, but I had her, and I pummeled her in every spot I could find. "Now, clean this damn house up and get my dinner ready. And if so much as one morsel ain't right, I'm gonna try my best to kill you."

As we sat at the dinner table, I talked to Alisha like there was nothing wrong. I told her about my day and all the fun stuff Eric and I had done. I never shared with her the type person Eric was because it seemed hypocritical, you know? She'd never understand anyway. Alisha held her head down when I talked to her. Submissiveness, I guess. Chewing my steak that she'd cooked to near perfection, I glanced over at her and realized her jaw seemed to be hanging slightly. Maybe she couldn't talk. Her right eye was so black that it shone blue and looked swollen shut. I didn't know how to say sorry for anything, so I didn't even address her injuries. Did the slave owner go out to his slaves after whipping them and offer to tend to them to make them feel better? She'd be alright.

About an hour later, I wanted sex. I wanted Alisha to cum all over me while sitting on my face. I felt somehow that our lovemaking reminded her that I really did love her and that I'd do anything for her. I'd rescued her from a life of nothing and exchanged it for a life of luxury. She'd been with a girl or two before me, but they weren't about shit. Then, while we were still trying to get to know each other, she fucked this guy and turned up pregnant. I told her if she wanted any kind of future with me, she was going to have to get an abortion. The fucker was pissed off with me, but I dared his ass to come up in here and start some shit with the sheriff.

Anyway, Alisha still wasn't talking to me, but I really didn't need her for talking. I kissed on her and took off her shirt. I rolled her nipples through my fingers, trying to get them to

perk up. That seemed to take forever. She didn't try to return my kisses or anything. I started to kick her ass again just
so we'd have an understanding, but I wanted to get my freak
on. I got on top of her and pumped my groin into her pelvis
as hard as I could to get a moan or something out of her.
That nut came right on.

See what I mean? I'm laying here with a broken jaw and two
black eyes. My back is sore, and my neck feels like a piece of rubber
that's been stretched out of shape. When she was on top of me, I
couldn't feel a thing. I can barely move my mouth enough to frown,
let alone speak. I need to go to the hospital, but I wouldn't even
know what to say. I can speak but not very well. I could've talked
back to Lorraine while we were at dinner, but I was so upset with her
that it will probably be a day or two before I say anything to her. I've
been thinking about packing my shit and getting out of here the
minute she drifts off to sleep. But where would I go? I sure as hell
can't show up at Grandmomma's looking like this. She'd catch a cab
over here and kill Lorraine in her sleep. I found some hydrocodone
in the medicine cabinet, and I have an ice pack sitting on my face
right now while I'm stretched out across the bed in the guest room.
I'm going to lie here for a few minutes until the throbbing stops. I
have to be back in the bed before she wakes up.

At two in the morning, my work pager went off. It was
Eric. I called him back on his cell and found out he was back
at the station.

"Lorraine, we've been called to cover the three A.M. shift.
You need to get your ass on over here."

Putting on my blues gave me this sense of authority. I
strapped on my holster, which I kept next to the bed, and
noticed Alisha's side of the bed was empty. I called out to her
but didn't get an answer. I checked the guest room next to
our bedroom, but she wasn't in there. I also looked in both

bathrooms on the second level. She wasn't in either one of them. Adjusting my belt, I took my shoes with me downstairs. Peeking into the guest room right off the kitchen, there she was extended against the bed. My first mind was to wake her up and ask why she wasn't in our bed, but I couldn't do that to her. I knew I'd hurt her. I leaned over and kissed her on the forehead. Her bruises were so horrible that I caught myself flinching as I scanned her body for the marks I'd made.

When I got outside, I looked at my cruiser that was so black that it looked blue against the moonlit sky. I propped myself against the hood and looked at my home and the damage I'd done to the one in it. I owed her more than what I'd given her. I have a problem, and I need to fix it. Opening the car door, I saw the message indicator on my cell phone blinking. Couldn't be nobody but Eric. I plopped down in the driver's seat and phoned Eric to tell him I was on my way.

I met him standing outside the station drinking a cup of coffee. Before getting out, I thought to myself about how cool Eric and I were. He'd told me if I ever needed to talk to him about anything he'd be there for me. He had issues with Blacks, but he dealt with me. He was a male chauvinist pig, but he was cool with me. So maybe, if he knew I was gay, he'd overlook being a homophobic jackass. No matter what way I rolled, I was still his partner, and as brothers in the fraternal order, he was obligated to me.

The reason I had to come in, so I found out, was that there was a tip about this cat selling guns in the downtown area, and they wanted extra patrols. I didn't have a problem with it. Shit, that meant overtime. Eric and I parked along the same alley where we'd found those cross-dressers a while back. As we sat there in the alley, the beating I'd given Alisha started fucking with me. I couldn't believe I was having a conscience about it.

"What's on your mind, Lorraine? You know I can read you like a book."

I sat flipping the cap on my Zippo. "I'm good, Eric."

"No, Holmes, something is on your mind."

Click-click. Click-click. I contemplated what I wanted to say and how to say it. Eric was my boy. "Eric, you and I been friends a long time, right. Best buds, right?"

"Yeah, yeah, of course," he said, nodding.

"I can trust you with my life, right?"

"Yeah. What's going on, Lorraine?"

Click-click. Click-click. I swallowed the lump in my throat and blurted out, "I'm gay."

Eric sat there for a minute, staring at me. He turned and looked out the window. I waited for some kind of reaction from him. "Let's get out and walk. We don't need to be talking about something like this in the squad car."

"OK."

We both got out and started walking through the alley. Suddenly, I felt a crack against the back of my head. I hit the ground. The blows came one right after the other. I couldn't catch my breath, nor did I ever have a chance to fight back. Spitting blood through my teeth, I tried to stand but was kicked back down to the ground. I fell face first and landed on top of my hand. Eric's blows were relentless. A couple of times I thought I was dead but had been forced to wake up. In writhing pain, I rolled over and reached for my gun.

"Try it, and I'll blow your fucking brains out," he said calmly.

"Man, what you doing? I thought . . ."

"All this time you been playing me for some fool." He kicked me again.

"It's not like that, Eric. I swear." Dazed and now afraid for my life, I crawled to the nearest structure I could find and tried to sit up. I knew something was broken. Every time I moved, it was like I was leaving a trail of bones behind me. It felt as if every part of me had crumbled. Trying to focus, I managed to make out Eric coming toward me with his piece in his hand. He reached for my radio and disconnected it, tossing it into the dumpster by the car.

"Eric, wait," I whispered as I coughed blood into my fist. My other hand clinched my ribs, trying its best to keep them in place. "Please don't . . ."

"Please don't what?" Eric asked harshly, kicking me yet again. He had that same fury in him the night he'd watched the cross-dresser being beaten to death. "You expect me to listen to a fucking nigger faggot? Give me a fucking break. I should shoot your ass and leave you here to die, but I'm not going to fuck up my career with some shit like that. As far as I'm concerned, though, you're dead to me." Then he whipped out his pale, White dick and sprayed me with urine from the top of my head to the tips of my shoes. To top off his tirade, Eric spit in my face, and as I felt his warm, coffee-saturated saliva ooze down my cheek, I watched him drive off in the patrol car signed out to me. From that point forward, there was no telling where my career or my life would end up.

As the sky began to lighten and as I continued to bleed from my head and mouth, I wiggled my fingers until I could get enough movement in my hands to reach my cell phone. I needed to do whatever possible to disappear from that alley before someone discovered me. I dialed home for Alisha to come and get me. Seemingly talking through her teeth, she agreed and came right on.

"Lorraine, you've got to go to the hospital," she said when she saw me.

"No, I can't go there. Take me home."

"But, you . . ."

I gave her a look she'd never forget. "I said take me

home." There was no way in hell I was going to fall up in the hospital with this uniform on. Besides, Alisha looked like she'd had a run-in with a punching bag. If anything, she needed to go to the hospital more than me. "I need to get out of this uniform before I do anything."

"OK."

On the way home, I told Alisha what had happened. I don't know why I expected any sympathy from her. She had her own battle with a madwoman who she had to deal. If the both of us walked into the emergency room all banged up, the staff would've called the station, and all my shit would be out. Ain't no telling what they would've thought. When we got to the house, I instructed Alisha to pull into the garage, shielding us from the sunlight and our nosy-ass neighbors. "I want to take this uniform off before I go in the house."

"OK," she mumbled. Alisha hadn't asked many questions, nor had she said much of anything to me despite my ordeal.

In the mudroom, I took off my uniform, exposing my bruised and battered body. I went into the bathroom and stared at my reflection in the mirror. Alisha stood in the doorway, looking at me with tears in her eyes.

"I need some privacy, Alisha. Can you take my uniform and put it in a garbage bag for me?"

"Yes, I'll get it. Do you need bandages or something?"

I couldn't believe she was trying to be helpful given all I'd done to her the night before. "No, that's alright. I'm cool."

I closed the door and lowered the toilet seat cover and gently rested my aching body on the stool. There was no doubt in my mind that I was going to quit the force. Eric had a calculating way of doing things, and I'm sure he'd come up with his story to cover his ass and why he had the cruiser. Looking down at my dirty hands, I saw that my left thumb was broken and so was my left pinky finger. I recall him step-

ping on those while I was trying to crawl to safety. My lips
were puffy, and as I slid my tongue across my upper teeth, I
noticed that one of them was loose. My injuries didn't seem
all that bad. I'd probably be sore a while. Every time I
thought about Eric's blows to my face, I had flashbacks of my
blows to Alisha. There was a knock at the door.

"Um, I have some bandages for you and a couple of ice
packs." Alisha never did what I told her to do, but this time I
wasn't mad.

"Thank you," I said softly as I gazed into her eyes. I was
hoping to see that she was OK with things. Instead, I saw
something different. Alisha came into the bathroom with a
hand towel, some bandages, ice packs, alcohol, peroxide,
and a bottle of pills. First, she ran some warm water in the
face bowl and poured some of the alcohol into the water.

"It's going to burn a little, but I need to get some of this
dirt off."

I didn't say a word. I simply let her do her thing. Gently,
she rubbed my face with the towel, cleaning the scratches
and scars on my face and forehead. After rinsing the towel,
Alisha washed my hands and even took the time to get the
dirt from underneath my nails. "Take your T-shirt and bra
off. Oh, and take one of these."

"What's that?"

"A painkiller," she mumbled. "You need it."

I didn't argue, but I only agreed to take half of one of the
pills. Once I had the bra and shirt off, I saw the extent of the
damage. There were bruises from the top of my chest all
the way down to my lower torso. My back was painfully sore,
but I could handle it. I worked out extensively, so I knew I'd
make it through this. Alisha delicately massaged alcohol into
my skin and rubbed it over my entire upper body. Afterward,
she wrapped me with Ace bandages and put Band-Aids on

my wounds. I felt like a new woman when she was done. I looked at her still fighting through her own pain and took her hand in mine.

"Let me take you to the hospital. I'll be fine here since you've played doctor on me."

At first she didn't say anything, but, to my surprise, she agreed.

As we approached the stop sign at the end of our street, Alisha opened a piece of folded paper and said, "I don't want you to take me to the hospital. I want to go to this address."

I recognized the address because I'd dropped off so many women there, and given what I'd put her through, I didn't blame her one bit for wanting to go. "Are you sure?"

"Yes, I'm sure. I already have a bag packed in the trunk. I was actually planning to be gone when you got home," she said tearfully.

"I see." I made the left turn and drove her to Chicago. When we arrived at the gate, Alisha told me she didn't want me to go in with her. It was the end of the road for us.

One week later

"My name is Lorraine Webster, and I am a perpetrator of domestic violence." I hated being put on the spot, but I knew my turn was coming, so I spoke up like they expected us to do in group therapy.

THE DEACONESS

The fire must've started in the kitchen where I'd been fry-
ing chicken. I remember stopping to see the Redskins
score on their final drive of the last quarter. As I stood outside the house with the fire department spraying water in
what used to be my bedroom, I didn't recall turning off the
grease.

I called Pastor Tucker from a neighbor's house and told
him my house had burned to the ground. The fire had
spread so quickly that I didn't have a chance to run upstairs
to grab any clothes, money, or my Bible. He and his wife,
Ruby, came over to pick me up and asked if I had anywhere
else to go.

"No," I said. I don't have any family here."

"We didn't think you think you did," Pastor commented.
"We're going take you on home with us and make sure you
get what you need to start over."

Mount Canaan Baptist Church was my home away from
home. I'd joined one Sunday after Pastor Tucker had
preached about all God's children being sinners, and that it
was His son, Jesus, who would save us from eternal damna-

tion. I was thirteen years old and knew I didn't want to go to Hell. Walking up the aisle, I felt everybody's eyes on me. Tears started streaming down my face, and there was this burning in my soul that led me to believe that everything was going to be alright. But then, I met Sonya three Sundays later at a dinner on the grounds. Dressed in her white usher uniform, she looked like an angel to me. I don't know if it was because she smelled like fresh honeysuckle or if it was because she didn't seem as harsh as the other older ushers.

A frisky adolescent, I was considered a tomboy even though I wore little frou-frou dresses my aunt picked out for me. Instead of singing in the choir or making cakes for the bake sales or preparing for life on the Mother Board, I wanted to hang out with the deacons. I was in the room when they prepared communion, and I stood with them when the doors of the church were opened. On Wednesdays, I'd sneak out of Bible study and slip into the deacon's meeting. It was almost like being in the barber shop, if you ask me. They talked about stuff that the women of the church didn't need to hear, like which sister in the choir had the biggest behind. Anyway, back to Sonya.

That Sunday Sonya brushed past me with a piece of watermelon she was taking to Pastor's table. She winked at me, and for some reason, that made me feel funny inside. On her way back toward my table, I was eating some collard greens and didn't notice the juice running down my face.

"You're drippin'." She laughed as she pulled her handkerchief from her pocket. It was the same one she'd used to dry the tears of Miss Turner when the spirit had touched her during the service. *Praise God.* Sonya touched me, and then our eyes met. She cupped the lower part of my face with her left hand and wiped my mouth and chin with her right hand.

"There," she said. "That's better."

When she leaned over, I couldn't help but look down into her bosom and see "them." And they were pretty, too. I didn't know what I was doing, but something inside of me recognized it. *Was it sin?* After that, I didn't see Sonya for another week or two, but when I did see her again, that feeling was still there. This time, though, I imagined what she looked like completely naked.

On my seventeenth birthday, the deacons surprised me and gave me my first pair of white gloves. They did this presentation in front of the congregation and told me I could start helping pass the offering tray. Over the years, I'd served the Lord in only the best ways I knew how. Mount Canaan was a small church with about two hundred members, and no good deed, by anyone, went unnoticed. At the end of service that same day, I saw Sonya standing in the foyer and went over to say hello.

"Miss Sonya, it's good seeing you this fine Sunday."

"Good seeing you, too, Trudy. Got any plans for your birthday?" By this time, Sonya was twenty-five.

"No, ma'am, I don't have any plans. I'm going to go home and get me a plate, then I'm probably going to catch a football game or two."

"Oh, well, that sounds fun. This is the only fun I get. I have to go to work in a couple of hours. The devil's work is never done."

"What you mean?"

"Come on outside, and I'll tell you." I swung open the door for her, and as she walked out, I smelled those honeysuckles again. In the sun's brightness, we headed for a tree about a hundred yards from the church.

"I'm a stripper. I work at the club down on Waterson."

I was dumbfounded. *A stripper?* That explained the sexy lingerie I kept seeing underneath her usher's uniform.

"Wow," I said. There was nothing I could really say. It wasn't for me to judge her. "I mean, Miss Sonya, you do what you have to do."

She seemed uneasy at this point, and the last thing I wanted was for her to feel uncomfortable. "Trudy, don't tell nobody, OK?"

"Oh, I'm not. We all got secrets, and yours is safe with me."

Sonya hesitated before she said good-bye. She was looking around us and all through the trees to make sure no one was around. "You want to come down to the club for your birthday?"

Oh, Jesus.

"I can get you in if you tell me what time you're coming."

For an opportunity to see those breasts she'd dangled in my face a few years before, I'd miss the games and take whatever chance I had to.

"Um, you sure I won't get caught?"

"Don't worry about all of that. I got you."

"I'll be there around five. Is that too early?"

"No, that's perfect."

The bus was never on time during the weekends. I got to the club closer to six. When I got there, this big, burly guy was standing at the door. He was checking me out from head to toe. "You Trudy?"

"Yes," I said shyly.

"A'ight. C'mon in."

Cigarette smoke filled the air, and the smell of liquor reeked from every man I passed. The fog from the smoke was so thick that I could barely see the four shiny poles extending from the ceiling and stopping at the floor. I didn't listen to a lot of secular music, but I recognized R. Kelly when I heard him. As the intro to "Bump 'n' Grind" started, I found an empty table right in front of the stage. It was the only one in the smoke-filled room. Then, I saw her. Sonya entered the stage with three other women, and all of them were naked. Her face was covered in devil's paint—makeup— and unlike what I'd been taught to believe about it, her face looked beautiful. Slightly uneasy about what was before my eyes, I studied her graceful movements and envied her ability to work a pole as she did. The gyrations of her private area made me perspire and fidget in my seat. The next thing I knew Sonya was standing directly in front of me and had taken my hand and placed it on her breasts.

"Happy Birthday," she whispered to me. She made motions with my hand that I had only imagined. When she glided it across her stomach and into her crotch, I froze. There that feeling was again, and I liked it. *Lord, have mercy.*

When I turned thirty, Pastor Tucker and the deacon board did something they'd never done in the history of the church. They voted in their first deaconess: me. No one but Sonya knew about my birthday outing thirteen years earlier. She'd left the church five years ago to pursue a career as an exotic entertainer in Las Vegas. I never let anyone know I was bothered by that because Sonya and I maintained a really good friendship. It was easy to see that she felt comfortable enough with me to share her private life. I liked her, in that way, but refused to ever let her know it.

My first night at Pastor's house was busy. The house had been my aunt's, and I inherited it when she died. I had to call the insurance company and what few friends I had to tell them about the fire. Most of them offered me a place to stay, but there was no way I was going to leave town and abandon Mount Canaan. I loved that church and everybody in it. Pastor Tucker, now in his late fifties, had remarried since his first wife died from pneumonia. Miss Ruby, as we all called her, was almost twenty years younger than her husband and was a firecracker. By that, I mean she's a real looker. I think the dresses she owns are all either black or red, and, when she wears those red ones, it's like Satan himself buys her wardrobe. Watching her roam through the house, I noticed all of her lounging clothes were also in either black or red.

The next day my body started trying to tell me I was coming down with something. My chest was hurting, and a terrible cough kept me irritable most of the day. Pastor suggested I might have inhaled a bit of smoke from the fire, and he was probably right. Miss Ruby said that it sounded like I was coming down with a little cold.

"I've got something that will knock that cold right on out."

While I was sitting in the den with Pastor, I heard a lot of commotion coming from the kitchen. Glasses clanking, water running, kettle whistling. A few minutes later, Miss Ruby emerged from the kitchen with a cup of smoldering liquid.

"Here's a hot toddy for you."

Never a liquor drinker, I almost threw up when I took the first sip. "Oh, God. What's in this?"

"A little something to make you feel better. You should get a real good night's sleep with it."

"I appreciate your help, but I don't drink. What's in this?"

"Oh, a little tea, some lemon, and few other things that you don't need to know about. You'll feel better in a few days."

My first mind was to not drink it because I absolutely detested the smell and taste of liquor. "I'll take my chances with Sudafed or something."

Then Pastor spoke up. "Trudy, drink the toddy. It's not going to hurt you. Trust me."

I drank the toddy, and not long after the last sip, I was ready for bed.

*　*　*

Over in the night, I was awakened by the lack of air. The
room was so dark that I couldn't even see in front of me.
Part of me was still in such a fog from the toddy that I had to
fight for my bearings. The more I struggled, the sooner I realized someone was on top of me kissing my face and neck. I
couldn't wiggle or shout, my movement and air constricted
by this obstruction on my chest. The funny thing was that
there was an overwhelming smell of honeysuckle filling the
air in the room. I managed to free my hands from underneath what now felt like a woman's body. She ripped open
the pajama shirt that Pastor had given me and tasted my
breasts. *Lord, Jesus.* I caressed her with my hands, and as my
palms hugged every curve, the rest of my body fell limp. I
was asleep again.

The morning after, I woke up to find the smell of honeysuckle gone and my pajama shirt intact. Nothing in the
room was out of place. The only thing that seemed out of
order was my mind. I'd never dreamed about a woman like
that. When I got to the kitchen, Miss Ruby was pouring coffee for everybody. I sat down at the table and drank a swal-
low. There was an irresistible hint of cinnamon and vanilla
in it, a combination I loved.

"How'd you sleep, Trudy?" she asked.

"I slept OK." Still bewildered at my dream, I didn't have
much else to say and wanted desperately to get back to making my life seem normal. Pastor took me to the bank to with-
draw some money so I could buy clothes and toiletries. I'd
been wearing men's suits for the longest time, but no one
knew it because I dressed them up with ladies' blouses.
Confused about what made me feel right, I chose not to
wear perfume or cologne. After we finished our errands, we
headed back home to find Miss Ruby still in the kitchen.

"You must live in the kitchen, Miss Ruby. You in here every
time I see you."

Turning a bit red in the face, she chuckled. "I have to keep that man of mine fed. I like to keep busy in here. An idle mind is the devil's playground."

"You're right. It sure is." I coughed.

"You still coughing?"

Holding my hand to my mouth as I spewed all kinds of germs into my palm, I replied, "Yeah. It's not as bad as it was yesterday."

"I can't tell. You need another hot toddy. That's what you need. After dinner, I'll make you one."

I didn't have the strength to argue with her. "OK, Miss Ruby. Thank you."

That night, lying there in bed, I was sleeping like a log, and then that feeling of being robbed of my air supply came over me again. Opening my eyes, I looked up into the breasts of a thief in the night. She was riding me like the Lone Ranger rode Silver, and all I could do was lie there in splendid bliss. Honeysuckles filled my nostrils again, but tonight they acted like poppies and put me in a comalike slumber. For the next three nights, this happened to me, and each time I'd refused to believe I was dreaming. Morning after morning everybody in the house went on about their business, ignoring me and my concern about these wild dreams.

One day Miss Ruby came into my room and asked me if I was feeling better. I informed her that I'd been having trouble sleeping and wasn't sure what could be causing it.

"Miss Ruby, what's in your hot toddies? I know you said tea and lemon, but . . ." I'd paid attention to her hair since I'd been living with them, and there was never a strand out of place.

"Are you having an upset stomach over in the night?"

"Well, no, nothing like that."

"Is your head hurting?"

"No, I can't say it does."

"Then I wouldn't worry about it. It's probably that old cold you got that's giving you fits."

I wanted to believe that she was right, but with the state my body was in during the middle of the night, something else was going on. After deacons meeting the next evening, I drank another hot toddy, but I popped two Vivarin to keep me awake. I sat up all night reading my Bible and praying. At about 3:00 A.M., I went to the bathroom and had this strange feeling that I wasn't the only person awake in the house. I heard many sounds—crickets singing, the house settling, wind blowing, and sometimes I swear I heard someone moving about in the house. When I was done, I peeped out my door into the hallway. I didn't see anyone, but I did smell honeysuckle.

Puzzled as to where this fragrance was coming from, I ventured into the kitchen to get a glass of water and took a moment to walk through the house to check things out. As I approached the living room, the fragrance became stronger.

Just as I was about to turn on the light, a voice whispered, "She keeps farting. I had to come out of there and spray some air freshener. All I could find was this stuff Ruby gets from her cousin out in Vegas." It was Pastor standing in the front room by the window trying to get air. "I'm sorry if I woke you. I keep telling her she can't drink milk like she used to."

"No, sir, I was up doing some reading. You didn't disturb me."

"Let's go sit outside for minute." He opened the door and gestured for me to walk out ahead of him. I might've acted like one of the deacons, but Pastor still treated me like a lady. We sat in the swing. "You been feeling alright, Trudy?"

I couldn't lie to Pastor. "No, I haven't lately. Something's been bothering me." I was going to tell him about Sonya and me. "You remember that usher named Miss Sonya?"

He sat for a minute and pondered my question like he really had to think about who I was talking about. "Yeah, yeah, Ruby's cousin. She's out there in Vegas now working as . . ."

"An exotic dancer?"

"Call her what you want. I say she's stripper," he laughed.

"OK, well, she and I, we . . ."

"Andy!" someone yelled through the house. "Andy!"

Pastor got up and hurried inside the door. "Hush, woman. You're going to wake up the whole neighborhood. Me and Trudy just sitting out here talking."

Miss Ruby came to the door and winked at me. "Trudy, you need to be getting some sleep, don't you?"

"I guess so. I'm about finished reading my scriptures. I'll probably be up another hour or two." The Vivarin had my hind parts wired.

"OK, baby. I'm going back to bed now." Even at night, Miss Ruby's hair was in place. It was tied up when she came on the porch, but, even in rollers, it was together.

Tired as I don't know what, I dragged myself into the kitchen the next morning and found Miss Ruby beating eggs. Goodness, she was beating them so hard her head was shaking, but her hair stayed in place. She was a good cook, and I could see why Pastor was so crazy about her.

"Good morning, Trudy. How you feeling this morning?" she asked.

God, please forgive me for this lie. "Good morning to you, too. I'm feeling much better. Sat up last night and read some scripture. Meditated a little bit." Really, I felt like I'd been run over by an eighteen-wheeler. My eyes were burning and felt like they had pins in them. I went to the refrigerator to get some orange juice and noticed bottles of gin, vodka, and cognac on the counter. I poured my juice and sat down at the table.

"Pastor was telling me that Miss Sonya is your cousin."

She stopped beating those eggs and slowly looked up and out the window. Then she responded, "Well, she is. You know her?"

I didn't know what to say, but I wasn't going to lie this time. "Yes, ma'am, I know her. I met her some years ago at the church."

"Aw, well, that's nice," she smiled. "Sonya and I are first cousins. Shoot, we're more like sisters, though." Then she cackled, "She gave me my first kiss. Was good, too!" Regaining her composure, she inquired, "When's the last time you saw her?" She seemed troubled.

"Oh, Miss Ruby, it's been a while."

She got a little quiet on me, but then she said, "She was here about three . . . four weeks ago. Brought me some of those nice-smelling perfumes I wear."

I needed to leave. "Oh, OK then. I'm going to get out of your hair and go get dressed for work."

My job as a substitute teacher was enough for me to have a few dollars in my pocket. I've never wanted for much. My relationship with the Lord kept me richer than any employer ever could. On Sundays, I gave my ten percent, and the Lord blessed me for it.

A lot of folks have often asked me if I was ever going to get married, but I never had a satisfactory answer for them—or myself, for that matter. I recalled that afternoon I saw Miss Sonya's breasts and the show that I got on my seventeenth birthday. Feeling like that about another woman's body was not normal, but I'd accepted that it was how God had made me. Maybe these dreams I'd been having were manifestations of those desires. Maybe I was acting out in my dreams what I really was feeling in my mind. Perhaps talking it over with Pastor would put my mind at ease. Early in the afternoon, I met up with him at the church.

"Pastor, you got a minute?"

As he was reading through the mail that was about to be forwarded to the church secretary, he glanced up at me and said, "Sure, sure, come on in and have a seat."

The palms of my hands were sweating profusely as I rubbed them against the sides of my pants. A fairly stocky woman, I humbled myself and sat down across from him. I'd been able to tell him every and anything in the past, but this would be a bit different since I was about to tell him I craved the flesh of a woman.

"Pastor, I've been having these dreams here lately where I can't breathe. It's like someone is sitting on top of me and taking advantage of my body."

He laughed. "Oh, a wet dream? Women have those, too."

"No, it's not like that. It's like a woman's body is pressed against mine, and she's—" I leaned into his desk— "having sex with me."

Pastor laid down the mail and reclined in his chair until the top of it rested against the wall. "And what are you doing in these dreams?"

"Well, I'm not doing anything. I'm just lying there. She's unbuttoned my shirt, and . . . "

He sat tapping the tips of his fingers from both his hands together and asked, "How long have you been having these dreams?"

Clearing my throat, I answered, "Since the fire."

"I see," he said. "You should probably lay off my wife's hot toddies for a night or two. That liquor has probably got your head all screwed up."

"Pastor, it's not just the dreams I want to talk to you about."

"Well, what else is it?"

"You remember the other night I was asking about Miss Sonya?"

"Yeah?"

"Well, I was sort of liking her when she was here."

"Hell, who didn't?" he laughed. "That was a whole lot of woman right there."

Pastor was funny. "I'm ashamed to admit that, but it's the truth."

"Look, Trudy. My first mind is to tell you that you going to Hell for thinking the way you do, but from what I know and have heard about some people in our church, you'd have plenty of company when you got there."

We both laughed because he was certainly right. "I know, but—"

"Let me finish. Most pastors would do everything they could to try and change you, but I'm not in the changing business. That's the Lord's job. What I *am* supposed to do, though, is tell you that He loves you."

"So, what, you're saying this feeling is OK?"

"No, I'm not saying that. You know what the Bible says. What I'm telling you is that you're human and do whatever it is you need to do to be happy."

"Thank you, Pastor."

Reassured that my feelings were OK, I went back to the house and prepared for bed. I was exhausted and still had a bit of a cough. In the kitchen, I found Miss Ruby and asked her to make me one last hot toddy. She obliged, and I returned to my room.

I did all I could to fight sleep for a while but didn't have much luck. It seemed like the minute I blinked I was out like a light. I didn't even get a chance to drink the toddy. Maybe two hours into my sleep I was awakened by this thud on my chest. It was a warm body scented with . . . honeysuckle. Those same curves in the hips and thighs were there, and this time I felt my own body's temperature rise. She had aroused my passion, and instead of resisting in any form or fashion, I returned the heavy kisses and maneuvered myself from beneath her. I rolled her over and gave her what she'd been giving to me. Sliding one hand between the bed and her neck, I pressed my lips to hers and then to her breasts and saturated her chest with kisses. Lying there, she slithered like a serpent against the mattress with the back of her head buried in the pillow. I spread open her legs and laid one kiss right after the other along the rest of her body. My lips had never tasted anything so tantalizing. Gently, I positioned a finger inside of her, and I listened to her moaning softly against my chest. *My Lord.* I felt things within her body I never knew a woman had. My motions were quick, but her responses were quicker. When she climaxed, she was quiet, and I tumbled from her body and rolled to my side. That was no dream.

Feeling refreshed and like I'd slept for days, I arose to a brighter than usual day. My pajamas were intact, and I struggled to understand what had gone on. My bed was no more disheveled than normal. When I got to the kitchen, there Miss Ruby was mixing batter for fresh blueberry muffins. Just as I was about to open my mouth to speak, Pastor walked in and grabbed her from behind. He said, "Ruby, what's wrong with the back of your head? You ain't got a curl in sight."

The cost of an outing to the strip club on a Sunday: $25.

The cost of a box of Vivarin: $5.

The cost of realizing I worked Miss Ruby over so tough that I messed up her hair: priceless.

QUICK-DRAW McGRAW

Irolled off her and gasped. "Whew, that was good." My heart raced like the engine of a Ferrari, and my dew was greater than what any Bounty towel could handle. Erica's loving was like a glass of Hpnotiq—you had to take a double shot to make sure shit so good was real. Rolling over on my side, my body quivered like a newborn puppy. I covered myself as protection from the elements, keeping my cold sweat under control. I felt Erica's glare burning a hole in my back. I'd done it again . . . Quick-Draw McGraw.

Have you ever noticed that the orgasm you have while on top is more intense and more egotistically developed than the one you have while on the bottom? It's like, on top, you're doing the fucking and are working your best to make her scream and moan. You feel like a knight on a stallion out for your next conquest, and when you've conquered it? *Oh-my-God.* This surge of energy racing up your back rests in your loins. I wonder if guys feel like that when they shoot off. When on the bottom, though, you're getting fucked while trying like hell to help her reach climax. You're massaging her breasts—with your tongue or either your fingers. You combine those efforts with gentle but quick smacks on her booty cheeks. Her ass is situated between your legs at an angle so you can be clit-to-clit without becoming disjointed. But the minute I feel her against me like that . . . I cum. That's what it's like with Erica and me.

I'm not sure if anybody else has ever done this, but I cheated on my girl with this young lady I met at Pride. The minute I saw I her, I knew I was going to have her. She came in with a group of girls from Jersey, I think. We were staying at the Wyndham City Center Hotel right outside of George-town. It was the host hotel, and all the boys were staying there, too. It wasn't like it was in the A-T-L where all the guys were in one hotel and almost all the girls stayed in another. Everybody was under one roof, and sometimes, I couldn't deal with it. The fellahs? They didn't care who saw them making out with each other. But Erica wanted to stay there, so I made the best of it.

Her name was Shatera, and I knew she saw me when I was looking at her. Because she didn't feel too well, Erica had al-ready gone up to the room. I think she ate something on the way up from North Carolina that made her sick. While I was waiting on the bellhop to get our car registered with the valet, I turned my back to the bell stand and watched every move that girl made. She had on low-rider jeans and a baby-doll T-shirt. I was standing there with this T-shirt on that read, YOUR GIRLFRIEND WANTS ME. I saw Shatera chuckle and show me love by winking at me.

The instant I decided to make my move, the bellhop gave me my ticket. As I grabbed my bag from the chair next to the bell stand, I felt her watching every move I made. I ac-knowledged her by tipping my hat before getting on the el-evator.

Erica was almost blue in the face. She'd been throwing up and looked like she didn't have an ounce of energy left. I gave her a cold towel for her head and the garbage can in case she couldn't make it to the bathroom. "You want some ginger ale, baby?"

Lying on her side with her head hanging off the side of the bed over the trash can, she whined, "Yes, please. I feel so sick right now, boo. I'm sorry."

"Don't worry about it," I said as I walked over and kissed her forehead. "I'm going to run downstairs to the bar and get your drink for you."

"Thank you," she whispered.

Shatera and her friends were still in the lobby when I got downstairs. They were hanging around shooting the shit. I walked over to the bar and asked the bartender for a ginger ale. He gave me a glass that was a smidgen taller than a shot glass, filled it with ice, then poured the drink into it. "Can I have a bottle of it or something? I need a little more than this."

The muthafucker looked at me with a shitty-ass smile and said, "There's a convenience store around the corner."

"Thank you," I snapped. I refrained from showing my ass. Quickly turning around, she was standing in my space.

"Hi. My name is Shatera."

Shocked was an understatement. "Oh, hi, nice to meet you." I didn't know whether to shake her hand or lick her face. She was so fucking sexy. "I'm Egypt." We shook hands.

"I rushed over here to keep you from clicking on him."

"Oh, well, he owes you a word of thanks because I was about to step all up in that ass."

Shatera stood there with titties the size and shape of two tennis balls. "I can walk with you to the store if you want."

"You're not going to check into your room?"

"Oh, I already have. I'm in a room by myself because we made our reservations at different times, and then the person who was supposed to come with me canceled at the last minute."

"OK. You can join me if you want."

While we were walking, I noticed she had a tattoo in the small of her back. It was of a dragon, of all things, whose tail touched the top of the crack of her ass. I dropped back a couple of steps to watch her hips work the back of her jeans, and Shatera instantly became someone I had to have.

"Why are walking so far behind me? I can't talk to you if you're way back there."

"Aw, no reason. I walk a little slow sometimes."

"Well, catch up." She laughed. "Why do you need a big bottle of ginger ale anyway?"

"Eri—um, I need some to mix with my . . ." I couldn't lie. "It's for my girl. She's up in the room sick and wanted some ginger ale."

"Oh, no." She sighed. "I hope she's going to be alright."

"Girl, I don't know. She didn't look too good when I was up there. We think it's something she ate."

"I hope she feels better before the weekend is over. It would be a shame to miss Pride. Is this your first time coming?"

"No. We came a couple of years of ago, and it was really nice. What about you?"

"To be honest, this is my first time, but I didn't come to participate in the festivities. I came to get laid."

I choked on my spit. "What?" She'd said it so calmly.

"You heard me. I came here to get me some . . . to find someone who would fuck my brains out and make me come until Monday morning when it's time to check out."

"Dayum. I'm scared of you."

"What? Because I know what I want and am not afraid to ask for it?"

"Well, well, yeah," I replied like a little schoolgirl. "With so much stuff going around, aren't you afraid of catching something?"

"Duh, have you ever heard of dental dams?" she said as she whipped one out of her pocket.

"I have, but—"

"But what? Men can go off on wild weekends and fuck strangers but women can't?"

"No, I wasn't staying that. It's just that . . . Never mind."

Approaching the store, I saw she'd grown extremely interested in my comment, or lack thereof. She was studying me like a book. When I came out of the store, she asked, "Tell me what you mean, Egypt."

I put the two-liter drink under my arm and contemplated as to where this conversation was going to end up. "There's nothing wrong with wanting to get your groove on. Absolutely nothing at all."

"So, why do you seem uncomfortable?"

At this point, so many thoughts were running through my mind. First, I was thinking about what Erica would say about me walking to the store with a strange girl. Second, I was thinking why, out of all the women in the lobby, did Shatera pick me to run up behind. Third, I was wondering if I was going to get caught. And fourth, I was wondering if Shatera would let me hit it. After all, it wouldn't take but a minute. Right? "Don't pay any attention to me. I'm old fashioned." I was starting to tell lies. That's not a good sign. Lies lead to betrayal then to sex.

"Meaning?"

"I like to get to know a woman before we have sex, but that's just me." I should've been ashamed. I did it with Erica within two days of meeting her.

"Not many around like you anymore. Most women like to hit it and quit it."

We'd reached the entrance to the hotel, and I knew Erica needed that ginger ale. "Shatera, I have to get this to Erica. It was nice talking to you."

She looked defeated. The chipper, inquisitive tone she'd had earlier was gone. "OK, same here. Uh, if you want to continue our conversation, I'm in Room 509."

I tried to block that out, but it went in one ear and embedded itself in my memory.

Later in the evening, I was lying in the bed curled up around Erica who was in a comalike sleep. The ginger ale had seemed to settle her stomach, but while my arm was draped over her abdomen, I could still feel it rumbling. Before she'd drifted off, she said she was most likely going to stay in the room the entire weekend. I didn't mind that because, for me, it was all about her feeling better. Going out and having a good time was no fun if she wasn't going.

By 9:00 P.M., I was about to fucking lose my mind. Those hip-hugging, low-rider jeans wouldn't go away, and, if it wasn't that, I was seeing dragons dancing over my head. Erica was still asleep, and I was starving from hunger. I got up and put my clothes on, snatched up the room key, and headed for the door.

"Where you going?" she said softly.

Shit! I froze in my tracks and turned to her. "Aw, poo-poo, I didn't mean to wake you. I was going to run downstairs and get a bite to eat. They're having some kind of mixer with chicken wings, meatballs, and . . ."

"*Ew!* Never mind. I don't want to hear about food. Have fun," she murmured as she hugged her pillow and drifted back off to sleep.

Instead of pushing a button, I got on the elevator and stood there waiting for it to move. Any idiot would know you'd have to choose a floor in order for it to move. I knew that, but my problem was whether to push "L" or "5." Reaching for numbers, I was stunned when the elevator began moving and the doors opened up to the fourth floor. A group of fellahs and a couple of chickenheads got on. The men smelled like they'd just jumped out of the shower and into buckets of their favorite colognes, and the girls' looks were enough for me not to care what they smelled like. We reached the lobby, and the other riders got off. But I didn't. I pushed "5" and said a prayer.

Room 509 had so much music blasting from it that Shatera sounded like she was auditioning for *American Idol* or something. I knocked at the door and waited. What was I doing? I thought maybe she didn't hear me, but as I felt the urge to walk away, the music stopped. Cracking the door enough to see who it was, Shatera gave me a gigantic grin. She opened the door enough for me to see that she was dressed in a pair of short shorts and a push-up bra. "Hey, I was hoping it was you. Come on in."

The scent of Victoria's Secret fragrance, Halo, invaded my nostrils with fierce familiarity. I recognized it because Erica used to wear it when we first met. Shatera had to have taken a bath in it, used the lotion and the body spray, and then sprayed on the perfume. This was truly overkill for me.

"Dayum, you got it smelling all good in here," I said, thinking I was going to gag.

"Thank you. It's my favorite." She closed the door behind her and ducked into the bathroom before coming out into the room and taking a seat on the bed. "You want something to drink or eat?"

"No, I'm fine." After looking out the window into the streets below where it seemed that Black gay people from all around the world were congregating, I sat on the bed. Shatera came and sat beside me. I noticed she had an outfit lying across the other side of the bed. "So, what are you about to get into? Going out?"

"Yeah." She hesitated. "I'm about to hit a party or two with my girls."

"Oh, that sounds like fun."

"It's alright unless something better comes along," she said, running her hand along my thigh.

Moving an inch or two away from her, I sensed a sudden change in the energy around us. Her legs were glistening with oil, and there were speckles of glitter spread across her breasts. I couldn't help myself when I leaned over to kiss her shoulder. I closed my eyes and my heart started racing. I kissed her again . . . and again . . . and again until I'd caressed the length of her arm. Next thing I knew, I had her pinky finger, then her ring finger, her middle finger, her forefinger, and finally her thumb in my mouth. I pressed the palm of her hand to my face with one of my hands, and I took the other and reached around her waist to pull her to me. Extending my hand around to the small of her back, I noticed her body fall weak to my touches. She slumped over into me as I spread my hand over the dragon. Had I found her spot?

Shatera angled herself toward me, opening her legs, entangling me in them. I raised myself from the bed so I could press my body against hers in some kind of way. I crawled between her thighs, lifting her left leg to the heavens.

"Aren't you going to take off your clothes?" she asked.

Shit, I'd forgotten. I was feeling so good that I didn't need to take off my clothes. I grabbed hold of her breasts and gently held up her bra. They were firm. As I flicked my fingers around her nipples, her moans began to bounce against the walls. I wasn't about to stop and risk losing this moment. Soon, I realized, that after several minutes of this escapade, I hadn't cum. I couldn't seem to get enough of her. Shatera rested her leg around my waist as I worked my magic. Her face contorted as if I were inflicting pain. She gasped then sighed. "I'm cumming, Egypt. I'm cumming, Egypt. I'm cumming."

Breathing like a pit bull at this point, I couldn't, for the life of me, stop fucking her. And she, still dressed in her shorts, kept cumming one right after another. Nearly ten minutes had passed before I released myself. With Erica, it had only taken a minute or two. Thoroughly disgusted with myself and now drenched with the scent of another woman's perfume, I got up and immediately left the room. I'm sure Shatera understood.

Back on the second floor where our room was, I was running the lines for my lies in case Erica was awake. I slid the key into the slot and watched the light turn green. The lights weren't on when I opened the door. With the covers pulled over her head, Erica was still asleep. In the closet was a bag for clothes that needed to go to the cleaners. I removed it from the hanger and carried it into the bathroom with me. Quickly, I stripped and stuffed the clothes into the bag. I didn't need the T-shirt any longer, and the jeans were replaceable. My panties, damp with my passionate lubricant, were tossed in the sack, too. I hopped in the shower and lathered my body with every bar of soap I could find. Even as the water washed my impurities down the drain, I didn't feel as if I'd really cheated. We were in our clothes, and nobody exchanged bodily fluids—not even through a kiss. My mission was to get that perfume off my body because Erica hadn't worn it in years.

The one thing I can't seem to understand is why it took me so long to cum with Shatera when, in the blink of an eye, I'd bust a nut in Erica. I managed to slip out of the room and disposed of my clothes in the nearest receptacle. Upon returning to the room, I climbed back into the bed and once again curled up around my baby. Images of the dragon were no longer in my head, and I didn't give a damn about lowrider jeans.

Question: Is it really cheating when you keep your clothes on?

WET

Ass and titties in a multitude of showers in the middle of the afternoon while you're sipping on some Alizé or gulping a Miller Lite or munching on a platter of hot wings from the snack bar. Women with booties in every flavor of an assorted bag of Jolly Ranchers come through here. We got apple bottoms, peach-shaped, got 'em like cherries and plums. Imagine watching a girl take a shower while you lay back in your seat and fantasize about that water beating her skin, and you can't help but notice the shit she can do with her hands. . . . grinding that pole. Whoever heard of such nonsense? No damn body. And that's why I started Soft 'n' Wet Afternoons.

I'm Mz. Vicki, the founder of Soft 'n' Wet afternoons—the biggest and best once-a-month all-girl party on the East Coast. Haters refer to me as Big Pimpin'; I don't care for that stigma. My relationship with my girls is far from that. Big Daddy? Nope. It's not like that either. Campaign Save-a-Ho? Sometimes.

There are so many people who hate what I do, and I say they feel that way because they don't understand it. Other people believe I sleep with my girls to try them out. This ain't no damn kat house. Let me explain. I consider women dancing for women to be entertainment. Our female patrons see these girls as fantasies beyond their wildest imaginations. Men, though, see them as pieces of meat. They want to know if they'll give head, if they can take them home, and if they can fuck them. That dog don't hunt here. I charge their asses double just to come in and sit at a table wayyyyy in the back, and security is on standby to escort their asses right out if they get to acting stupid. Before I am anything to these women, I'm simply another woman who understands the shit that comes along with being a woman. I understand what it's like to have to feed your kids. I understand what it's like to want something so bad, but no one gives a fuck about you getting it but you. I understand what it's like to be sick and not have a dime to go to the doctor or to pay for the medicine, and I understand what it means when the whole world wants to call you a ho but all you're doing is doing what you gotta do to get done what you need to get done.

I love the ladies, and the ladies love me because I take care of them—no matter what.

Brown Shuga

Terika told me about how, when she was a little girl, she used to have to sleep over her aunt's house because her mother worked crazy hours. When it was time for her bath, her aunt insisted on bathing her and sometimes she just got on in the tub with her. Terika said she didn't feel like anything was wrong with that, and she was even OK with sleeping with her. But then, one night, her aunt grabbed her and pulled her on top of her and rubbed her innocence against her body. It happened only twice; yet, Terika said she distinctly remembered feeling a sensation that didn't feel terribly bad. Up until the moment she told me, no one knew about that ugly time.

The day she showed up at The Edge where we were going to do our first party Terika was drunk. She was two hours early, and the smell of liquor was heavy on her.

"You been drinking, Terika?" I asked.

"No, Vicki, I haven't," she said, stumbling to take a seat at the bar.

She was a friend of a friend, and I'd opened my big mouth and told her she could dance for me at Wet. Terika was going through some things. That terrible time with her aunt had come back to haunt her, and she was trying to fight the urge to kiss a woman.

"Terika, I'm not about to let you go out there drunk. We're not going to start that."

"I had a couple of wine coolers before I left the house. That's all."

I walked up on her and sniffed her. "You've had more than that. I'm not letting you on stage until you sober up."

Then she had the nerve to try and get an attitude. "Look, I'm here doing you a favor. I don't have to dance."

Taking a seat on the stool next to her, I posed this question to her. "Do you realize how many women would kill to have this job? I got fifty messages on my machine from girls with kids to girls needing money for college tuition. One girl owes her dealer some money and is willing to come in here and suck dicks or eat pussy if she can."

"And your point?"

We were an hour from opening. "I don't need this shit. I can have somebody in here in your place before the first customer sets foot in here. That's my point."

Deep in turmoil, I watched the pain on her face that she'd tried to mask with the liquor. Beneath her issues, Terika was really a sweet, brown-skinned young lady of only twenty-one years. I had a stage name for her.

"Did you come up with a name yet?" I asked.

"No, I haven't given much thought to it."

"Well, I got one for you. Brown Shuga."

Terika sat there for a minute as if she wasn't sure if that would suit her. "How you get that?"

I arose from my stool and embraced her shoulders from behind. I leaned into her left side, pointing at the mirror surrounding the stage. "You are a beautiful, brown woman with a sweetness you need to share with all these D.C. lesbians that's about to come in here. I want you to know you don't have to worry about anybody bothering you as long as you're with me. I got you."

Tears streamed down her cheeks, and she picked up a napkin from the bar and wiped her face. "OK, Vicki. Where's the dressing room?"

I gave her a hug and a kiss on the forehead and led the way.

By 5:00 P.M., Wet was jumping. Outside, there was a line three blocks long, so we couldn't let anyone in until people started coming out.

Brown Shuga, dressed in nothing but a silver G-string, stood tall in her matching stilettos as she popped her ass to the music. I'd made her wait for two hours and let her watch the other girls make her money. I wanted Terika sober when she finally got a chance to display her talents. She, with that cherry-shaped ass, wrapped her pussy around that pole like caramel on an apple. Women were throwing dollar bills at her like Skittles, and we couldn't pick up the money fast enough. Once she was done, she ran to the dressing room. I went after her to offer my congratulations, but instead of seeing her smiles of joy and accomplishment, I saw tears.

"What's wrong, baby?"

Brown Shuga was distraught. "She's out there."

"Who's out there?"

"My aunt."

"What?"

"She's out there sitting at the bar. I can't go back."

"Tell me where she's sitting, and I'll take care of it."

"Over by the showers." And she burst into tears.

I went back out into the club and immediately recognized her aunt because they had the same eyes and facial features. "Excuse me," I said.

"Yes?" the older woman responded. The only way I knew she was a woman was by her chest, which was bigger and more inflated than mine.

"One of my dancers isn't comfortable with you being here."

Staring into space as she swished her drink around in her mouth, she replied, "Oh really? And who might that be?"

"Don't go there. You know who I'm talking about. I'm going to have to ask you to leave."

"Bitch, you better step off. I ain't going nowhere. Terika needs to get a grip."

I wasn't in the mood for starting shit. I knew there was a calmer way to handle the situation. "I tell you what," I whispered into her ear. "Terika and I had a talk a while back about you and your problem with keeping your hands to yourself. She's done you a favor over the years by not saying shit about what happened between the two of you."

"Girl, I was young and stupid when that happened. Ain't nobody going to even believe her."

"Oh, is that an admission of guilt?"

The woman chilled for a minute. "Look, I don't want any trouble. I—"

"Just leave, and don't ever come back. If you do that for me, we're done."

She got up and left, and as far as I know, she's never been back.

Chantico

Sheba was standing in the checkout line at Giant when I first laid eyes on her. In her basket, she had three blocks of cheddar cheese, a dozen eggs, a box of Cheerios, three gallons of milk, a jar of peanut butter, two bottles of Juicy Juice, three cases of formula, and a toddler baby boy. She looked like she was about to pop with her belly poking out from beneath her sweatshirt. Dexter, the little boy, kept throwing his bottle out of the basket, and she, with all the energy she could muster, kept bending over to pick it up. Yes, I looked at her ass every time she bent over, and I quickly discovered peaches come in a variety of shapes and sizes.

The next time he tossed the bottle out of the basket I stooped down and picked it up for her. "Thank you so much," she smiled. "I need to beat his ass, but I ain't trying to have this baby in jail."

"Honey, he's just being a baby," I said, handing the bottle back to the toddler. "When are you due?"

"Yesterday," she said. "They're going to introduce labor next week if she don't come."

"Induce, you mean?"

"Yeah, whatever. Girl, I'm so tired."

"I bet you are. You seem to have your hands full." Her breasts, although full of milk and some extra weight, had potential. "Here, let me help you." After I paid for my milk and butter, I took her groceries and carried them out of the store for her.

"Where's your car?" I asked.

"Oh, I don't drive. I took the bus over here."

I was shocked. She was in no condition to be riding the bus and fooling with a stroller, a baby, and four bags of groceries. "Uh, if you don't mind, I'd like to take you home to help you out. This is a bit much for you to be trying to handle all by yourself."

"No, thank you. I can manage. We don't live that far from here."

"I understand that, but my conscience won't let me leave you like this. Please, I promise I'm not a psycho or anything. I only want to help."

Dexter had fallen asleep in the basket, and with the bulky stroller and the groceries, Sheba knew she needed my help. "OK, if you really don't mind."

"Great."

Getting in the car was a chore because I didn't have a car seat for the baby, and she barely had enough room to buckle herself in the seat belt let alone stick Dexter in there with her. "My place is only ten minutes from here. Right up on Bladensburg Road."

"OK, no problem." While we were riding, I knew it was uncomfortable for her. She finally ended up taking the seat belt off. I didn't want to pry, but a nice-looking lady like her couldn't have been alone. "You don't have anyone around to help you, a boyfriend, husband, or something?"

"My girlfriend left me after I got pregnant. She paid all the bills, bought the groceries, paid the rent, and took care of Dexter because he's hers. I was fooling around with this guy one day in the park, and it just happened. No rubber, nothing. She kept up with my periods better than I did and noticed when I'd missed one. Sure enough, I was pregnant. When I told her, she said she was leaving. She left, took all the money, and left all the bills and her son. At the end of the month when I went to pay the rent with some money I'd saved, the lady at the rental office asked me if I was there to pay all three months we were behind or if I was paying just one month. I gave her every penny I had and explained the situation to her.

"Not at all supportive of the fact that I'd had a girlfriend, she did sympathize with me being pregnant and that my girl-friend had left the baby behind. She put me on this program where I pay only five dollars a month. Then I went to the food stamp office and got on welfare. They set me up with WIC, food stamps, and a check that barely covers the neces-sities."

"They didn't say anything about Dexter not being your child?"

"They see what they want to see and ask what they want to ask. To them, he's a foster child."

"I see. So you don't have a job?"

"No. I can't work. I don't have nobody to keep Dexter. Stop right here at the corner. My apartment is over there." She pointed to the back of the development where there weren't any parking spaces.

I was impressed as hell because this girl was making it de-spite her circumstances. I knew women who had cars, jobs, and no kids, but were trifling as all get out. "Um, you take care of you and the baby. I'll get the groceries."

"OK, thank you."

I went to the back of the car and retrieved her bags. As I approached her side of the vehicle, I realized she was mov-ing a bit slower than before. "Anything wrong?"

"Well, I think my water just broke."

This wasn't what I'd planned for the day. I was on my way home to bake a cake and cook some turnip greens, ribs, potatoes, and peach cobbler.

"What?"

"Ooooh, I'm so sorry about your seats," she said as she held tightly to Dexter.

"Tell you what. Give me your key, point me to where your place is, and I'll run in and put the groceries away. Is there a car seat in there for Dexter?"

"Yes. It's in the closet in my bedroom."

I hurriedly trotted in the direction of her apartment, found it, and, when I opened the door, I stepped into the cleanest house I'd ever seen. I ran to the kitchen and put all the refrigerated items away. Then I jetted for the bedroom to get the car seat. On my way out the door, I noticed a framed piece of paper on the wall. Sheba had graduated from the University of Maryland.

Sitting in the hospital room, I held Dexter in my arms as Sheba slept. The nurse had brought the baby in but didn't leave her since her mother was asleep. She'd been named Nikita Renee Young. I didn't get to see much of her when they rolled the bassinet in, but I could tell she had a head full of hair.

"Are you the grandmother?" the nurse asked.

Now what was I supposed to say? "No, I'm a friend of the family."

"Oh, OK. Let me know if you need anything and tell her to buzz us when she wakes up, and we'll bring the baby down to her."

"I sure will."

Sheba was in a semi-private room, which was all Medicaid's doing. While I was in her apartment, I realized she didn't have much, but she was working the hell out what she had. I put Dexter down and walked over to the bed to see if I could wake her.

"Hey," I whispered.

At first she didn't move. After I called her a second time, Sheba started, slowly, trying to stretch. "Hi."

"How you doing?"

A bit fuzzy, she answered back, "I'm OK. A little sore. Where's the baby?"

Gently rubbing her thigh, I told her, "They brought her in while you were sleep and said to buzz the desk, and they'll bring her back. Is there anyone you want me to call for you?"

She pushed the nurse's button. "No, it's just me and Dexter. My family doesn't live here, and we don't talk much anyway."

"Oh, I'm sorry to hear that. Do—"

"Look, Ms. . . . I don't even know your name."

"It's Vicki. My friends call me Mz. Vicki."

"Mz. Vicki, thank you so much for your help today. I'm sorry you got all caught up in my drama."

"No need to apologize for life. Besides, I believe everything happens for a reason."

"True. This is so true." There was a knock at the door, and the nurse peeped her head around the corner.

"Miss Young? I have a visitor for you." She smiled.

Nikita was the spitting image of her mother as I watched Sheba hold her firstborn. "Sheba, I'm going to—"

"How'd you know my name?"

"Well, aside from hearing you talk with the nurses, I saw it on your degree at your apartment as I was walking out."

"Oh, that."

"Oh, that? You have a degree from the University of Maryland. Why aren't you using it?"

"Long story."

"I understand. I'm going to leave you alone so you can spend some time with the baby." I watched her with Dexter in one arm and Nikita in the other. "Sheba, do you mind if I take Dexter with me? You don't have any way to take care of him up here."

She couldn't argue with me and blew sighs of frustration. "He don't have no clothes, or . . ."

"Chile, I have money. Don't worry about him. Get yourself some rest. He'll be fine. By the way, I gave the nurses my number for when you're ready to go home. You're going to need a ride."

The two days Dexter was with me, I felt rejuvenated. His energy helped me to work through my own complacency. Sheba called me and tried her best to get me to let her take a cab from the hospital, but I wasn't having it. Although Dexter and I had been having a fabulous time, I knew he missed Sheba. I rolled him in his stroller up the walk of the hospital, and when he saw Sheba sitting in the wheelchair waiting by the entrance, he kicked his little legs in delight. I let the two of them sit and entertain each other while I went back to get the car.

On the way back to her apartment, I said, "I took it upon myself to get a few things for you and the kids while you were in the hospital. I've already put them in the house for you, if you don't mind."

"Mz. Vicki, you shouldn't have. I'm going to have to pay you back."

"No, you don't. I just want you to be able to take care of those babies. Speaking of which, I wanted to ask you a question."

"What's that?"

"Would you be interested in coming to work for me once you're back on your feet? Trust me, it's not a conventional type of job, but I guarantee you will be able to tell the food stamp office to kiss your ass after only a month of work."

"Really?"

"For real."

"What kind of work do you do? You never told me."

"I'm a promoter. On the last Saturday of the month, I give these all-girl—"

"Wait a minute. You talking about Soft 'n' Wet Afternoons?"

"Yes. I run that."

"Get the fuck outta here. My girl and I used to go there. I loved it, but she didn't care for it."

"I would like for you to come dance for me at Wet."

Sheba sat in deep thought for a moment, and then said, "I can't dance, Vicki."

All that ass she had? She had to be kidding. "You're playing, right?"

"No. I'm what one would call rhythmically challenged."

"I wouldn't worry about that. You got a bangin'-ass body, and I got some girls that'll teach you what to do. Besides, it's just like fucking without the sheets and the bed."

She looked in the backseat at the kids. "I don't know, Vicki. I have two kids now, and—"

"Exactly. You have two kids."

"I don't have a sitter."

"Yes, you do. My little cousins ain't doing shit on Saturday afternoon. They're fifteen and sixteen and wouldn't mind making some extra coins. Don't worry about paying them. I got that."

"Vicki, I don't know what to say. I've got a college degree, and—"

"Look, this isn't a permanent thing. I don't expect that of you. This opportunity will help you to make some crazy money on the weekends while you look for a nine-to-five during the week. What do you say?"

Sheba was looking at me like I was her fairy godmother or something. "Can I think about it for a couple of days?"

"Sure, you can. I'm going to stop at Starbucks and get something to drink. Want something?"

"No, I'm fine. Thank you."

I don't know why I had this craving for hot chocolate. It

was in the middle of the afternoon, and the weather was a bit warm for March.

"May I help you?" the person at the counter asked.

"Yeah, give me a cup of hot chocolate, please."

"OK, coming right up."

Most times when I go to Starbucks, I get a decaf white chocolate mocha. Today, though, I wanted a simple cup of hot chocolate.

"Here you go."

I took a sip and was like, "Damn, what is this? I asked for hot chocolate."

Puzzled, the server said, "That's what I gave you."

"This is not hot chocolate. It tastes like freaking melted chocolate."

"Ma'am, that's what it is actually. What you might've wanted is hot cocoa. What I gave you is called Chantico."

"Chan . . . what?"

"*Chan-tee-co.* Do you want me to exchange it?"

"Hell no. This is divine." Three of these a week, and I was destined to get diabetes. "Thank you. I've never experienced anything like this."

When I left the coffee shop, I couldn't wait to let Sheba taste my find. I approached the car and saw Sheba nursing the baby. I'd never paid much attention to her other features, especially since I focused so much on her booty and titties. She was really a beautiful girl, and as I studied her as Nikita drank from her voluptuous fountain, I knew what her stage name would be.

Cranking the car, I swallowed this lump in my throat so I could get my thoughts out. "Sheba?"

"Yeah?"

"You wouldn't be completely naked. You know that, right?"

Putting her breast back inside its cup, she said, "That's not

what I'm worried about. It's all those people looking at me.
I'm not used to that."

"You'll get used to it. They're respectful of your body, and
they'll look at you like a dream they wish would come true."

"It's a lot of money?"

"A lot. If you shake that ass good enough, you can easily
make a grand or two all in the same day."

"What am I going to call myself? Sheba isn't what I call a
stage name."

"Actually, I have a name for you."

"What is it?"

"Before I tell you, I want you to taste something. Here."
She took a sip of the hot liquid.

"Damn. What's that?"

"It's Chantico."

"What?"

"Chantico, and that's what I think your name should be.
You're chocolate, and when you're all warm inside, you'd
make an enticing drink."

"Wow, that's creative. I like it."

Sylk

One afternoon after a hellacious show, I caught a glimpse
of Sylk massaging her breasts. That wasn't really unusual in
the dressing room, but for Sylk, it was. She wasn't big on
masturbating or touching herself. The women watching her
apple-bottom-shaped behind loved her because she could
clap her butt cheeks like a spasm out of control. Of all the
girls in our repertoire, I loved Sylk. As I don't make it a point
to become intimate with my girls, Sylk and I had shared a
moment or two.

The business side of Wet kept me from having physical

relationships with the girls because I was providing them a space for entertaining and not a space as an open meat market. If I were denying the public of an opportunity to purchase sex that should never be for sale, then I'd be a hypocrite, and that's not what I'm about. The personal side of Wet kept me from having a lover because every woman I met was always so jealous of the dancers. I fed them, I clothed them, and I gave them money when they needed it. If I knew of a party in a city where we could get there by car within a few hours, I offered them chances to make some extra cash by dancing for unsuspecting crowds. The ones who wore the crown of Miss Soft 'n' Wet had it extra good since they got all the glitz and glamour associated with being a queen, half-naked or not. I made a way for them when there seemed to be no way at all.

Sylk had skin so smooth it almost disappeared against your fingertips. The crowd loved her because she could massage the pole with her body without ever touching it. Sounds far-fetched, but it's the truth. One night after we'd closed for the night I saw her standing outside the club still waiting for her ride.

"Sylk, what's up, baby girl? Why haven't you left yet?"

Standing on the curb wearing a lightweight cloak, she giggled lightly. "He's running a little late."

I knew she was living with this man called Stony, and it was no secret that he loved being in bed with two women. Sylk was his main squeeze, but when trying to attract other women into their threesome, he disrespected her often by making her feel worthless. He kept her clothed, but he mostly did that to make idle promises of such luxuries to those other women. Many of the girls at the club stayed away from Sylk because they knew she was bi.

"Come on and get in. I'll take you home."

We arrived at her house to find all of the lights off and no sign of Stony.

"Shoot, he has the keys with him."

What kind of shit is that? "Well, you can come home with me and call him when you think he's home."

"OK."

Before stopping at the house, I made a quick run to the liquor store to pick up a bottle of Bacardi for some daiquiris. Unlike the other girls, Sylk didn't smoke or drink. While I ran in, she sat in the car and waited for me to return. I got back in and found her crying. "What's wrong, baby?"

Wiping the tears from her eyes, she inquired, "Do you ever get lonely, Mz. Vicki?"

I couldn't lie. "All the time."

"How's that, and you have all this going on?"

"I guess I get so caught up in trying to give love that I completely forget I need love, too."

"God will bless you one day for it," she said, reaching for my hand.

"Honey, he blesses me every day."

In my home, no one was ever a guest. I asked Sylk for her cloak, and when she gave it to me, I saw she hadn't undressed from Wet. Her body was like something I couldn't describe. The grapefruit-sized breasts atop her chest made me take a shot of that Bacardi without the strawberries. I walked over to her and asked her why she was still crying. She told me she was worried about me and the fact that I never got any love. "Sylk, I'm fine."

"No, you're not," she said, kissing me around my mouth as if she were looking for the proper angle in which to stick her tongue inside.

I accepted her kisses but kept my hands from touching

her. I stuck them in my pocket to prevent temptation. Finally her kisses landed in my mouth, and I didn't reject them. Before I got into any trouble, I stopped it. "I think you need to call Stony, Sylk."

She looked at me with puppy-dog eyes and agreed, "Yes, I probably should." She disappeared to the kitchen and called him. He told her he was on his way.

I went into my room and pulled some sweats from my drawer. "Here, put these on." I couldn't believe I'd turned down someone who was willing to love me for a change. But I was flattered that it had even crossed her mind.

Sylk kissed my hand, extended in front of her. "I love you, Mz. Vicki."

"I love you, too."

That afternoon I did something I had never done in the history of Wet. I sent all of the girls, with the exception of one, out into the club. Once the room was empty, I closed and locked the door. The amazing thing about Sylk was that you could see right through her emotions. I walked over to her and sat down on the dressing table, face to face. "What's going on?"

Her fear made her speak up quickly. "The other day when I was in the shower I felt these knots on my left breast, and just now I found one on the other one."

"On both of them?"

"Yes," she said, gasping. "I don't know where they came from."

"You don't have to say another word. First thing Monday morning I'm taking you to a friend of mine who's a gynecologist." I knew she didn't have any health insurance, so I was going to do all I could to help her out.

I called Juanita at home that Sunday and requested, as a favor, an appointment before business hours on Monday.

When I picked Sylk up, she was trembling like a leaf. Wearing the same sweats I'd given her Saturday night at my house, she got in the car and asked if I had a cigarette. That was nothing but nerves because she knew I didn't smoke.

"It'll be OK, sweetie," I assured her.

Since Juanita's office was in Georgetown, she told us to get there by 6:30 to avoid traffic. When we arrived, she had already created a chart for Sylk and told her to undress from the waist up. "I'm going to do a breast exam before we do the mammogram."

"You can do the mammogram here?"

Juanita beamed. "This is a state-of-the-art office. We can do everything right here onsite. There's a radiology department in the back."

"Cool."

"Vicki, you coming?" Sylk asked.

I lagged behind on purpose. I wasn't good at handling bad news.

"Right behind you."

The exam room was typical. Sylk laid across the table, and Juanita put a sheet across her chest. "OK, Sylk, raise your arms above your head for me. This won't take long at all."

Sylk rested each arm on both sides of her head on a pillow. Juanita gently massaged her left breast as Sylk looked out the adjacent window. I watched Juanita's every move until I saw her stop. Then she glanced over at me.

"Sylk, how long has this lump been here?"

"Awhile."

"I see."

Juanita switched sides and examined the other breast. Again, she stopped and glanced over at me. "And the same with this one?"

"I found that one on Saturday."

"These are pretty large masses. I'm going to go ahead and do the mammogram myself." Helping her up from the table, she gave Sylk a new sheet. "Wrap this around you and follow me."

The three of us walked down the long hallway in silence until we came to a room filled with machines. Sylk asked, "Will we know something right away?"

"I hope so," Juanita answered. "How have you been feeling lately?"

"Well, I've been kinda out of it. I haven't been eating much."

"OK," she said. "I need you to follow my instructions. Don't worry. This will be over in a jiffy. Once we're done, you can go back to the examination room and wait for me."

After the test, Sylk and I sat waiting for almost forty-five minutes before Juanita arrived with the test results. She asked Sylk if she wanted me to stay with her. "Yes, of course," she said. Juanita's normally pleasant demeanor had become serious. "What's wrong?" Sylk asked.

"Sylk, from what I can tell there's chance you might have breast cancer. Those masses are huge and need to be removed. I hope you have time to stay here awhile. I'm ordering blood work and a couple more X rays. I'll need you back here in the morning for your MRI. Everything will be done here in the building, so you won't need to worry about going from place to place. I'm also going to do a biopsy."

Sylk had a blank look on her face. "So you mean I'm sick?"

"Yes, dear, but I won't know how sick until I see the results of the blood work and the MRI. I don't mean to scare you, but one thing Vicki knows about me is that I'm direct."

Throughout the rest of the day, I provided whatever support I could by making Sylk laugh to keep her mind off things. Juanita came in to visit with us before the last X ray was done and said she'd be present at the MRI.

* * *

For every day of Sylk's chemo, I was there. I moved her in
with me because Stony wasn't about shit and wasn't giving
her the attention she needed. The vomiting and the hair loss
gave her the most grief because most times she had no control over it. I got her a wig, but she refused to wear it. I was
able, however, to talk her into cutting her hair low enough
so she wouldn't have to worry about maintenance. At Wet we
took up donations for six months for breast cancer aware-
ness in her honor. Ten percent of the money went to the
Mautner Project, and the rest went to Sylk. We collected over
a hundred thousand dollars with the girls chipping in an
extra five thousand they took from their own pockets. As
part of their shower performances, the girls started doing
erotic self-exams to educate and to entertain.

Oh, as for Sylk, we had a couple of scares, but she pulled
through and is now cancer-free. It took her a minute to get
her groove back, but you can still catch her working that
pole on Saturday afternoons at The Wet.

THE CIGARETTE

Imagination. Webster defines it as "the act or power of forming a mental image of something not present to the senses or wholly perceived in reality" or simply put, "a creation of the mind."

If I had a dick for a day, I'd fuck the brains out of my stuffed-shirt coworker who comes in every day with this I'm-better-than-you-I-hate-my-job-my-husband-won't-give-me-head attitude. Her tailored pantsuits are the envy of the office. She wears tight skirts that ride up her thigh when she bends over or sits down. On summer days, she's bare-legged in the sexiest sandals that Nordstrom sells. Her blouses hug every dip in her upper body as each curve bulges from the seams. Her breasts, well, all I have to say is that she should invest in those little things that make your nipples disappear, but when I hear her raspy voice against the walls of our office, that *dick* of mine stands at full attention.

When I walk past her office, I catch a glimpse of her and slap that image across my memory. I take it with me to the ladies' room where I can find a stall to just . . . think. Behind those closed doors, I stand over the toilet gripping it, stroking it. Then, there are footsteps. I hold my breath with *it* lying there in my hand. The water starts running, and peeping through the crack in the bathroom door, I see her. I open the door with it still rock hard in the palm of my hand. She runs for the door and locks it. With her hand stretched against my pole, she caresses it. "What do you want me to do for you, baby?" I ask. She never utters a word.

One of her legs wrapped around my waist and the other in the air, I enter her. In those Nordstrom sandals, her toes curl up toward the sky, and when I shoot off, we pant like wild dogs in heat.

If I had a dick for a day, how could I get through it without leaving my legacy? I'd have to make me a baby. I'd dig through all of my junk drawers and glove compartment to find the number of the one woman who made my heart stop. Meeting her at the beach, just before sunset, I'd buy her an ice cream cone and watch her taste every swirl. We'd sit on the shore with our feet buried in the sand, arm in arm. After the sun set and the moon casted its reflection over the ocean, I'd turn to her and passionately plant my seed.

If I had a dick for a day, I'd go to the men's department and buy the sexist draws I could find. Then I'd go home, saturate my body in Vaseline and head straight for the strip club . . . and ask for a job. I've always wondered what it was like to be a Chippendale. I'd watch the ladies throw their panties at me, climbing on the stage to get a kiss. There'd be that one girl I couldn't take my eyes off.

Grooving my way through the crowd, I'd make my way to her and twist my hips in front of her. Eye to eye, I'd pull her from her seat and press her body against mine so she could feel my wood. Breathing heavily, she'd rest her head upon my chest as her heat warmed my passion. I'd fall faint as she stuck her hand inside . . . with everybody watching.

If I had a dick for a day, I'd make a way to fuck every woman I've ever thought to have sex appeal, pizzazz, and the cum theory. I'd prove my theory that you don't have to be a man with a dick to work over a woman's pussy. If you blow or lick on her right, she'll cum no matter what you got hanging below.

Now, imagine that.

About the Author

When you do what your passion is—your passion being what God gave you the zest and talent to do—the rest falls into place.

Divine destiny is what motivates mother, daughter, author Laurinda D. Brown to do what she does—write novels that portray real people in real life situations. "Growing up in Memphis, TN, and graduating from Howard University exposed me to the diverse sides of human nature and gave me the oportunity to observe people and their situations. I wrote to work through my own emotions, to find explanations for other people's circumstances, and to try to humanize thier idiosyncrasies. Writing expresses my take on the world."

Laurinda's books include Fire & Brimstone, the 2005 Lamda Literary Award finalist for Best Debut Lesbian Fiction, and Undercover.

The author currently resides with her two daughters in Hampton Roads, Virginia, where she continues to write about life—not lifestyles. She firmly believes that one day we will love one another not for what we are, but for who we are.

My Woman His Wife

By Anna J.

I magine that, imagine that, imagine that, imagine . . .
At 5'2", 136 pounds, dark chocolate skin, and almond eyes, sexy Monica is standing over me topless, in a red thong, and giving me one hell of a show. My girl is popping it like she's trying to get rent money and only has two days left to scrape it up. You would think there's a pole in the center of the bed the way she's rotating and grinding her body to the beat of the music.

My eyes are fixed on hers as she does a sensual butterfly all the way down until the lips of her tunnel kiss my stomach, leaving a wet spot where they landed. She bends over and a tattoo spelling her name in neat cursive peeks out over the band of her thong. She takes her right nipple into her mouth and caresses the other as she continues to move to the beat of the music. Her body seems to shimmer as light from outside lands on her skin.

Stepping off the bed, she bends over to remove her thong, afterwards hooking it onto my foot. A dildo magically appears as she crawls toward me. My legs spread invitingly when her lips make contact with the space behind my right knee. I hear R. Kelly hyping it up with the guitar, making the love of my life sweat just a little.

Well, the second love of my life. While I'm laying here, legs spread eagle and playing with my clit, I can't even get into it because I know I should be at home with my husband and two kids. I could just get up and go, but I don't feel like the drama and tears I have to see every time I'm ready to leave. I know in my heart that I have no damn business being here in the first place, but I was thinking with my pussy in anticipation of all the wonderful orgasms I would have. Shit at home died down a long time ago, but it wasn't until I found myself lying here looking up at another woman's breasts did the guilt set in.

It wasn't supposed to be like this. I knew I should be at home making love to my husband, but he wasn't producing multiple orgasms like Monica. She does things with her tongue no one has written about yet. She has ways of making me explode that my husband has no idea on how to find that spot, and I can forget about him lasting all night. The five minutes he gives me I can do myself. I need satisfaction that my own hands don't produce, and Monica gives me what I need without any questions.

I don't want to have to tell my partner what I want. After all these years, he should already know what makes me cum. If you're going to hit it from the back, put a finger in my asshole or leave a handprint on my ass cheek. Take it with one of my legs on your shoulder while you use your thumb to play with my clit. While I'm riding, take both of my nipples into your mouth at the same time. Do something besides pound me all hard for five minutes then roll over and fall asleep.

Then, if that wasn't enough, this fool wanted to invite company into our bed. And that's why I'm in this mess now.

It all started about two months before the twins' fourth

birthday. It had already been eight months since my husband and I had so much as fondled each other, let alone had any actual sexual contact. He had been on my last nerve about having a threesome with some hoochie he'd met, and I was about tired of hearing it. All I got was five minutes. What was he gonna do? Break it down to two and a half minutes between the both of us? He must have been suffering from too much radiation from sitting up in that news station all day or something. And what the hell was this girl and I supposed to do? She could munch all the carpet she wanted to, but I DON'T GET DOWN LIKE THAT!!!

Back in the day, my husband and I made love constantly. It was nothing to be bent over the kitchen counter getting served from behind. He would be stroking me from the back with one finger playing with my clit and the other in my asshole, while kissing my neck and talking dirty to me all at the same time. I would ride him in the dining room chair until my legs hurt, and he would then pick me up and lay me on the table, devouring me from feet to head, and not necessarily in that order. He liked for me to hold my lips open so my clit stood right out as he simultaneously sucked on it and fingered me with three fingers the way I liked it.

All of that stopped for one reason or another, and I didn't feel like him or this girl he was trying to sell me on. It got to the point where this fool started leaving notes around the house, practically begging me to jump on board. One night he tried to show me a picture of the girl, and I just snapped. What part of "no" didn't he understand, the "n" or the "o"?

"Babe, just hear me out," he said, pleading on his knees at my side of the bed. "You won't even listen to what I have to say."

I remembered the days when he would be on his knees on my side of the bed, only my legs would be thrown over his shoulders as his lips and tongue would have me squirming and begging for mercy. But right then, the sight of him was contributing to my already pounding headache.

"James, I done told you fifty thousand damn times that I'm not doing it, so why do you keep asking me?"

He didn't even realize that I was ready to bust him in the head with the alarm clock. Why wouldn't he just go to sleep?

"Because you're not keeping an open mind."

"Would you want me to bring another dick into the bedroom?" I asked.

He looked at me like I was crazy and got up to go lay on his side of the bed.

That shut his ass right up, if only for a second. I was so damn tired of hearing about this Monica chick, I was ready to just go ahead and get it over with. This entire scenario was making me sick to my stomach. What his dumb ass didn't realize is I might have went along with it just to please him, but I'd be damned if I would be pressured into doing anything I wasn't down for.

"So, is doing it in the bedroom the problem?" he asked in a desperate voice.

"What? Didn't I just tell you I didn't want to talk about it?"

"I'm just saying that if your concern is bringing her into our home I could easily get us a room over at the Hyatt or the Marriott."

"James, how do you even know this girl? What kind of shit are y'all into over at T.U.N.N.?"

I'm guessing this fool couldn't see the big ass pile of salt on my shoulders. If we were in a cartoon, steam would've been coming out of my ears at that point.

"My buddy Damon hooked it up for me. It's his wife's sister or something like that. They do it all the time."

That only made me wonder what kind of freaky shit her family was into. I don't know too many people just putting their own flesh and blood out there like that.

"What do you know about her, James? This chick could be HIV positive for all we know. There is no cure for that!"

"We would all be using protection," he said as if he was offended. Shit, I'm offended he won't let it go.

"Will she be putting a condom around her mouth?" I asked. "Semen and saliva can carry the same shit."

"Here you go taking the conversation to another level. Why can't you just relax and enjoy life for once? It's only this one time."

"What I'm about to do is enjoy this six hours of sleep. Goodnight!" And with that, I turned my behind over and went to sleep.

Of course it wasn't over. When I woke up, James was in the shower. As much as I hated to go in the bathroom while he was in there, I figured if I could at least brush my teeth, I could shower real quick and be out the house before he had a chance to come at me with some bullshit. I was hoping he wouldn't bring this Monica shit up at 6:37 in the morning because I would hurt him.

By the time I was done brushing my teeth and cleansing my face, James was stepping out of the shower. Through the mirror I peeked at his toned body, and semi-erect penis. At the age of thirty-two, standing at least six feet three inches, he still had the body of a college football player. He's definitely well endowed, but what difference did it make if he was only good for five minutes? He caught my eye as he was drying off and a sly smile spread across his face as he covered his midsection with the towel and went into the bedroom. I hopped in the shower and lingered a little longer because it was his morning to get the kids ready.

When I stepped out of the streaming water and into our room, I could still smell his Cool Water cologne. That made me wet instantly, but he'd never know. I'd just as soon please myself than waste my shower on a few minutes with him.

After putting my outfit together and plugging in the electric curling iron, I was finally able to sit on the bed and moisturize my skin. Out of the corner of my eye I noticed a single yellow rose on my pillow and a piece of heart-shaped chocolate with "I Love You" printed on the foil resting next to it. I smiled, but continued to rub my Happy by Clinque body lotion into my skin.

I loved my husband, and maybe we could talk about this entire threesome thing later.

Surprisingly he had nothing to say at breakfast. He smiled a lot, and that just pissed me off. Not that I had any conversation for him, but his being quiet made me nervous. At least if he was talking I'd know how to vibe off him. He just sat there smiling the entire time, and that just made me suspicious.

When I started gathering my stuff up to leave for work, he already had my briefcase and files along with my lunch stacked all nice and neat in the passenger seat of my 2003 Blazer. I got a kiss on the cheek, and he even offered to take the kids to childcare for me. Something was definitely up, and I wasn't at work for five minutes before I figured it out. I was looking through the files that I was supposed to be working on over the weekend when a hot pink folder that I don't remember having before caught my eye. When I opened it, a 5x7 photo of Monica was pasted to the left, and a three-page printout about her was on the opposite side. I was too shocked to be offended.

The pages included her date of birth, zodiac sign, likes and dislikes, a copy of her dental records, last HIV test results, and the results of her gynecologist exam, which I was glad to see were all negative. Her address and phone number were also included, along with directions on how to get to her house from my job off Map Quest. I had to laugh to keep from being pissed because I was sure my husband was going crazy.

If that wasn't enough, further inspection produced a key card from the Hyatt and an invite to meet him and Monica at the hotel restaurant for dinner. A note, handwritten by James, said the kids would be at his mother's house, and I should be at the hotel by seven. I put everything back in the folder, and went to my first meeting of the day. I didn't even want to think about that right now, and I had a few choice words for James later on.

When I returned to my office for lunch, I opened my door to at least three hundred yellow tulips crowding my space. On my desk sat a bouquet of tulips and white roses mixed in a beautiful Waterford crystal vase. My secretary informed me that they were delivered only ten minutes before I got there, and the card could be found next to the vase on my desk. I was too overwhelmed to think clearly and mechanically walked over to my desk to retrieve the card. It was in a cute yellow and white envelope to match the flowers, and was written with a gold pen. It read:

Jasmine,
    You must know that you're the love of my life, and there is nothing in this world I wouldn't do to make you happy. This one time I want us to be happy together. Please reconsider . . .

                                    Love Forever,
                                      James

Attention Writers:

Writers looking to get their books published can view our submission guidelines by visiting our website at:
www.QBOROBOOKS.com

What we're looking for: Contemporary fiction in the tradition of Darrien Lee, Carl Weber, Anna J, Zane, Mary B. Morrison, Noire, Lolita Files, etc; groundbreaking mainstream contemporary fiction.

We prefer email submissions to: candace@qborobooks.com in MS Word, PDF, or rtf format only. However, if you wish to send the submission via snail mail, you can send it to:

Q-BORO BOOKS Acquisitions Department
165-41A Baisley Blvd., Suite 4. Mall #1
Jamaica, New York 11434

*** By submitting your work to Q-Boro Books, you agree to hold Q-Boro books harmless and not liable for publishing similar works as yours that we may already be considering or may consider in the future. ***

1. Submissions will not be returned.
2. **Do not contact us for status updates.** If we are interested in receiving your full manuscript, we will contact you via email or telephone.
3. Do not submit if the entire manuscript is not complete.

Due to the heavy volume of submissions, if these requirements are not followed, we will not be able to process your submission.

LOOK FOR MORE HOT TITLES FROM
Q-BORO
B O O K S

TALK TO THE HAND - OCTOBER 2006
$14.95
ISBN 0977624765

Nedra Harris, a twenty-three year old business executive, has experienced her share of heartache in her quest to find a soul mate. Just when she's about to give up on love, she runs into Simeon Mathews, a gentleman she met in college years earlier. She remembers his warm smile and charming nature, but soon finds out that Simeon possesses a dark side that will eventually make her life a living hell.

SOMEONE ELSE'S PUDDIN' - DECEMBER 2006
$14.95
ISBN 0977624706

While hairstylist Melody Pullman has no problem keeping clients in her chair, she can't keep her bills paid once her crack-addicted husband Big Steve steps through a revolving door leading in and out of prison. She soon finds what seems to be a sexual and financial solution when she becomes involved with her long-time client's husband, Larry.

THE AFTERMATH
$14.95
ISBN 0977624749

If you thought having a threesome could wreak havoc on a relationship, Monica from My Woman His Wife is back to show you why even the mere thought of a ménage a trios with your spouse and an outsider should never enter your imagination.

THE LAST TEMPTATION - APRIL 2007
$6.99
ISBN 0977733599

The Last Temptation is a multi-layered joy ride through explorations of relationships with Traci Johnson leading the way. She has found the new man of her dreams, the handsome and charming Jordan Styles, and they are anxious to move their relationship to the next level. But unbeknownst to Jordan, someone else is planning Traci's next move: her irresistible ex-boyfriend, Solomon Jackson, who thugged his way back into her heart.

LOOK FOR MORE HOT TITLES FROM

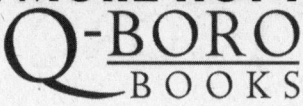

Q-BORO BOOKS

DOGISM
$6.99
ISBN 0977733505

Lance Thomas is a sexy, young black male who has it all; a high paying blue collar career, a home in Queens, New York, two cars, a son, and a beautiful wife. However, after getting married at a very young age he realizes that he is afflicted with DOGISM, a distorted sexuality that causes men to stray and be unfaithful in their relationships with women.

POISON IVY - NOVEMBER 2006
$14.95
ISBN 0977733521

Ivy Davidson's life has been filled with sorrow. Her father was brutally murdered and she was forced to watch, she faced years of abuse at the hands of those she trusted, and was forced to live apart from the only source of love that she has ever known. Now Ivy stands alone at the crossroads of life staring into the eyes of the man that holds her final choice of life or death in his hands.

HOLY HUSTLER - FEBRUARY 2007
$14.95
ISBN 0977733556

Reverend Ethan Ezekiel Goodlove the Third and his three sons are known for spreading more than just the gospel. The sanctified drama of the Goodloves promises to make us all scream "Hallelujah!"

HAPPILY NEVER AFTER - JANUARY 2007
$14.95
ISBN 1933967005

To Family and friends, Dorothy and David Leonard's marriage appears to be one made in heaven. While David is one of Houston's most prominent physicians, Dorothy is a loving and carefree housewife. It seems as if life couldn't be more fabulous for this couple who appear to have it all: wealth, social status, and a loving union. However, looks can be deceiving. What really happens behind closed doors and when the flawless veneer begins to crack?

LOOK FOR MORE HOT TITLES FROM

Q-BORO
BOOKS

OBSESSION 101
$6.99
ISBN 0977733548

After a horrendous trauma. Rashawn Ams is left pregnant and flees town to give birth to her son and repair her life after confiding in her psychiatrist. After her return to her life, her town, and her classroom, she finds herself the target of an intrusive secret admirer who has plans for her.

SHAMELESS- OCTOBER 2006
$6.99
ISBN 0977733513

Kyle is sexy, single, and smart; Jasmyn is a hot and sassy drama queen. These two complete opposites find love - or something real close to it - while away at college. Jasmyn is busy wreaking havoc on every man she meets. Kyle, on the other hand, is trying to walk the line between his faith and all the guilty pleasures being thrown his way. When the partying college days end and Jasmyn tests HIV positive, reality sets in.

MISSED OPPORTUNITIES - MARCH 2007
$14.95
ISBN 1933967013

Missed Opportunities illustrates how true-to-life characters must face the consequences of their poor choices. Was each decision worth the opportune cost? LaTonya Y. Williams delivers yet another account of love, lies, and deceit all wrapped up into one powerful novel.

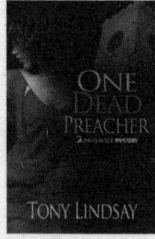

ONE DEAD PREACHER - MARCH 2007
$14.95
ISBN 1933967021

Smooth operator and security CEO David Price sets out to protect the sexy, smart, and saucy Sugar Owens from her husband, who happens to be a powerful religious leader. Sugar isn't as sweet as she appears, however, and in a twisted turn of events, the preacher man turns up dead and Price becomes the prime suspect.